BRIAN FL'
EXIT SIR J

BRIAN FLYNN was born in 1885 in Leyton, Essex. He won a scholarship to the City Of London School, and from there went into the civil service. In World War I he served as Special Constable on the Home Front, also teaching "Accountancy, Languages, Maths and Elocution to men, women, boys and girls" in the evenings, and acting in his spare time.

It was a seaside family holiday that inspired Brian Flynn to turn his hand to writing in the mid-twenties. Finding most mystery novels of the time "mediocre in the extreme", he decided to compose his own. Edith, the author's wife, encouraged its completion, and after a protracted period finding a publisher, it was eventually released in 1927 by John Hamilton in the UK and Macrae Smith in the U.S. as *The Billiard-Room Mystery*.

The author died in 1958. In all, he wrote and published 57 mysteries, the vast majority featuring the super-sleuth Antony Bathurst.

BRIAN FLYNN

EXIT SIR JOHN

With an introduction by
Steve Barge

DEAN STREET PRESS

INTRODUCTION

"I let my books write themselves. That is to say, having once constructed my own plot, I sit down to write and permit the puppets to do their own dancing."

DURING the war, Brian Flynn was trying some experiments with his crime writing. His earlier books are all traditional mystery novels, all with a strong whodunit element to them, but starting with *Black Edged* in 1939, Brian seemed to want to branch out in his writing style. *Black Edged* (1939) tells the tale of the pursuit of a known killer from both sides of the chase. While there is a twist in the tale, this is far from a traditional mystery, and Brian returned to the inverted format once again with *Such Bright Disguises* (1941). There was also an increasing darkness in some of his villains – the plot of *They Never Came Back* (1940), the story of disappearing boxers, has a sadistic antagonist and *The Grim Maiden* (1942) was a straight thriller with a similarly twisted adversary. However, following this, perhaps due in part to a family tragedy during the Second World War, there was a notable change in Brian's writing style. The style of the books from *The Sharp Quillet* (1947) onwards switched back to a far more traditional whodunnit format, while he also adopted a pseudonym in attempt to try something new.

The three Charles Wogan books – *The Hangman's Hands* (1947), *The Horror At Warden Hall* (1948) and *Cyanide For The Chorister* (1950) – are an interesting diversion for Brian, as while they feature a new sleuth, they aren't particularly different structurally to the Anthony Bathurst books. You could make a case that they were an attempt to go back to a sleuth who mirrored Sherlock Holmes, as Bathurst at this point seems to have moved away from the Great Detective, notably through the lack of a Watson character. The early Bathurst books mostly had the sleuth with a sidekick, a different character in most books, often narrating the books, but as the series progresses, we see Bathurst operating more and more by himself, with his thoughts being the focus of the text. The Charles Wogans, on the other hand, are all narrated by Piers Deverson, relating his adventures with Sebastian Stole who was, as per the cover of *The*

Hangman's Hands (1947), *"A Detective Who Might Have Been A King"* – he was the Crown Prince of Calorania who had to flee the palace during an uprising.

While the short Wogan series is distinct from the Bathurst mysteries, they have a lot in common. Both were published by John Long for the library market, both have a sleuth who takes on his first case because it seems like something interesting to do and both have a potentially odd speaking habit. While Bathurst is willing to pepper his speech with classical idioms and obscure quotations, Stole, being the ex-Prince of the European country of Calorania, has a habit of mangling the English language. To give an example, when a character refers to his forbears, Stole replies that *"I have heard of them, and also of Goldilocks."* I leave it to the reader to decide whether this is funny or painful, but be warned, should you decide to try and track these books down, this is only one example and some of them are even worse.

Stole has some differences from Bathurst, notably that he seems to have unlimited wealth despite fleeing Calorania in the middle of the night – he inveigles himself into his first investigation by buying the house where the murder was committed! By the third book, however, it seems as if Brian realised that there were only surface differences between Stole and Bathurst and returned to writing books exclusively about his original sleuth. This didn't however stop a literary agent, when interviewed by Bathurst in *Men For Pieces* (1949), praising the new author Charles Wogan . . .

At this stage in his investigative career, Bathurst is clearly significantly older than when he first appeared in *The Billiard Room Mystery* (1927). There, he was a Bright Young Thing, displaying his sporting prowess and diving headfirst into a murder investigation simply because he thought it would be entertaining. At the start of *The Case of Elymas the Sorcerer* (1945), we see him recovering from "muscular rheumatism", taking the sea-air at the village of St Mead (not St Mary Mead), before the local constabulary drag him into the investigation of a local murder.

The book itself is very typical of Brian's work. First, the initial mystery has a strange element about it, namely that someone has stripped the body, left it in a field and, for some reason, shaved the body's moustache off. Soon a second body is found, along with a mentally-challenged young man whispering about "gold". In common with a number of Brian's books, such as *The Mystery of The Peacock's Eye* (1928) and *The Running Nun* (1952), the reason for the title only becomes apparent very late in the day – this is not a story about magicians and wizards. One other title, which I won't name for obvious reasons, is actually a clue to what is going on in that book.

Following this, we come to *Conspiracy at Angel* (1947), a book that may well have been responsible for delaying the rediscovery of Brian's work. When Jacques Barzun and Wendell Hertig Taylor wrote *A Catalogue Of Crime* (1971), a reference book intended to cover as many crime writers as possible, they included Brian Flynn – they omitted E. & M.A. Radford, Ianthe Jerrold and Molly Thynne to name but a few great "lost" crime writers – but their opinion of Brian's work was based entirely on this one atypical novel. That opinion was *"Straight tripe and savorless. It is doubtful, on the evidence, if any of the thirty-two others by this author would be different."* This proves, at least, that Barzun and Taylor didn't look beyond the "Also By The Author" page when researching Flynn, and, more seriously, were guilty of making sweeping judgments based on little evidence. To be fair to them, they did have a lot of books to read . . .

It is likely that, post-war, Brian was looking for source material for a book and dug out a play script that he wrote for the Trevalyan Dramatic Club. *Blue Murder* was staged in East Ham Town Hall on 23rd February 1937, with Brian, his daughter and his future son-in-law all taking part. It was perhaps an odd choice, as while it is a crime story, it was also a farce. A lot of the plot of the criminal conspiracy is lifted directly into the novel, but whereas in the play, things go wrong due to the incompetence of a "silly young ass" who gets involved, it is the intervention of Anthony Bathurst in this case that puts paid to the criminal scheme. A fair amount of the farce structure is maintained, in particular in the opening section, and as such, this is a fairly unusual outing for Bathurst. There's also a fascinating snapshot of history when the criminal scheme is revealed. I won't go into details for obvious reasons, but I doubt many readers' knowledge of some specific 1940's technology will be enough to guess what the villains are up to.

Following *Conspiracy at Angel* – and possibly because of it – Brian's work comes full circle with the next few books, returning to the more traditional whodunit of the early Bathurst outings. *The Sharp Quillet* (1947) brings in a classic mystery staple, namely curare, as someone is murdered by a poisoned dart. This is no blow-pipe murder, but an actual dartboard dart – and the victim was taking part in a horse race at the time. The reader may think that the horse race, an annual event for members of the Inns of Court to take place in, is an invention of Brian's, but it did exist. Indeed, it still does, run by The Pegasus Club. This is the only one of Brian's novels to mention the Second World War overtly, with the prologue of the book, set ten years previously, involving an air-raid.

Exit Sir John (1947) – not to be confused with Clemence Dane and Helen Simpson's *Enter Sir John* (1928) – concerns the death of Sir John Wynward at Christmas. All signs point to natural causes, but it is far from the perfect murder (if indeed it is murder) due to the deaths of his chauffeur and his solicitor. For reasons that I cannot fathom, *The Sharp Quillet* and *Exit Sir John* of all of Brian's work, are the most obtainable in their original form. I have seen a number of copies for sale, complete with dustjacket, whereas for most of his other books, there have been, on average, less than one copy for sale over the past five years. I have no explanation for this, but they are both good examples of Brian's work, as is the following title *The Swinging Death* (1949).

A much more elusive title, *The Swinging Death* has a very typical Brian Flynn set-up, along with the third naked body in five books. Rather than being left in a field like the two in *The Case of Elymas the Sorcerer*, this one is hanging from a church porch. Why Dr Julian Field got off his train at the wrong stop, and how he went from there to being murdered in the church, falls to Bathurst to explain, along with why half of Field's clothes are in the church font – and the other half are in the font of a different church?

Brian's books are always full of his love for sport, but *The Swinging Death* shows where Brian's specific interests lie. While rugby has always been Bathurst's winter sport, there is a delightful scene in this book where Chief Inspector MacMorran vehemently champions football (or soccer if you really must) as being the superior sport. One can almost hear Brian's own voice finally being able to talk about a sport that Anthony Bathurst would not give much consideration to.

Brian was pleased with *The Swinging Death*, writing in *Crime Book Magazine* in 1949 that "I hope that I am not being unduly optimistic if I place *The Swinging Death* certainly among the best of my humbler contributions to mystery fiction. I hope that those who come to read it will find themselves in agreement with me in this assessment." It is certainly a sign that over halfway through his writing career, Brian was still going strong and I too hope that you agree with him on this.

Steve Barge

CHAPTER I

Mr. Walter Medlicott, solicitor and sole surviving partner of the long-established firm of Medlicott, Stogdon and Medlicott, stood and looked gloomily through the glass of his office window. He commented inwardly upon the atrocious weather conditions which prevailed on this December morning in the small market town of Aldersford. Although fog and frost held the country in a relentless grip, the main street was thronged for the reason that Christmas was but a matter of a few days ahead.

"Give me June and July," he muttered to himself as he made his way back from the window to his official desk. As he slumped into his old-fashioned chair, the clock of St. Clement's, the parish church of Aldersford, struck eleven. Mr. Medlicott sat silent in his chair for the space of some minutes, frowning heavily at the various inoffensive, inanimate objects connected with his profession which lay upon the desk in front of him.

Then he rose, still murmuring to himself, and walked to the window again. From where he stood he could look across the road and see the light of the blazing fires which shone from the windows of the 'Lion', opposite to his offices. This sensation of physical comfort cheered him and once again he turned and walked back to his desk— this time in a slightly better frame of mind.

He was a short, plump, middle-aged man, a little stiff in manner, perhaps, undoubtedly pompous when the occasion was suitable, with sandy hair and a pair of mild, kindly eyes. He had been born and bred in Aldersford, was the leading solicitor in the little country town and almost the leading solicitor in the county. Of more recent years, one or two firms had taken their stand and bid for rivalry, but Medlicott's, now in their seventh generation, had withstood the challengers and reigned in Aldersford even more indisputably than ever before.

Mr. Medlicott picked up the current issue of *The Times* and regarded it moodily. Three times he adjusted his glasses, moved in his chair and frowned at the different columns of the newspaper. Adderley, his managing clerk, had formed the opinion for some two or three days that the 'Guvnor' had something on his mind, and could he have seen him now he would have considered the opinion more firmly foundationed than at any previous time of their acquaintance. At last, Mr. Medlicott pushed back his chair, thrust the fingers of both hands into the lower pockets of his waistcoat, kept them there for some few seconds, removed his right-hand fingers and reached forward with them to the inter-departmental telephone. He unhooked the receiver.

"Oh—Adderley," he said, "bring me in the Wynyard deed-box and the December 'A.B.C.'"

Having delivered himself of this instruction, Mr. Medlicott sat back in his chair again and replaced his right hand in his waistcoat pocket with the air of a man who had crossed the Rubicon and, at the same time, taken an irrevocable decision.

2

Stephen Adderley was tall, thin and hatchet-faced. He had been with 'Medlicott's' since the days of his early youth. Of but moderate ability, he possessed, nevertheless, the quality of reliability. Or, at least, so Walter Medlicott had always found and always believed. Adderley had married young, lived in the village of Magdalen Verney, a few miles from Aldersford, liked the cinema, the theatre, and the public-house, and on Sundays officiated with a somewhat unusual solemnity as a sidesman at the village church of Magdalen Verney where as a boy, and later as a man, he had sung in the choir.

He placed the black tin box marked 'Sir John Wynyard' on his chief's desk and offered the current issue of the 'A.B.C.' to his outstretched hands.

"Thank you, Adderley." Mr. Medlicott took the 'A.B.C.' and looked somewhat abstractedly at the ceiling before turning again to his managing clerk. "For the next hour, Adderley, or rather shall we say—until after lunch—I am not to be disturbed. Understand! I am not to be disturbed *on any account*. And please don't leave the office until you've seen me."

The last three words of the penultimate sentence had been heavily emphasized.

"Very good, sir. I understand. I'll see to that, sir. You can rely on me."

"Er—thank you, Adderley. Er—then that's all right . . . You may leave me now."

Adderley made his exit and closed the door behind him. Mr. Medlicott cleared a space from the daily batch of letters which still held a place on his desk and then went over to his private safe and to the drawer therein which contained the key to the 'Wynyard' box. He found the key he needed and went back to the desk. He unlocked the box. His eyes were still anxious and troubled and more than once his hands trembled. He removed the papers at the top of the box. Two large envelopes marked in each case with the word 'Will', a copy of *The Times* with the obituary column heavily blue-pencilled, a large, rather florid memorial card in purple print intimating a funeral service at the parish church of a place called Montfichet, and then, underneath these, a bulky green file of correspondence, marked on its outside cover, 'Wynyard'.

He had by this time reached the object of his search. Right at the bottom of the black tin box lay a small envelope—of the normal shape and size which is in everyday use. The flap of this envelope was sealed in three places and the envelope itself had scrawled across it 'John Wynyard'. For the first time on this cold and foggy December morning, a slight smile played on the face of Mr. Walter Medlicott. For some few fleeting seconds the smile remained as he held the envelope and weighed it, as it were, on the palm of his hand. A curtain had been rolled back in his mind and he savoured the lost years of time. But the smile faded, almost at the instant of its birth, and the frown came back to its former possession of his features. Mr. Medlicott tossed the small envelope on to his desk, pushed his chair back, one might have thought almost angrily, and walked back to his old position at the window. He thrust his hands deep into his trouser-pockets.

A brewer's dray had drawn up and was unloading its large and cumbersome barrels into the cellar of the 'Lion' and he could just see the figures of the draymen with their flapping aprons as they flitted to and fro, up and down the inn's cobble-stoned courtyard. Twice, as he stood there, Walter Medlicott gave a shake of the head—but suddenly he shrugged his shoulders and turned away.

"No," he murmured to himself—"no. I must act as though Roger were alive. He would not have hesitated. Any other course is unthinkable. Any other standard impossible. Though, God knows, it goes against the grain to do so. Why on earth did this have to happen now? And to me of all people?"

The frown left his face and was replaced by a look of resolute determination. Seated at his desk, he rubbed the palms of his hands softly together. Taking up the sealed envelope, he deliberately broke the seals and removed the enclosures. Then, very similarly as he had before when he had spoken to Adderley, he leant forward and pulled the Post-office telephone towards him. With the other hand, he began to turn the pages of the 'A.B.C.' Or, in other words, Mr. Medlicott had signed his own death-warrant. Just as surely as he had ever effected anything. The time, be it noted, was 11.53 on the morning of Saturday, December the twenty-second.

"I want you to get me this number," he said . . .

3

Elisabeth Grenville sank back in the cushioned corner of her first-class compartment and crossed her legs with a sigh of luxurious relief and contentment. She felt singularly blessed to have got even as far as she had. Fog, frost, ice and snow she regarded as a quartette of abominable desolations and it was just her cursed luck, she argued to herself, to be forced to travel on a Christmas Eve of all days under such appalling conditions. It was certainly very sweet of Catherine Poulton, née Wynyard (who was by way of being a distant cousin), to have invited her to High Fitchet for Christmas, but at least the weather might have played up gallantly for her and assumed its most cheerful Yuletide face. At any rate, thought Elisabeth, the worst was over and, of course, Catherine would have a car waiting for her when she reached Colbury. Once at High Fitchet she could snap her fingers at the very worst show the weather could possibly put up for the next week, and abandon herself thoroughly to all the delights of Christmas at a house-party in the country.

Nick Wynyard would be there—she had rather tender feelings for Nicholas since she had seen him hoist a flag for Oxford at the Inter-Varsity sports the previous Spring—Catherine's cousin, Helen Repton, whom she had met on two previous occasions and who had a special job of some kind at no less a place than Scotland Yard and, of course, a host of other distinguished and, without doubt, charming people. With the one exception of the atrocious weather the prospect she viewed was altogether delightful to her, and Elisabeth nestled again against the upholstery of her seat and cherished a fervent wish that the train would soon start and another stage of her journey to High Fitchet be well and truly launched.

She caught a half-glimpse of herself in the compartment window and what she saw increased the sense of contentment that had now begun to take possession of her. For Elisabeth was good to look upon in this latter half of her twentieth year. She was superbly turned out, her mist of red-gold hair crowned a pair of exquisite sapphire eyes in a face delicately elegant in colour and almost impertinently and unrepentantly lovely. Elisabeth averted her gaze from the window to her tiny lozenged wrist-watch and noted with some degree of impatience that the time was already a minute past the scheduled time of the train's departure. And she still had, most unusually for these times, the compartment to herself. No—this wasn't so—for precisely as she registered the thought, the door of the compartment opened and a middle-aged man got in. Her companion was obviously a gentleman. He selected the corner-seat opposite to her, placed a largish suitcase on the rack, seated himself comfortably, took off his gloves and then carefully assumed a pair of horn-rimmed spectacles. Elisabeth, almost mechanically, glanced at the time, and the guard, just outside on the platform, waved his flag and blew his whistle. Mr. Medlicott—for it was he—smiled at Elisabeth and nodded.

"Yes, I agree with you. I know what you're thinking. I'm afraid I cut it rather fine."

Elisabeth noticed that his voice was both pleasant and cultured and she found her fullness of comfort returning to her.

"Almost *too* fine," she answered.

"I know," he laughed back. "But it wasn't altogether my fault, you see. My taxi from Paddington had bad luck all the way, lost all the fights with almost monotonous regularity, and then finally—just to do the thing properly—wound itself up in a real great-grandfather of all traffic jams. So I plead bad luck, not guilty and then good luck."

Elisabeth turned her full sapphire battery on to him. "Yes. It might have been worse. After all—you did what you wanted to do. You did *catch* your train."

Mr. Medlicott looked at her with undisguised admiration. "My dear young lady," he said, "it might have been *considerably* worse."

The implication was obvious. Elisabeth almost blushed as the train gathered speed, but a year's training stood her in good stead and by a supreme effort she averted the calamity.

Mr. Medlicott turned towards the window and looked out. "We aren't being favoured," he remarked, "in the matter of the weather. I've been travelling since eight o'clock this morning. Fog—practically all the way. Nothing worse!"

"It seems," said Elisabeth, responding to his mood, "that weather of this sort is usually dished up for us at Christmas. It's become an institution—like turkey, Christmas pudding and mince-pies. As for sunshine—we never seem to get any."

The train had run into a belt of fog and was slowing down. A little bit later it gave a convulsive sort of shudder and stopped altogether. Elisabeth peered anxiously through the window.

"I do hope," she said, "that we aren't going to be too frightfully late."

Mr. Medlicott smiled at her. It was a nice, charming, friendly smile. He seemed to have shaken off the worry and depression which had hag-ridden him over the week-end. "I'm rather afraid," he replied, "that you're going to be disappointed. I fancy that we're bound to be late. As a matter of fact, it was my original intention to have caught the train before this one. The 2.17. So I'm afraid that I'm well behind schedule. Will it be terribly awkward for you? If we are very late, I mean?"

Elisabeth nodded emphatically. "My worry's transport," she answered. "Where I'm going to is five miles from the station. There *should* be a car for me. But I can't very well expect a car and a chauffeur to wait for me hours and hours in this vile weather, can I?"

The train took unto itself life and began to crawl forward again. Mr. Medlicott's eyes twinkled at her through his glasses.

"Well, that's by way of being a coincidence! Because I happen to be in exactly the same position."

Elisabeth put her book down on the seat beside her. "Don't tell me," she said rather mischievously, "that you're going to High Fitchet? Because that would be rather *too* much of a coincidence."

Mr. Medlicott's eyes opened wider. "But, my dear young lady," he replied in amazement, "I most certainly am."

4

Elisabeth's laugh tinkled through the compartment. It was a most musical accompaniment to the complete stopping of the train, which in some particularly clumsy manner seemed to jerk itself to a petulant and most self-willed standstill.

"Well," said Elisabeth rather breathlessly, "how remarkable! And to think that we two people should choose the same train and the same compartment to travel down by."

Mr. Medlicott's mood changed. "These things *do* happen," he remarked portentously, "and after all—it's not so . . . er . . . wizard . . . as it may appear . . . at first blush. After all—we're two people travelling to the same place on the same day. Our routes are identical. So why at some place on that route . . . shouldn't we meet?"

Elisabeth looked a little doubtful. She didn't feel prepared to accept the logic of the argument. It was her nature to taste disillusionment when unusual incidents achieved sudden metamorphosis and embraced the commonplace.

"When you put it like that," she said, "I suppose . . . in a way . . . it does make some sort of a difference."

"Of course it does. But seeing that we're going to spend Christmas in one another's company, how about a spot of mutual unloading? Let's introduce ourselves properly. I think that's most definitely indicated."

The sapphires got to work again. "You begin," she said, a trifle primly.

Mr. Medlicott nodded acceptance of her proposal. "That's right. I will." He leant forward towards her and the train, as though in entire approval of the arrangements they had just made, began to move on again. "My name's Medlicott. Walter Medlicott. I live at a little town called Aldersford. You may have heard of it. In Warwickshire. I'm a very old friend of the Wynyard family—in addition to being their solicitor. And I'm spending Christmas with Sir John Wynyard, for the principal reason that he was good enough to invite me the day before yesterday, on the telephone. I think that's about all—oh—there is one other thing—I suppose I ought to tell you—I'm a bachelor."

Elisabeth's head went to one side in appraisement. "That sounds," she said demurely, "as though the invitation from Sir John were rather sudden."

Mr. Medlicott's kindly eyes twinkled again. "Perhaps it was—in a way. But you must remember, as I told you, that Sir John Wynyard and I are very old friends. Much closer than the usual solicitor and . . . er . . . client. That explains a very great deal." Mr. Medlicott laughed.

"Isn't it a little surprising and . . . er . . . unusual," said Elisabeth, "for Sir John Wynyard at High Fitchet, in the county of Essex, to have a solicitor in Aldersford, in the county of Warwickshire. Two places that are miles and miles apart?" The sapphires now were both mocking and mischievous.

"That also," replied Mr. Medlicott smilingly, "is easily explained. You listen to me. Earlier generations of Wynyards—six or seven—I'm not sure which—resided at a little place called Magdalen Verney, which is but a few miles from Aldersford. It was Sir John's grandfather, Sir Christopher Wynyard, who bought the High Fitchet estate in Essex. He was a restless man. My ancestors have served the Wynyards for generations. Now—how's that? Have I satisfied all the terms of your equation?"

Elisabeth laughed again. "I'll say you have. You've come through with full marks and all your colours flying. And now, I suppose, it's my turn to unburden myself."

"It most certainly is," asserted Mr. Medlicott with solemnity. "And I'm all attention."

"Mine'll be quite short, I'm afraid. I'm not in the least important. I'm a sort of distant cousin of the Wynyards. My name's Elisabeth Grenville."

She stopped—and as she did so—the Colbury express did likewise. She also caught a look in Mr. Medlicott's eye. Almost as though, she thought hurriedly, her name had not been unfamiliar to him. She found herself still hesitating.

"Go on," he said, "it's a good name. I've always revered the memory of the great Sir Richard."

"Well," she continued, "there isn't a lot more. When Catherine was married last spring to Henry Poulton, she asked me to be one of her bridesmaids. That seemed to bring us together a bit—she said she'd be going home for Christmas and that she'd wangle me an 'invite'. I'm at an Art School in town. There you are."

"Yes," said Mr. Medlicott almost absent-mindedly, "there I am. *Hinc illae lacrimae.* So you're Elisabeth Grenville—eh? A third cousin of the Wynyards? Yes. I remember hearing about your branch of the family."

Elisabeth noted the numeral. She hadn't told him that. Mr. Medlicott went on. "Grenville—eh? Very strange—indeed. That I should meet you like this. Especially considering—" he broke off rather abruptly. "Reminds me," he continued (and Elisabeth thought a trifle inappositely), "of an old tag that I read somewhere when I was a boy. Can't think where. Let me see now! How did it go? It'll come to me. I've an excellent memory. For some things. But I have to chase it sometimes." He cocked his head to one side. "I've got it. 'Copplestone with Grenville strive—while both families be alive.' Yes—that was it. Don't quite know what it means or what it's got to do with you. But there you are. I just happened to think of it. I'm like that."

Elisabeth tinkled her laugh again. "Oh—I've heard of that! I know it quite well. I've often heard my father repeat it. There's an old legend extant in the two families that there'll always be a blood-feud or something of that sort between the Grenvilles and the Copplestones. You know—a fight to the death. You see—just as we're distant cousins of the Wynyards, the Copplestones are distant cousins of us."

"I see," nodded Mr. Medlicott, "so that's the explanation, is it?"

"That's the explanation," added Elisabeth—"and fancy you knowing about it. But I expect the Wynyards heard of it from us and you must have picked it up from the Wynyards. Don't you think that's probably the explanation?"

"Very likely," agreed Mr. Medlicott. "As I said just now, most things have a logical explanation if we can only find it."

With a series of grumbles and growls, the train got under weigh, and as it did so Elisabeth saw her vis-à-vis look up. Two people had just passed along the corridor, which was on Elisabeth's left. She just had time herself to catch a glimpse of a man with a brown beard and then all her thoughts were brought to a summary halt by the expression on her companion's face. She felt impelled to translate her observation into a definite question.

"Why—what's the matter?" she asked—"you look as though you've seen a ghost!"

Mr. Medlicott recovered himself and shook his head. "Not quite. Not a ghost. No—no—far from that. But I rather fancy that I know one of those two men who passed. If I'm right—he's on his way to High Fitchet as you and I are. But I'm not certain—he'd almost passed from my line of vision when I caught sight of him. I saw him only side face. But we shall know all in good time, my dear. By Jove—we seem to be really moving at last. Perhaps we're running clear of the fog."

Elisabeth nodded and settled herself down in her seat as cosily as she could. She picked up her book from the seat beside her.

"What is it?" asked Mr. Medlicott with an indication of his head. "What are you reading?"

Elisabeth answered by showing the book to him. "Do you know it?"

Mr. Medlicott's features demonstrated something like delight. It was the *Summa* of St. Thomas Aquinas. "My dear young lady," he exclaimed once again—"do I know it? Do I *know* it? When I first read it I loved it. Positively revelled in it. But that's a good many years ago now." He shook his head. "Many more than I care to remember—if you'll forgive the cliché."

He sank back in his corner seat and became reminiscent. "I was about twenty-five at the time. Been down from Oxford about three years. And I had asked a good literary friend of mine to prescribe for me a Scheme of Reading. You know—you get the urge for that sort of thing when you're young. He did. Just five books. No more. Five only. I'll tell you what they were. I feel sure I can remember them." Mr.

Medlicott closed his eyes. "Butler's *Analogy*, Coleridge's *Confessions of an Enquiring Spirit*, Newman's *Apologia*, St. Augustine's *Confessions* and that one you hold in your hand—the *Summa* of St. Thomas Aquinas. They all made a tremendous impression on me and I've been eternally grateful to my mentor for what he did for me. To my mind, they represent the real line along which Christianity must ultimately be defended. But there—I fancy that I'm quoting Butler himself."

Mr. Medlicott opened his eyes and leant forward again towards Elisabeth. "If I may, I'll borrow that down at High Fitchet. Just for an hour or so. There are one or two passages in it on which I'd very much like to refresh myself. May I?"

Elisabeth assented willingly. "Any time—Mr. Medlicott. I shall be only too delighted. It's a bit heavy, perhaps, for a railway journey. But I'd started it and I wanted to finish it."

She put a used envelope between the leaves to mark her place and replaced the book on the seat. The desire to read had left her. The train was now travelling fast. Mr. Medlicott looked at his watch.

"If we keep this up—and we seem to have cleared the fog somewhat—we shouldn't be more than an hour late. So we should get to Colbury by about six o'clock."

"Too late," murmured Elisabeth lugubriously. "I'm tired already. And by that time I shall be both frightfully hungry and horribly thirsty. And, in addition to all those, probably—exceedingly bad tempered."

Mr. Medlicott chuckled and became benevolent. "Well then, I suggest that you adjust the first of all those conditions *now*. Have a sleep, my dear young lady—don't mind me. And don't worry about not waking up in time. I promise to wake you—should it be necessary—when we get to Colbury."

Elisabeth looked at him and under the influence of fog and frost suddenly decided to take him at his word. She curled up as cosily as she could. Elisabeth slept! It is perhaps a matter for wonderment that her sleep was untroubled. For—had she but known it—she was so close to Terror and Tragedy! So close to Death and deaths—so close to the menace of 'Mr. Levi'!

5

When Elisabeth woke up, she smiled a little whimsically. For by this time Mr. Medlicott too had dozed off. The compartment by now had warmed up, the heating-system was evidently working well, the train was running rhythmically and Elisabeth felt deliciously cosy and comfortable. She glanced at her wrist-watch. It was just five o'clock. According to Mr. Medlicott's calculations, they had only about another hour to travel. It will be funny, she thought to herself, if I have to wake him up. Considering what he said to me. Being a man—how he'll hate it! Still—there was plenty of time yet. Elisabeth took her book again, found her place and made another attempt to read. But concentration was difficult in the circumstances, and after a time she tried to look out of the window. They were running across a belt of comparatively open country where there was no sign of fog at all. On the contrary, sleet was falling, and the white flakes, becoming grey as they descended, seemed to her like handfuls of chill welcome tossed petulantly down to earth by certainly jealous and perhaps angry gods. They curled towards the moving train and licked the windows of the carriages in their thousands, and as Elisabeth looked at them she heard—and shivered when she heard—the monotonous whine of the wind, the whine which at times turned into a long shrill screech—and then—away in the far distance, the steady unsubdued swish of the sea.

Oh—to be inside High Fitchet, folded in warmth, lulled by light and cosseted in creature comforts! The train was moving splendidly now and as Elisabeth leant back in her comfortable corner seat and half closed her eyes, the regular beat of the engine and the locking thud of the carriages as they devoured the miles of line almost brought her to sleep again. By an effort, however, she remained awake and at ten minutes to six, there was a slight stirring opposite to her and Mr. Medlicott emerged from his doze. He listened—she wasn't quite sure in her mind what he was listening to—and then sought the time again.

"I thought so," he remarked—"running into Colbury. And I shan't have to wake you up after all."

"Just now," Elisabeth laughed, "I thought that the boot was going to be on the other leg. You seemed well away in the land of slumber."

"Did you? Ah—no—I'm like the dogs, you know—I always sleep with one eye open."

Mr. Medlicott straightened himself, put on his gloves, shrugged his shoulders as though he had suddenly come over cold and was trying to get warm, and began to whistle. He whistled on a note of pessimism, Elisabeth thought, and the notes came flatly from between his teeth. She imagined he meant it to be Coleridge Taylor's 'Willow Song', from the 'Othello' suite, but the resemblance, if indeed there were any, was only occasional and, she feared, achieved by accident much more than by design.

The train suddenly began to slacken speed. It passed over a succession of points, curved round, straightened itself again, and then Elisabeth saw with relief that they were running into a station.

"Here we are," said Mr. Medlicott, abandoning his musical effort—"Colbury! And now bright lights, good food—and better drink."

He began to move impedimenta from the racks—first Elisabeth's—then his own. "I'm still worried about transport," said Elisabeth. "Do you really think there'll be a car for us? We're ever so late."

"If there isn't a car," replied Mr. Medlicott jovially, "I'll see that there soon will be. You leave all that to me."

"How?"

"Oh—there'll be a 'phone-box knocking about somewhere. There may even be a venerable 'taxi' kicking its dilapidated heels in the station-yard—for all we know. I have a distant memory of having once seen one there once upon a time—in the dim and distant past."

The train stopped. Mr. Medlicott helped Elisabeth out. They struggled across the platform into the booking-hall. No porter proffered help. They were engaged in putting up notices which read "Give the railways a square deal". The trip took some minutes. And as Elisabeth came through the booking-hall and peered into the darkness, with the sleet chilling and lightly stinging her cheeks, she was just able to see three or four people stepping into a big limousine. There were certainly two men and a woman—and she felt certain that one of them was the brown-bearded man she had seen in the corridor of the train on the journey down. She turned disappointedly to Mr. Medlicott and plucked him by the sleeve.

"There you are," she said, "we're slow. Too slow to catch cold. Too slow to be last, as Nick Wynyard said to me once. You saw what happened. There goes the transport to High Fitchet. And you and I, my dear Mr. Medlicott, are still standing here in the cold like a couple of mutts. 'The orphans of the storm'," she added bitterly—"in more ways than one."

Mr. Medlicott was stung to instant rejoinder. "My dear young lady," he said, "if that's a car from High Fitchet—all well and good. If it's come down to the station once, it can surely come again. And I'll damned well see that it does! Come on—we'll take the cases and find a telephone somewhere—and then we'll have it all fixed up in a brace of shakes. You rely on me."

"The man is actually talking sense," replied Miss Grenville.

6

Mr. Medlicott was as good as his word and found a telephone kiosk just outside the station. She could hear his voice. She noted with many degrees of thankfulness and gratitude that it had taken upon itself a cheery tone. When he emerged to her, he was smiling broadly.

"Everything's all right," he announced gaily. "I got through to High Fitchet and spoke to Quentin. You were quite right—the car had come from the house. And according to what Quentin thinks, it was probably intended to pick *us* up. But there you are. We can't reasonably complain that they've done what I believe is known as the 'dirty' on us. *I* should have caught the earlier train and *your* train was over an hour late. That's what's thrown the arrangements out of gear. Anyhow, Quentin says he'll see that it's turned round when it gets there and comes straight back for you and me. So there's nothing wrong with that, is there?"

Elisabeth nodded and at once essayed mental calculation. "High Fitchet's five miles from here—isn't it?"

"Yes. A little over, I should say, rather than under. Say about eleven miles for the car to do—there and back. Let me see now. Shouldn't be longer than twenty minutes to half an hour. If Quentin does his stuff as he's promised. You can shift in a car along these country lanes—believe me."

"It's jolly dark," remonstrated Elisabeth.

"All the better," countered Mr. Medlicott—"nothing on the road to worry about. Let's get back into the station, find a comfortable seat and wait. It'll be warmer there than here." He picked up the suitcases and they made their way into Colbury station again. "You've met Quentin, of course?"

"Oh—yes. But only once. That was at Catherine's wedding. He comes of age sometime next year, doesn't he?"

"Yes; April. Easter Monday, I fancy. Nice boy. I'm his godfather, by the way. Like his father. *And* like Catherine, of course. A bit more balance perhaps than Nick. More sober-headed. Nick takes after his mother. He's the odd one. At least, that's my opinion. Lady Wynyard was a Heseltine. Gets his games skill from her rather than from Sir John. Steady old file, Sir John. Books with him before brawn, every time. I'm pretty sure that he'd have much rather seen Nick an academic success than pull off a 'Blue'. Ah well—that's Life. Things seldom go as we'd like them to."

"All the same," said Elisabeth, semi-combatant, "I think I prefer Nick to Quentin."

"Very likely," returned Mr. Medlicott complacently, "and I've nothing to say against it. Nick's good points are in the front of the shop-window. Quentin's aren't. If you know what I mean."

For some absurd reason, Elisabeth felt herself growing a little angry. Not furious—merely nicely angry. Who was this old fogey, after all, to patronize her opinions? Because that was just what it sounded like. On the point of continuing the contest, for that was how she considered it, her ears caught the sound of a car in the distance. Mr. Medlicott heard it, too. He turned to her and his smile melted all her antagonism.

"I think so," he remarked, "our car for a certainty."

His opinion was soon confirmed. The limousine which Elisabeth had seen before swung into the station-yard and pulled up. The uniformed chauffeur got out and came towards them.

"Are you the young lady and gentleman for Sir John Wynyard's place?"

"Yes," replied Mr. Medlicott, "and I can't say how glad we are to see you. You've been quicker than I expected."

The chauffeur held open the door and Elisabeth got in. The cases were seen to, and Mr. Medlicott joined her. She could hear voices not very far away. A man shouted. Elisabeth resigned herself to a sensation of luxury.

"Thank God, all that's over," she murmured.

Mr. Medlicott made no reply. She turned to him. He was staring in a most strange way out of the window—staring apparently into the cloak of darkness through which they were travelling. In some extraordinary manner, he seemed to have been transported into another world.

"I said," repeated Elisabeth, "thank God that's over."

Mr. Medlicott seemed to force himself back to existence. He shook his head as though he hadn't properly heard what Elisabeth had said. His face was white and strained and anxious. It was as though he had seen something or somebody through the window of the car which had frightened him badly.

"'Over,' you said, Miss Grenville. But it's not over. On the other hand, I'm afraid that it's only just begun."

With this cryptic remark he sank back into his seat and relapsed into silence. Elisabeth, seeing how things were, made no further attempts at conversation.

When the car reached High Fitchet and the chauffeur came round to open the door for them, Elisabeth was destined to receive yet a second shock. For as Mr. Medlicott alighted and turned to assist her, she noticed that his hands were trembling. More than that even— he was hardly able to control them. Thus she and Walter Medlicott came to the Wynyards at High Fitchet.

CHAPTER II

1

CATHERINE Poulton and Quentin Wynyard, her brother, came to meet them in the big hall of High Fitchet. Catherine rushed to Elisabeth and Quentin took Mr. Medlicott under his care. Gooch, the chauffeur, carried the suitcases into the hall.

"Leave them there, Gooch, for the time being," said Quentin Wynyard. "I'll see that one of the maids takes them up to the bedrooms. I shall want you for another job in a few moments, so don't disappear."

"Very good, sir," replied Gooch. "I'll remain here."

Quentin turned to Mr. Medlicott. "Well, how are you, sir? Haven't seen you for a year or two now, but I'm blessed if you seem to grow any older, despite the dancing years. What a day—eh?"

Quentin was tall, thin and slender. His fingers were as sensitive as his face. "My father told me that he wanted to see you directly you showed up. As a matter of fact, we expected you before. But, of course, I made that clear to you on the 'phone just now."

"That's all right, Quentin. Don't you worry. I lost the train that I intended to catch. The fault was entirely mine."

"We've put dinner back till half-past seven in view of the fog, but I'll see mother about sending some tea into you, when you're closeted with father. What do you say? Shall we dash along?"

Mr. Medlicott acquiesced in all the arrangements and Quentin bore him off to Sir John Wynyard. Meanwhile Catherine had carried Elisabeth off to her room. Catherine was the eldest of the Wynyards—twenty-three. Like Quentin, she was tall and slim. With brown eyes of striking frankness and friendliness. She was blessed, too, with a glorious colouring—like a moss-rose—and this was her greatest asset in the beauty column. She wore her hair cut unusually close, but her head was well shaped and the style suited her admirably. Also—she invariably wore very English-looking clothes.

In the previous March she had married Henry Poulton, a man many years older than herself, and with very valuable interests on the Stock Exchange. Why Catherine should have chosen him as a life-partner was not outstandingly obvious to those who saw Henry Poulton for the first time. In the early fifties, he was thin, tall and excessively round-shouldered. He had little physical grace of any kind. His knees were bent, his feet were awkward and clumsy and his walk was more of a shamble than anything else. He was an inveterate cigarette-smoker and his long fingers were generally brown-stained with nicotine. At the same time, these fingers were strong and supple and his arms unusually muscular for a man of his build and physique.

He seemed to have a great affection for his young wife and as, also, he was possessed of a considerable income, Catherine, no doubt, was much happier than many people might possibly be inclined to think she was.

"Tell me, Catherine," said Elisabeth, as they sat down in Catherine's bedroom and which for the holiday was to be Elisabeth's, "who's here? I'm almost wildly excited and longing to know who my Christmas companions are going to be. I've been thinking about it all the way down from Liverpool Street. Even before I found myself sitting opposite to the ancient family solicitor, Mr. Medlicott. That was a coincidence, wasn't it, he and I landing up opposite to one another in the same compartment like that?"

"I'll say it was," replied Catherine. "Quentin was in fits over it when old Medlicott got on the 'phone just now. He came straight over to me and told me all about it. But you want me to tell you about the others. Let's see now. Where shall I start?"

Elisabeth waited for it. "There's the family, of course, to begin with. Daddy, Mummie, Nick, Quentin, Henry and I. You've met all of us. We were all at my wedding in the Spring. Then there's Aunt Amy, Daddy's sister. The only one he's got living. I don't think you've met her. She wasn't at the wedding. She would have been, of course, if things had been normal, but the poor old dear was just convalescing after a pretty vicious attack of pleurisy. She's not a bad sort. When you know her properly. Forbidding exterior, quaint get-up and quite a bark. But as usual in these cases, the bark's much worse than the bite—believe me, Elisabeth. Then there's Helen Repton, another cousin, on Mummie's side, who's actually employed at Scotland Yard of all places. But don't let that put you off. She's a thoroughly nice girl with loads of 'it'. I understand she's doing quite well for herself at her job. Expected to be a Commandant or something—one of these days."

Catherine paused in her recital and favoured Elisabeth with a grin of camaraderie. "Crime certainly won't pay at High Fitchet this Yule-tide with Helen Repton on the premises."

"I must remember that," said Elisabeth solemnly, and entering thoroughly into the spirit of her cousin's remark. Catherine proceeded with her list of guests.

"Let me think, now. Who is it comes next? Oh—I know. Perhaps our most distinguished guest. From some points of view, certainly. Percival Comfit, the novelist with faded spouse attached. Have you read any of his stuff? Very much Italian renaissance period. I expect you've heard of *The Gilded Cardinal.* He's a quaint bird—really, our Percival. Languid and drooping. And frightfully absent-minded. Always reminds me of Gilbert and Sullivan. You know! 'If you walk down Piccadilly, with a sunflower or a lily, in your mediaeval hand.' That sort of individual. Cynthia—that's the aforementioned spouse—is very faded and too, too self-effacing altogether. Just a loyal chorus to Percival—not merely most of the time—but *all* the time. Never once have I heard her even hint at anything like disagreement with what Percival has said."

"How do you come to know him, then?" enquired Elisabeth. "Has Nick or Quentin picked him up anywhere?"

"Oh no—nothing like that. He's a neighbour of Daddy's. Actually, he's his nearest neighbour. Bought three old cottages, just there by Montfitchet Mill, about six months ago, and had them converted into one. You know the idea. I haven't been there myself, but from all accounts that have reached my ears, the people responsible have made a pretty good job of it. Some people rave about it. Mummie's read a couple of Percival's books—she hasn't the least idea, probably, what they're about—but thought it would be a wizard idea to ask the Comfits for Christmas. So we did. Then there's Ebenezer Isaacs."

"Heavens!" ejaculated Elisabeth—"what a name! It can't be his real name surely? Not in a place like High Fitchet."

"I'll bet it is," replied Catherine. "And so will you when you clap eyes on him. And quite a character, believe me. Wants seeing to be really believed. Tons of 'boodle'. City magnate. Chairman of 'Amalgamated Industrials'. *And* a bachelor, my pet. Quite a chance for you, if you set your little cap at the appropriate angle and trim it as only you can. He isn't a day older than sixty-five."

Elisabeth, remembering Catherine's own essay into matrimony, thought that this was by way of a dirty crack and hitting just a wee bit below the belt. But Catherine Poulton prattled on.

"There are a lot more to come. We've quite a house full—I can tell you. Alfred Lillywhite—his wife Myra, he's a fellow director of Daddy's in timber—you've heard of the people, I'm certain. Anglo-Swedish Timber Combine. Gregory Copplestone—*the* Doctor Copplestone—conductor of the famous Orpheus Orchestra—and his wife, Lydia. At least, mother swears it's famous. Personally—I've never heard of it."

Elisabeth cut in. "Copplestone! Well, of all the extraordinary things! Now that *is* a coincidence! The Copplestones are cousins of the Grenvilles, something like the way we're cousins of yours. Mr. Medlicott and I were actually discussing it on the journey down here."

"Well, cousins or not—Gregory Copplestone's here, my dear, with his wife Lydia, and there's nothing you can do about it." She continued almost laconically. "Then there's another family—people Mummie met at her hôtel in the summer. When she was staying at Looe in Cornwall. Charles and May Stansfield with son, Guy. The old boy's in flour ('ur,' my dear). The boy's about my age. Haven't seen much of them yet—haven't had a chance. They blew in by car only about half an hour before you did. Nice little bus, too. That's about the bundle, I fancy. No—I've forgotten darling Quentin's contingent. No less than three authentic 'lovelies'. Any one of whom would cheerfully consign the other two to the stake or something with boiling oil in it. Quentin's collected them during the past year in various—probably questionable, if the truth is known—hunting-grounds. Their names are Ann Waverley, Virginia Proud and Clarice Irving. Ann and Virginia are blondes—Clarice Irving's a brunette. Quentin evidently believes there's safety in numbers. What he'll probably discover before very long is that there's a darned sight more safety in a judicious exodus. There you are, my dear Elisabeth, that's the complete record of the High Fitchet Christmas personnel in this present year of disgrace."

Catherine surveyed her finger-tips with an air of complacent satisfaction. Elisabeth looked round the bedroom.

"I suppose," she said demurely, "that I'd better be dolling myself up for the evening 'eats'."

"Well and truly spoken, Miss Grenville," returned the daughter of the house—"but I should have told you. Owing to the fog and the various late arrivals, dinner's not till half-past seven."

2

As Elisabeth came down to dinner a few minutes before half-past seven, on this most memorable Christmas Eve, she ran into Catherine again—this time in the company of husband Henry. Henry did his quick little shamble towards her and greeted her effusively. His wiry hair stood up straighter than ever as a result of the effort, and his pale face coloured. Elisabeth hoped that the colour was induced more by pleasure at seeing her than by an inroad of his customary nervousness.

As they went into dinner, following on various introductions, she just found time to whisper to Catherine: "Quentin's got three 'lovelies' here, you say—what about Nick? Isn't his quiver reasonably full, likewise?"

Catherine regarded her with mock indignation. "That's good, I must say—coming from you of all people. If you knew all, you'd think yourself highly honoured, I can tell you."

For the second time that day, Elisabeth was perilously close to blushing. But she recovered herself to answer carelessly: "O.K., Catherine, my girl, if that's the way it is, I can take it."

When they had all drifted in and Lady Wynyard had performed all the introductions that either hadn't been or had been left over and Elisabeth found time to sort things out a little, she discovered that Catherine's smoke held a certain amount of fire and that she was seated between Nick Wynyard and—of all other people—Mr. Medlicott! But Nick's place was still empty.

Elisabeth thought matters over and was by no means displeased at the arrangement as she saw it. All the same—why wasn't Nick Wynyard in his place? If Catherine's hint had solid foundation, he wasn't making too good a start. Elisabeth glanced at her hostess and at once saw that Lady Wynyard was troubled. She kept giving quick, anxious looks towards Nick's seat and then at the chair at the head of the table. Then Elisabeth realized that Sir John Wynyard also was absent. But suddenly Lady Wynyard's face cleared and to Elisabeth's relief, both Sir John and Nick Wynyard bustled in. Sir John waved to her so she evidently was the only person he hadn't yet encountered. Nick came to her eagerly, pressed her hand hard, murmured "You look wonderful—my dear," and Elisabeth sat down to dinner feeling deliciously hungry, delightfully interested and radiantly happy.

Nick began to talk to her—almost confidentially—he made the most conventional remarks sound terribly important—and then Elisabeth formed the judgment—a trifle belatedly perhaps—that it would be shockingly bad form on her part to neglect entirely her other dinner companion, the faithful Mr. Medlicott.

3

But the solicitor from Aldersford was a long way from gaiety. His first mood of geniality which Elisabeth had known in the train had been shed and he still retained that mantle of depression . . . almost one might say of fear . . . that Elisabeth had first noticed about him when they had been coming away from Colbury station. Now, while dinner was being served, he responded to Elisabeth's advances with a complete absence of enthusiasm and seemed to hold precisely similar emotions towards those of his fair neighbour on the other side of him—Virginia Proud. One of Quentin Wynyard's pair of blondes.

In between Nick's sallies, Elisabeth was able to take stock of the house-party generally. The introductions before dinner had been a little hurried through sheer force of circumstance, and she was now, as she sat at dinner, in a much better position to do a spot of sizing-up than had been the case formerly. Nick, she thought, looked a trifle fine-drawn. He was dark, with a strong, powerful, sinewy frame. Raven-black hair, dark eyes, white even teeth, made him look less English perhaps than his younger brother Quentin did. Yes. Elisabeth summed up, Mr. Medlicott was right. Nick Wynyard takes after his mother—there were no two opinions with regard to that. He must be a Heseltine.

On the left of Sir John Wynyard, at the head of the table, sat Cynthia Comfit and Alfred Lillywhite. Elisabeth remembered that, according to cousin Catherine's version, the gentleman had co-interests with her host in a timber combine. He was fat and gross and folded his hands over his paunch. Elisabeth had already seen him doing it on several occasions. It was her first impression of Lillywhite—Alfred. He was eating now—and putting all his weight into every tackle. He had pale-blue eyes and was to himself, Elisabeth concluded, as Abelard had been to Heloise or Beatrice to Dante.

Elisabeth looked across at his wife who was seated at the other end of the table on the left of Lady Wynyard. Myra was thin and scraggy with rather prominent teeth. Elisabeth mused on the mysteries of matrimony. It was clear to her that Alfred was no judge of human beauty—except, probably, when he was shaving.

Cynthia Comfit, in Catherine's words, was 'the faded spouse' of Percival, the novelist. She was a tiny, mouse-like creature whose brown eyes were constantly seeking her husband and flickering and fluttering at him in unconcealed admiration and pride of possession. At every utterance he made, Cynthia smiled beatifically and then nodded her head in instant and immediate approval.

Next to Alfred Lillywhite came May Stansfield, her son Guy, and Virginia Proud. Charles Stansfield sat opposite to Alfred Lillywhite. 'The flour man', thought Miss Grenville as she endeavoured to place him. Charles Stansfield was tiny and insignificant—just a wee bit like the renowned Hawley Harvey Crippen. May Stansfield, his wife, as so often happens in marital pairings, was cast in absolutely the reverse mould and had, in a previous existence, been something, probably, of the eagle variety. She over-towered the little flour manufacturer as a daughter of Anak might have over-towered Tom Thumb. Guy, the son, seemed commonplace enough—but cheerful, affable, and although a trifle boisterous, perhaps, quite a good compromise on the part of his parents. Might have been a great deal worse, commented Elisabeth, as she stole a glance at Guy Stansfield and listened to Nick Wynyard.

Virginia Proud was next for Elisabeth's assessment. Just a pretty blonde with blue eyes. Not too much above the neck, if I'm any judge, was Elisabeth's assessment of her and then, before she could do any more stock-taking, she realized that her hostess was talking about Nick and almost *to* Nick.

"Oh yes," she heard Lady Wynyard say as she looked along the table, "Nick won the long jump at the 'Varsity Sports. Pretty comfortably, too. Beat the Cambridge first string by over a couple of feet. And talking of these things always makes me think of the very first time I ever went to 'Queen's'. My father took me, he was dead keen on 'Rugger', you see."

Myra Lillywhite leant forward to listen, but Alfred, of the paunch and complete self-satisfaction, plugged away stolidly at his sole.

"It was in 1908," went on Lady Wynyard. "Oh dear—I'm giving my age away. Or as good as. It was a positively atrocious afternoon. The whole of West Kensington was choked with a real London pea-souper. We don't get 'em like that now—even John will agree with me on that. When the ball went in the air, you just couldn't see it at all. Well, Daddy and I were rooting for Oxford and I know that I got tremendously excited about almost everything that happened. And then there occurred one of the most *remarkable* incidents."

Lady Wynyard's voice was so clear and emphatic that almost everybody at the dinner-table had ceased conversation and was listening to her. Probably everybody with the exception of Alfred Lillywhite. *Sole à bonne femme* took precedence of 'Varsity Rugger with him or any other variety—come to that! Lady Wynyard continued.

"'Grunt' Macleod, one of the Cambridge 'three's' and a Scottish cap, my dears, even at that age, 'dropped' from about half-way. It was an enormous kick! Really prodigious! Wanted to be seen to be believed. Well—the ball absolutely went up into the air—and completely disappeared! Just ballooned into the black blanket of fog and vanished! Absolutely! Until somebody in the crowd somewhere threw it back on to the field. Said it had dropped down into them out of what should have been the blue but was much more like the black. Now the real point about all that is this. Which is why I'm telling you the story. Not a soul knew if Macleod had dropped a goal—or not. I was simply palpitating with fear that he had! Because it would have put the 'Tabs' in the lead. And what *do* you think happened? The poor referee, of course, was just like all the rest of us. Hadn't the least idea of where the ball had gone. So he actually went up to 'Grunt' and said 'how was that "Grunt?"' and that *dear* boy said instantly, 'no goal'. Never hesitated. Wasn't it *sweet* of him? And did I breathe again!"

There were sounds of approval of Lady Wynyard's story, and Nick murmured "good for you, Mother. I don't know what I should have done without you."

And Elisabeth knew at that moment, for the second time, that Mr. Medlicott had been right. Nick was the son of Pamela Heseltine much more than of his father, John Wynyard.

"And who won the game eventually, Lady Wynyard?" The enquirer was Guy Stansfield.

"It was a draw—my dear boy! So you see what a difference it made—that dear Cambridge boy doing what he did. No matter how long I live, I shall always think of it as the *noblest* deed I ever saw."

Lady Wynyard fluttered in her seat and as Elisabeth caught Sir John's eye, he winked at her gracelessly. Mr. Medlicott was heard to remark to Virginia Proud.

"No, I'm no sportsman. I can't play outdoor games, I'm afraid. I can't even swim. Not a stroke." Previously he had seemed grave and preoccupied.

Nick uttered a whispered eulogy of his mother—concluding with "but all her geese are swans, you know. Never forget that when you're dealing with my mother."

Elisabeth smiled back at him and attempted to round off her little self-imposed task of fellow-guest stock-taking. Seated on Lady Wynyard's right the languid and drooping Percival Comfit certainly lived up to Catherine's description of him. Elisabeth fell to the smooth temptation of summing him up quickly. A poseur, she said to herself, if ever I've seen one. Such of his conversation as floated down to her struck her as precious, studied, and almost invariably artificial. He is full of, she decided, the affectation of the dilettante.

The next pair for her assessment, were the strange-looking man who had been introduced to Elisabeth as Ebenezer Isaacs and Miss Amy Wynyard. Genius, thought Miss Grenville, sheer genius on Lady Wynyard's part to have placed these two people together. Aunt Amy was a 'character' without a doubt. Determined, forceful and absolutely positive that her opinion of everything and everybody could be the only one which was correct, which mattered one whit, and which counted. At this moment she was laying down the law to Isaacs as Elisabeth looked across at her and he was listening both patiently and submissively.

Ebenezer Isaacs himself merits some small pen-picture. To Elisabeth Grenville he looked like a tall edition of Benjamin Disraeli, sometime Earl of Beaconsfield. His face was shrewd and calculating—but Ebenezer had something else besides. He possessed a strange, whimsical, almost fantastic brand of humour which manifested itself in unusual phrase and odd, bizarre descriptions and utterances. He was thin and spare and his oily-looking hair was beginning to say good-bye to him, but his frame was powerful and he would be an ugly customer to anybody who forgot his manners and spoke out of his turn.

Between Nick Wynyard and Percival Comfit was the dark, attractive Clarice Irving—rather nice, thought Elisabeth. Beyond Amy Wynyard—and here Elizabeth had a shock. For she was looking at the brown-bearded man she had seen in the train-corridor when she had sat in conversation with Mr. Medlicott. And then the lightning struck again, for shock number one was immediately followed by shock number two. Elisabeth realized that when she had been introduced to the company just before dinner, in some unaccountable way she must have missed the brown-bearded man and his wife, who was sitting five seats from him and on the right hand of their host. Also—she concluded—they must be Gregory Copplestone and Lydia Copplestone. Of all the unfortunate double coincidences. Copplestone looked distinguished and his wife both ordinary and distinctly *passée*—the usual state of affairs of matrimony at this stage, reflected Miss Grenville.

She would have to make their acquaintance quicker than soon—if only for the firmer future of the famous family feud. Three guests only now remained for her to think about. Or rather—two guests and Quentin Wynyard. Quentin, of course, she knew—and she wasn't sure whether she quite liked him or not. The girl to whom he appeared to be paying the more attention must be his other blonde—Ann Waverley. She was certainly a dainty little thing, full of charm and rather suggestive of the fragility of Dresden china. The pick of the Tempting Trio, decided Elisabeth.

The other girl, however, between Quentin and Gregory Copplestone, was of a very different type—and quite definitely an entirely different proposition for anybody to sum up. Of course, thought Elisabeth—this must be Helen Repton, the girl from the 'Yard'. Elisabeth studied her with unusual interest. She knew that Sir Giles Repton, Helen's father, was a fellow of History at Oxford, and that Helen herself had taken an Economics degree at London. Her face was the face of an intellectual—she was tallish, slender, with dark-brown hair and dark-blue eyes, and it was easy to see that Helen Repton would count in most places where there was any serious counting to be done. "I like her," concluded Elisabeth with definite conviction. "I'll get together with her, if I can. We ought to get on jolly well together, she and I."

But Nick was talking to her again, and she was scarcely answering—and Mr. Medlicott on her other side was still in the doldrums.

"Tell me, Nick," said Elisabeth turning to him—"who *is* that Mr. Isaacs? Next to your Aunt Amy. And why is he here?"

Elisabeth said that because she really wanted to ask about Gregory Copplestone without making it *too* obvious and the Gregory inquiry could come later.

4

"Isaacs?" said Nick—"Ebenezer Isaacs? He's big business—young lady. I'll say! Chairman of the big industrial combine that's just been formed. As a result of a recent merger on the grand scale. Now known as 'Amalgamated Industrials'. That's who he is." Nick grinned at her as he imparted the information. "Any the wiser?"

Elisabeth shook her head. "Afraid not. But you didn't tell me the other thing I asked you. You've only told me 'who'. *Why* is he here? I might be wiser if you told me that."

Nick frowned heavily at his Burgundy. "I'm dashed if I know *why* he's here. And that's the absolute truth. But the Guvnor's got a sound reason tucked away somewhere. That's a safe bet. He never does anything without a darned good reason. You can rest assured on that."

"I see." Elisabeth thought Nick seemed annoyed or even angry at not having been taken into his father's confidence, so she deftly shifted the searchlight from Ebenezer Isaacs on to Gregory Copplestone. "I'm sorry if I seem inordinately curious—but here's another one for you. Who's Gregory Copplestone and why's *he* here?"

All the time, of course, she knew what Catherine had told her, but she satisfied her conscience by persuading herself that all she wanted to do was just to compare notes.

Nick grimaced at her. "Why must you shove 'em down on my blind side? You've actually picked on the very two people in the whole room that I know least about. Copplestone? All I know is that he's a music wallah of sorts that Mother picked up at the B.B.C. in the early part of the year when she snaffled a studio invitation. Mother's like Quentin in that respect, you know. Always collecting people and carefully placing them in the snugness of her bosom. One day one of 'em'll turn out the wrong way and think she's Cleopatra. Sorry I can't supply any further details, Elisabeth."

"H'm! Rather interesting," commented that lady, "and I'll tell you why. You listen." She recounted the story of the Grenville-Copplestone tradition and recited the two lines of doggerel which Mr. Medlicott had revived for her in the train.

"I say—that's interesting," returned Nick Wynyard, "you two being chucked together like this. So entirely unexpectedly too. May even yet be a case of seconds out of the ring. What did the blighter say at your intro? How did he take it? Did his eyes flash black hate and vengeance?"

"That's the funny part about it, Nick. We haven't been introduced yet. He and his wife weren't here when your Mother was doing the honours. So we missed each other. Goodness knows where they'd got to."

"Necking some short ones, I expect, if the truth's known. Most of these musical johnnies have got a marvellous swallowing capacity."

"And here's something else," went on Elisabeth, "I *believe* I saw him in the corridor of the train as I came down. Just for a fleeting second as he passed by. But his wife wasn't with him. He had another man there."

Nick seemed more than ordinarily interested. "Oh—who was that? Anybody here now?"

"I couldn't tell. I didn't see the second man at all. He went by much too quickly."

Nick Wynyard gave her a sidelong glance. "Strange," he remarked, "still—there you are—Mother hooks up with some rummy blighters at odd times and divers intervals. One of these days we shall invite a couple of cut-throats for Christmas and a trio of fire-raisers for the August Bank-Holiday week. It's quite on the cards—the way she goes to work."

The dinner ran to its close. Mr. Medlicott seemed to perk up a bit and actually found time to address an occasional remark, not only to Elisabeth, but also to Virginia Proud.

"I'll tell you what," said Nick leaning over Elisabeth, "as soon as I get a reasonable chance after dinner, I'll get you introduced to Comrade Copplestone. I know you're dying to get stuck into him. All the canons of crime, scandal, etiquette and foul play are simply screaming for you two to get together."

"That's O.K. with me," replied Elisabeth demurely.

As she went into the lounge with the other members of her sex, she noticed Sir John Wynyard beckon to Mr. Medlicott and draw him gravely to one side. Had Elisabeth known it—the sands of the High Fitchet hour-glass were fast running down!

5

Lady Wynyard dispensed coffee in the lounge with the dignity of Boadicea and informed her guests that they were due for an "old-fashioned Christmas" in many respects. Not only was a special choir of carol-singers from the Parish Church due at 10 o'clock—"including the dear Vicar himself," but the waits, "all the way from Montfichet," were supplying a midnight performance for their particular benefit.

Elisabeth tried to attach herself to Helen Repton, but Quentin's trio of 'lovelies' bore down upon her and held her for their own until the moment came for the men to join the ladies. When the masculine invasion occurred, Elisabeth noticed that neither Sir John Wynyard nor Mr. Medlicott was present—and then, with a certain soupçon of pique, that Nick was also an absentee. This last mentioned state of affairs, however, was not destined to last long and her annoyance therefore was but short-lived. Nick came in. He was pale—certainly a good deal paler than was customary. And there was something else, too, showing on his face—besides the pallor. It wasn't worry or anxiety, Elisabeth concluded—it was something more like agitation. Yes—something had certainly upset Nicholas Wynyard since dinner. He made over to her and by an adroit body-swerve was just successful in heading off young Guy Stansfield.

"Where's Daddy?" asked Lady Wynyard, "can't he remember it's Christmas, just for once?"

Nick pulled himself together. He smiled across at his mother. "I think he's stopping behind—for a few words with his old china—Medlicott."

"China?" echoed Lady Wynyard vaguely, "I don't—"

"Skip it, Mother," said Nick genially, and seated himself between Elisabeth and Ann Waverley. No sooner, however, had he taken his seat than he jumped up again. "Oh—Lord—I'm forgetting. I promised to introduce you to the Copplestones." He bent over and took Elisabeth's hand. "I'll be squire of dames and lead you over to them. They're down the other end—with the Comfits and the Lillywhites. Waiting, probably, to exhibit their prowess at 'Postman's Knock'—or something. Come with me and we'll do the job properly. Everybody will exclaim—entirely spontaneously, as we make our way down the room—what a handsome couple."

Elisabeth gave him a playful push but took the extended hand nevertheless and allowed Nick to pilot her to the far end of the lounge. Gregory Copplestone and his wife were standing hard by the french windows. They had been talking to the Lillywhites, but the latter pair had moved away to join the Comfits. Nick went alongside with no overture.

"Oh—Doctor Copplestone," he said, "you and I have met. But here's a little lady whom you seem to have missed in your round of introductions and who's quite anxious to make your acquaintance."

Elisabeth saw a brown-bearded, foreign-looking man facing her. Trim of limb and shoulder—neatly made—but with inquisitively-boring eyes which looked all round you and through you at one central focusing. She saw, and acutely noticed, his fingers, before she really noticed his hands. The fingers were fat and podgy—and he was unable, it seemed, to keep them still or under control for any reasonable period of time. When he spoke, however, his voice, although on the punctilious side, was quite pleasant and well-modulated.

"Really?" he said, with a kind of exotic urbanity; "well now, that's very charming of her. It causes me to wonder. Who am I to merit so ... er ... delightful ... an ... er ... incident?"

"That's just what I said," responded Nick gracelessly; "but at any rate, here she is. My cousin, Miss Elisabeth Grenville ... Doctor Gregory Copplestone and Mrs. Copplestone."

The Doctor of Music bowed and his wife favoured Elisabeth with an expansive smile—both dental and labial. As Nick pronounced her surname, Elisabeth waited for what she considered would be the almost inevitable reaction. But to her surprise, none was forthcoming.

"My name then, Doctor Copplestone," she remarked a little nervously, "doesn't cause you anything in the nature of trepidation?" She smiled. The smile was intended as a pill-gilder.

Copplestone frowned heavily. He looked at his worst—no mean effort, either.

"Why—my dear young lady—I don't follow—should it?"

"Of course it should," she replied impulsively. But if Elisabeth didn't catch the look of wariness that flashed into Copplestone's eyes immediately after receipt of her reply, Nick most certainly did, and although he couldn't be absolutely positive on the second point, unless his eyes had deceived him, Mrs. Copplestone had made an abortive attempt to catch her husband by the coat-sleeve.

But Copplestone—undaunted—took another step into the unknown. "But why? I must confess that you have me at a disadvantage."

Nick was watching the exchanges closely now. There was something indefinable here which he couldn't understand. Elisabeth's next reply was ready enough but the words didn't come as quickly or anything like as pat from her as they had previously.

"Surely you're aware of the traditional feud which exists or which, at least, is said to exist, between our two families? Why, it's been going on for generations and generations." Nick was stark certain now that Copplestone (well out of his depth) was deliberately finessing and playing for time.

"Oh—that," he responded, "oh dear, dear—you did catch me on one leg, didn't you? I see—so that's what you meant? Of course—of course. And I didn't cotton on. Ha-ha! That's certainly one against me. Just fancy my not remembering that." The laugh which Gregory Copplestone produced as his accompaniment was a feeble specimen of its kind. Nick Wynyard decided to cut in.

"You've forgotten the old couplet, Doctor Copplestone. Most remiss on your part. Almost as well known to all of us here as the old Guy Fawkes rhyme. 'Guy, Guy, Guy—stick him up high!' But perhaps you've outgrown all that sort of thing."

Copplestone, the conductor of the famous Orpheus Orchestra, was by now even more uncomfortable. Two guns were more than he could stand. It wouldn't have taken a Philo Vance to see that.

"I'm afraid that must be the explanation," he remarked stiffly; "after all, there does come a time to most of us when we put away childish things."

Lydia Copplestone nodded an emphatic approval of her husband's remark. She had stood motionless since she had attempted to catch Gregory Copplestone's sleeve. But this was a line that she could not follow.

"Childish?" countered Elisabeth with mock indignation—"this isn't anything childish—believe me. It's cost the lives of many Copplestones and quite a few Grenvilles in its time. And very likely the tally isn't ended yet."

Copplestone shook off his mood and became the conventionally courteous again. He smiled cordially as he stroked his beard. "My dear young lady, God forbid! Let you and I, at any rate, live in charity together and set a good example not only to our ancestors but also to posterity."

He bowed to her gracefully. It was certainly his best and happiest moment. Nick decided that the moment had come for extrication. He was afraid that Lydia Copplestone was about to bow, too, and that would be more than he could stand. He whisked Elisabeth away on the pretext of a Bridge Four.

"Well, well, well," said the lady; "and what do you know about that?"

Nick fringed on profanity. "What a heel! His manners are about on a par with his standard of English. But I'll tell you what, Lillibet—the blighter knew no more about your family vendetta than my Guv'nor knows the form for the Grand National. Not so much. Which is just a *leetle* unusual—not to say disturbing. The mater certainly does find 'em! I'll hand it to her. Any old muck can trot in to High Fitchet on high-days and holidays and break bread with the Wynyards. Hullo, there's Dad and old Medlicott. They've come back. The parley's o'er. On with the dance! Or, as an alternative, let's come and have a chin-wag with Helen Repton. For Helen, let me tell you, is one out of the top drawer. I love every hair of her head."

Elisabeth was conscious of a tiny stab of jealousy at this tribute of admiration, but she riposted cheerfully. "And let me tell you, Nick Wynyard, that the drawer you *come out of* doesn't matter two hoots. It's the drawer you *get into*, before the curtains are drawn, that counts."

"Very sage," said Nick shaking his head solemnly but with his eyes full of good humour, "very Confucius! I shall have to pass that on—to certain lewd fellows of the baser sort—in one of my brighter moments. Come on, let's pin Helen down before we're deafened by 'Good King Wenceslas' from the village choir led by the short-sighted, red-nosed Vicar. And not conducted by the august Doctor Copplestone."

Nick and Elisabeth walked over to Helen Repton. "You two girls," he said . . . "and at a time like this. . . ."

<h2 style="text-align:center">6</h2>

Well—this book is not a detailed account of Christmas at High Fitchet. Christmas Eve passed, Christmas Day itself came and went. Boxing Day was a real cracker-jack of fun and games, and when the various members of the house-party crept to their respective beds in the early hours of the morning which immediately follows the Feast of Stephen, nothing of any consequence had happened—on the surface at least—to mar the general enjoyment of both the Wynyard family and their guests.

Elisabeth, as she lay in bed, gloriously tired, during those few rather exquisite moments which customarily precede the first lull to slumber, admitted to herself that it had been well worth while making the journey to High Fitchet for the acceptance of Catherine's invitation. It had really been the best Christmas in her recollection. There wasn't any doubt about it. Everybody had been kind to her. Sir John and Lady Wynyard had been most solicitous and equally charming. Quentin, Henry and Catherine, and, of course, Nick had been the very best of companions, and her comfort, happiness and entertainment, their first consideration.

The Comfits had proved quite attractive on closer acquaintance, the Lillywhites had become much more human, and even the Copplestones had done their best as people of infinite goodwill. The three girls whom Quentin had so courageously and perhaps indiscreetly invited, had been sociable and the reverse of 'catty'. Helen Repton had proved as charming as she undoubtedly was intelligent. The Stansfields had surprised Elisabeth by their complete willingness to fit in with everything and everybody. Amy Wynyard was the thoroughly good sort which Catherine had predicted, when you got to know her, and the somewhat mysterious Mr. Isaacs had actually emerged from his shell and proved one of the outstanding successes of the party by his skilful emulation of some of the highest skill usually associated with Messrs. Maskelyne and Devant.

"Jolly good," murmured Elisabeth sleepily to herself as she pulled the blankets up to her chin and curled her toes round the hot-water bottle—except perhaps the man she had met first of all—Mr. Medlicott. Now, poor old Medlicott had never once seemed to emerge from his shell and hit the high spots. All the time he had seemed unhappy, restless and generally under a cloud. Elisabeth had done her best to help him 'snap out of it', but on the whole the response she had received had been far from overwhelming. True, he had approached her late on the evening that had just passed with a request for the loan of the book she had promised to him—the *Summa* of St. Thomas Aquinas. When he had made the request she had run upstairs to her room to get it for him, with a feeling of intense pleasure that there was something which she could do for him. He had seemed so down in the mouth that she was delighted to have the opportunity of doing even a small favour like that for him. And he had appeared so terribly grateful to her when she had handed the book to him.

Poor old Medlicott, thought Elisabeth Grenville to herself in those moments when sleep was so ecstatically close to her. It's been a wizard Christmas—and it isn't over yet—there are still some more days to come! She was right. But had she been aware of what those days were destined to bring forth, Elisabeth would have been engulfed in horror.

CHAPTER III

1

SIR John Wynyard was found dead in his own writing-room on the morning of the 27th of December—to be more precise, about five hours after Elisabeth had drifted off to sleep. He was discovered by Carter, one of the maids, a few minutes before eight o'clock. His body was slumped across the writing-table with one shoulder—the right—strangely hunched, as though the dead man in his last moments had made an ineffective attempt to twist himself in some way.

But there were certain strange features connected with the circumstances of his death. In front of him were a fountain-pen, some sheets of High Fitchet note-paper and an open Bible. He was wearing, over his pyjamas, a dressing-gown with the girdle tied in front, and on his feet was a pair of ordinary bedroom slippers. The electric fire in his writing-room had been turned on and the left-hand corner of the dressing-gown had been burned by it, as also had been the outside of Sir John's left leg. The dead man's face was contorted as though he had been seized by a sudden spasm of some kind. His farewell to this mortal life had evidently been to the accompaniment of a certain amount of pain.

Carter, the maid who had found the tragedy, behaved much more sensibly and intelligently than might, perhaps, have been expected from a girl of her class and upbringing. She closed the door behind her quietly and with an entire absence of fuss made a straight track upstairs to find 'Mr. Nicholas'. She would spare her mistress, she decided, as much as she reasonably could. Carter went quietly and unemotionally to Nick's bedroom and tapped on the door. Three taps were necessary before she evoked response. At the third tap she heard Nick's voice.

"If that's a cup of tea—bring it in. Nothing could be more welcome."

Carter replied calmly: "No, Mr. Nicholas. It's not Morley—it's me—Carter. I'm sorry to disturb you, sir, but may I speak to you for a moment?"

"Hang on," said Nick, "while I chuck something on."

She heard him get out of bed and walk round the room. He came to the door but didn't open it. Carter knew what he was doing. He was putting on his dressing-gown. He had taken it off the hook on the inside of the bedroom door. She waited outside the door patiently. When Nick did open the door, he came and stood just outside.

"Now, what's all the trouble, Carter? It's not like you to come all over mysterious at this time in the morning without good cause and just reason. What is it? Frozen pipes?"

Carter shook her head in denial of the suggestion. "I'm sorry, Mr. Nicholas, to wake you up like this but it's your father. The master. I think he's been taken ill—or something. I'd like you to come downstairs to him."

Nick gave her a sharp, searching glance. "But . . . er . . . where's my mother? Isn't she with him? Did she send you to fetch me?"

"No, sir. It's not like that. The master's in his own room—downstairs. I want you to come, please, sir."

Nick looked a little bewildered before shaking his head. "There's something here I don't understand. All right. You'd better take me along to him, Carter."

"Yes, Mr. Nicholas. That's what I thought. That's why I came up to fetch you."

Nick suffered the girl to lead him downstairs. Fortunately, the coast was clear and they met nobody on the way. When they reached the door of the writing-room, Carter stepped to one side.

"Will you go in first, sir," she said, and retaining the quietude which had characterized her from the beginning she reached out and turned the handle of the door in order to give him entrance. Nick slipped into the room. His face blanched at what he saw. "Good God, Carter," he said, "he's—he's—" He went quickly to the body of his father and bent down over it. "He's not ill, Carter," he exclaimed, "he's dead! Look at him." Carter nodded—blankly. "Yes, sir. That's what I thought, sir. Why I came for you at once, sir." She stopped as though she had no more words and then added: "It's awful, sir, isn't it? To go like that with nobody with him—and at a time like this?" The tears in Nick's eyes were brushed away. But the maid—now that she had done her duty and her own crisis over—let hers flow unrestrainedly. Nick took a firm grip on himself and pulled himself together.

"Don't tell my mother . . . yet . . . Carter. Don't tell a soul. Leave it in my hands. I'll 'phone for Doctor Beddington to come over at once. That's all I can do, and that's too late." He motioned the maid to stand back by the door and sat down himself to use the telephone. "I'm sorry, Doctor"—she heard him say eventually—"but this is Nick Wynyard speaking."

2

Doctor Beddington arrived at High Fitchet within half an hour. He was a fussy, pompous little man with purplish-looking cheeks and a normally red nose which the bleak morning and chill wind had made even redder.

As arranged, Nick met his car a few yards from the house and took him into his father's writing-room quite unobtrusively. The time was just half-past eight and all the other inhabitants of High Fitchet, with the exception of the staff, were still seeking the seclusion granted by their respective bedrooms. Doctor Beddington lifted his eyebrows when Nick met him.

"What's the precise trouble, Mr. Wynyard? I understand it's the Dad. Nothing *too* serious, I hope? He seemed fairly fit when I last ran the rule over him."

Nick took the questions with ill grace. "Serious enough," he replied bluntly; "he's dead."

Even Beddington's pomposity broke down at the news.

"Good God! You can't mean that. Why—it's—"

"I can mean it, Doctor—and I do mean it. But have a look for yourself, Doctor. He's in here."

Nick opened the door of the writing-room, dismissed the faithful Carter, whom he had instructed to stand by, with a curt nod, and took Doctor Beddington in. The latter surrendered the position almost at once.

"Dear . . . dear . . . this is bad," he clucked; "yes . . . you're right. . . . I'm sorry to say . . . things couldn't be worse. Sir John's gone . . . poor fellow. Been dead some few hours by the look of him. Dear . . . dear . . . this is a bad business and no mistake. At this season of the year, too. My sympathy! To your dear Mother as well. And to all the family. Of course . . . of course. But those things go without saying."

Nick, who was thinking it a great pity that they hadn't, began to manifest certain signs of impatience.

"But, Doctor Beddington . . . please! I'm at a loss. At a complete loss. What did my father die of?"

There was no hesitation about Beddington's reply. "Oh—heart. No doubt about that, my boy. You knew he had a heart, didn't you? I've treated him for it for some little time now. Angina! He must have felt bad in the night and come down here. But I'm profoundly shocked all the same. I thought he'd hang on for a good many years yet. I had no idea that things had got so bad with him as they undoubtedly must have done. Nasty thing—angina. Very, very nasty."

"In that case, then, you won't need a P.M.?"

"Oh—no. Not at all. Don't you worry with regard to that. I can certify. No trouble at all."

He held out his hand for Nick Wynyard to take. "You know how I feel. My dear fellow! There's nothing I can possibly do."

Doctor Beddington went back to his car. He passed Quentin on the way. As the car moved off, the snow began to fall. And it lay where it fell—thick and heavy.

3

Lady Wynyard bore up splendidly after she had got over the first sharp shock of the bad tidings. And almost the first thing she said to her assembled guests was "Now, my dear people, I know exactly how you're all feeling. You think that you should make yourselves scarce at the first possible moment and leave us to the privacy of our sorrow. I know! That's how I should feel if the circumstances could be reversed. But please understand—I don't want you all to go away to-day. Please don't think of it. Especially in this dreadful weather. To-morrow—perhaps, some of you can slip away quietly—but please stay here with us to-day. I beg of you to. It will both help me and please me. You do understand, don't you?"

In these circumstances the guests acceded to the wishes of their hostess and stayed on at High Fitchet. The snow continued to fall until the early afternoon, when a quick change came over the weather and the sun decided to come out.

After lunch had been served, Lady Wynyard said to her guests: "Please do just what you feel you'd like to do. And don't worry about me in any way. John would have wished it. So don't be miserable and 'mopy'—it won't do him or me the slightest good."

Thus it was that in accordance with the expressed wishes of their hostess, several members of the house-party elected to take advantage of the weather change and go out into the open air. They were well rewarded for the decision. The sun was shining brilliantly and the country round High Fitchet had been magically transformed into a miniature Switzerland.

Helen Repton, Elisabeth and the three girls of Quentin's choice went for a five-mile walk to Swanley Bottom and back. Some of the elder persons of the party walked through Montfichet Woods as far as the Old Mill and saw the residence of the Comfits. Others chose to stay in the lounge, to read amongst other things, and it was getting on for five o'clock when they all reassembled. As tea was being handed round, Elisabeth noticed that Mr. Medlicott was absent. She had formed the habit of looking for him and spotted his absence as soon as she sat down. She mentioned it to Nick as he held out a tray of *petits fours* for her acceptance. Nick, however, was inclined to pay scant attention to the solicitor's absence.

"He's in his room, I expect. Perhaps he went out during the afternoon in one of the walking parties and didn't get back till a bit late. Bet your life he'll be down in a minute or two."

Nick was quiet and subdued—his father's death had affected him deeply. In his undemonstrative way, he had been strongly attached to his father and he had always clung to the belief (although he couldn't have said exactly why) that Sir John would live to the allotted span and even many years beyond. His death at this time and in such a manner, had been a shattering blow to Nick, and Elisabeth knew that he would feel it as a greater wound than either Catherine or Quentin would.

But the minutes passed and tea went on and five o'clock became half-past and there was still no sign of Walter Medlicott.

4

While Elisabeth was still thinking on these lines, Helen Repton came over and sat beside her.

"This is all pretty dreadful, isn't it?" remarked Helen, "to think that we're here as guests—and they're making us frightfully welcome too—when we know what's happened and the sorrow it must mean for all of them. I take off my bonnet to Lady Wynyard for the way she's faced her trouble. She's an absolute brick."

"I know," nodded Elisabeth in affirmation. "I agree, Helen, with all you've just said. And, by the way, had you noticed that Mr. Medlicott hasn't turned up for tea?"

"No—I hadn't," replied Helen, looking round the room. "Perhaps he's busy—as Sir John's solicitor, you know. There must be an awful lot of matters to do with the estate that will require clearing up."

"I don't think it's that," said Elisabeth; "at any rate Nick didn't seem to know anything about it just now when I spoke to him. He seemed more inclined to think that Mr. Medlicott had gone out for a walk somewhere and been delayed over getting back."

As she spoke, Nick came over to them. "Friend Medlicott's still absent from parade, I notice," he said quietly. "I hope he's all right."

"In what way do you mean?" enquired Helen, with arched eyebrows.

"Well," explained Nick, almost apologetically, "this morning's affair of poor old Dad gets on your mind and makes you apprehensive of ordinary things. You know what I mean, Helen. One tragedy comes right up alongside you and shakes you up and then something eminently simple occurs—and you find yourself, subconsciously perhaps, half-anticipating another. Just because your mind's got shoved into that groove."

"I see what you mean. And I suppose what you say's very largely true. But do you think it's serious enough," she spoke doubtfully, "for anybody to do anything?"

"How, Helen?"

"Well—surely he may be in his room. May have settled down for an after-dinner nap, perhaps, and fallen asleep so heavily that he hasn't awakened at the usual time. We were all pretty late getting to bed this morning, you know—and then there was the shock of your father's death on top of that."

"Yes. I expect there'll be a simple explanation before very long. All the same, I think I'll pop upstairs and make sure. It's Elisabeth's fault," he said with the ghost of a smile; "it was she who started me worrying over the old boy's absence."

"I think it would be a good idea, Nick," confirmed Helen Repton; "after all, Mr. Medlicott's not a particularly young man—and I understand he was a very old friend of your father's. The shock of his death may have upset him very much. Much more than anybody expected. Go and see how he is."

Nick nodded and walked quietly from the room.

"What train do you intend to catch in the morning, Elisabeth?"

"There's one a little after ten. I thought I'd try for it."

"I'll come with you, if I may. You won't come back for the funeral, of course?"

Elisabeth shook her head. "I don't think so, Helen. The women of the Grenville family usually give funerals a miss."

"I agree. It's a man's job. Well—it's a cliché—but truly—in the midst of life we are in death. Look—there's Nick come back. It doesn't look to me as though he's the bearer of good news. What do you think?"

Nick came up to them and shook his head. "He's not in his bedroom. I've established that fact."

"You're sure?" interrogated Helen, "you went in?"

"Even so, lady! I rapped on the bedroom door twice and got no answer. Then I tried the door to see if it were fastened or not. It was unbolted. So I went in. Nobody there. His suitcase is there and all his personal impedimenta seem to be in place so he evidently hasn't hopped off for good. Question remains, therefore, where the hell has the old bird got to?" Helen Repton looked thoughtful at Nick's news. "I think we ought to try to find out when he was last seen and by whom. He was at lunch with us, wasn't he?"

"Oh yes," declared Elisabeth; "I distinctly remember seeing him at lunch. I had excellent reason to. He sat next to me. Actually he spoke to me several times. Said how he liked boiling hot soup on cold days like to-day was. Said it *couldn't* be too hot for him. He was present at lunch all right."

Nick took up Helen's suggestion. He gestured to Quentin who happened to be passing close by. "I say, Quentin," he remarked in low tones, "Medlicott's not here. Hasn't shown up for tea at all. Miss Grenville pointed it out to me a few moments ago. Can you find out—quietly, mind you, no fuss—if anybody has happened to see him since lunch or has any idea what his intentions were? When you speak to the mater, do it as tactfully as you know how. If you hear anything, come back and report." Quentin looked a little startled. "That's funny! I hadn't spotted that he wasn't here. And I usually give an eye all round at meal-times. Too much on my mind, I suppose. I say—something else funny—I hadn't thought of that, either—you're Sir Nicholas now, aren't you? Just occurred to me. Hadn't struck me before. But I'll see what I can find out about Medlicott." Nick looked down at the two girls, but Quentin's remarks had, evidently, not reached their ears. Nick felt relieved. Somehow, what Quentin had said had annoyed him. He watched his younger brother as he mingled with the various groups of people. First the Comfits with Aunt Amy and the senior Stansfields. Then to Mr. Isaacs and the Lillywhites—then to Virginia, Clarice and Ann who were with Guy Stansfield and lastly to the group which comprised his mother, his sister and brother-in-law, and the two Copplestones. Quentin stayed for a few minutes in conversation with each group. He seemed to linger longest, Nick thought, with Ebenezer Isaacs and the two Lillywhites.

Nick bent down again to Elisabeth and Helen. "I asked Quentin to find out what he could with regard to Medlicott's movements after lunch. He's been sounding the different people. He's coming back. I rather fancy that he's been able to pick up something."

As he finished speaking, Quentin came up again. He pulled Nick to one side. "I haven't got much," he said, "but one definite thing I have managed to ferret out. From Isaacs of all people. According to him—Medlicott intended to go for a walk after lunch. Apparently what decided him was the sun coming out when it did. Same as with most of us."

Quentin spoke quietly to his brother, but this time both Helen and Elisabeth heard what he said.

"Did Medlicott actually tell Isaacs he was going for this walk?"

Quentin shook his head at his brother's question. "From what I can gather—not exactly. Isaacs says that—'he sort of hinted at it.'"

"He's no idea then, where Medlicott intended to go? In what direction?"

"No. I'm afraid he hasn't."

"H'm," commented Nick, "doesn't get us very far."

"Oh—but it helps," contributed Helen Repton; "assuming that Mr. Medlicott acted upon what he hinted to Mr. Isaacs, it does give us something like a starting-point. We're fairly safe in assuming, I think, that he did go for a walk."

"In a way I suppose it does," conceded Nick; "but the point is, or so it seems to me, what do we do now? In other words, where do we go from here?"

Helen looked at her watch. "It's just on ten minutes to six. Which, reckoning on normal time arrangements, means that Mr. Medlicott's nearly an hour and a half behind time. Now, how is he with regard to time as a rule? Can anybody tell me?"

Quentin shrugged his shoulders. Nick said simply, "Search me."

"Well, I think perhaps I can answer that question." The contribution came from Elisabeth. "Of course," she continued, "it relates only to since we've been staying down here. But he's *always* been punctual for meals. You can take that from me."

"Indicating?" queried Nick.

"How do you mean?" asked Helen.

"What I said just now, lady. Where do we go from here? It all comes back to that. In other words, are we to regard Medlicott's present absence as serious enough to warrant any special action on our part?"

There was a silence as the four members of the party thought over Nick's problem and weighed the 'pros' and 'cons'. The first of them to arrive at a conclusion was Helen Repton.

"Well," she said, "I've thought it all out carefully, I've tried to see all the probable—and even all the *possible* angles—and I keep coming back to the same conviction. I think, seeing what time it is and bearing in mind what Elisabeth has told us, that we ought to send search-parties out to look for him."

"You do?" said Quentin.

"I do. This is a fairly secluded spot—there are no houses particularly near—and if he went out for a walk in the country and was taken ill or slipped even and had an accident—well—the poor man's probably lying there now. And finding him quickly might mean all the difference between life and death."

Nick nodded. "I'm inclined to think you're right, Helen—hanged if I don't."

"Good. Now whom can you send, Nick? You can't very well ask any of the girls—although I'm perfectly willing to make one."

Nick looked round at the company. "Myself, Quentin, Guy Stansfield, Comfit, I should think would go—he knows the locality, you Helen—that's only five, isn't it?"

"How about the servants? Any of them available?"

"Can't very well ask old Cresswell—he's well over sixty—oh—there's Gooch—the chauffeur. He'd make one. That gives us six. Isaacs, Stansfield senior, Copplestone, Lillywhite—don't see any of them filling the bill."

"That's all right, then," said Helen emphatically; "six should do the job amply. Now what are the probable directions that a man like Mr. Medlicott would most likely take—if he did set out for a walk? In other words, let's organize the job as well as we can in the circumstances."

"Well," replied Nick. "I suppose there are three main routes a man might take starting from here. Out to Swanley Bottom, through the woods and round by Montfichet Mill and thirdly the walk across the fields past Blackforge Cottage to Sturton Ridge."

"We'll try to cover those three, then. Now, we've got three locals—you, Quentin, and Mr. Comfit—oh and Gooch—that's four—I forgot him—and two foreigners, Guy Stansfield and me. I suggest that Comfit and, say, Guy Stansfield cover the woods walk—because that's the way to Comfit's house and he probably knows it in the dark, Quentin and Gooch take the Swanley Bottom route, and you and I try the walk to Sturton Ridge. But they're only my suggestions. You can pick the bones out of all or any—I shan't mind. Now tell me what you think."

Nick shook his head. "No complaints—I can find no fault with your suggestions, Helen. I'm certain we couldn't better them. You can count me in on all that. I don't know what Quentin thinks."

He turned to his brother interrogatively. Quentin seemed to be weighing up the various points of the situation.

"I suppose that's as good an arrangement as any," he replied eventually, "but I was thinking of Gooch. We shall be two locals. Whereas in each of the other pairs there's only one. Oh—I forgot—there are four locals—we can't distribute them equally. No—seeing that's how it is, I've no objection. That will be O.K. by me."

"Right-o, then, Quentin. Get Comfit and Guy Stansfield over here. I'll tell them what we've arranged. Otherwise—keep it under your hat."

"I'll get ready, then," said Helen Repton, rising from her seat by Elisabeth, "because time's precious. Where shall I meet you, Nick?"

"We'll get away from the back of the house. Meet me by the big garage. What should we take, do you think?"

"Torches, some brandy, perhaps, in a flask—and I've another idea, Nick. Rather bright, too, I think."

"Spill it, St. Bernard," said Nick quietly. Despite his forced raillery his face looked worn and tired. The worry of the day, culminating as it had, was beginning to tell on him at last.

"Bicycles, Nick," said Helen. "Are there any spare push-bikes knocking about in the house?"

"How come?"

"If each pair that went out took a cycle—one of the two could wheel it—and if they *did* come across trouble, it would be a much quicker way of getting help. I was visualizing a broken limb, say. You know how brittle bones are in this weather and on this ground. And Mr. Medlicott's not exactly a young man. If he were lying anywhere like that, poor old chap, one of the pair could stay with him while the other rode back on the bike for suitable transport. You'd need transport for anything like a broken leg."

"Yes—that's pretty sound, Helen. I agree. Quentin's got a bike, there's an old one of mine knocking about somewhere and also, I'm pretty certain, an ancient one of Catherine's in the garage somewhere. You pop off and powder your nose—I'll pass the word to Comfit and

Stansfield—and meet you as arranged in a quarter of an hour from now. And God send we're on a wild-goose chase."

"I echo those sentiments," returned Helen, "but something in my bones tells me we're not."

5

Percival Comfit, looking by no means in love with life or even himself, which was unusual, set out with Guy Stansfield—the latter wheeling Catherine's bicycle. Nick and Quentin had fixed it that all parties, assuming they drew blank, should return to High Fitchet by 7.30 at the latest. They all left the house at 6.20 which meant an outward journey of thirty-five minutes before they turned for home. Helen agreed with them that this time should be ample for their joint purpose, as she argued that Medlicott, at his age, would not have intended to walk too far abroad at this time of the year. Comfit and young Stansfield took the path through Montfichet Woods, and naturally Comfit knew it, as Helen had insisted, like the palm of his hand.

Quentin and Gooch, the chauffeur, went the way of Swanley Bottom—Quentin Wynyard in charge of his own bicycle and Gooch walking a few paces behind him. The track here wasn't too good as but a small portion of it was on the level. The grass was hard and spiky and rimed with hoar frost, and now that the sun had departed on his mission of waking the brethren beneath the western sky, it was freezing hard again. The ground was treacherous and slippery in many places. Neither of the two men spoke much. Quentin was thinking how little it took to devastate a man's personal outlook, and Gooch was contemplating one or two of the niceties of what he always called to himself—'class distinction'. He had learnt the phrase during his service in the Air Force.

Nick and Helen took to the open fields that led to Sturton Ridge. To reach the ridge by way of Blackforge Cottage, it would be necessary for them to cross two open, fields each broad and wide, make their way through Welford Spinney and then traverse a third field which was usually under broad beans. Keeping close to the shelter of the hedgerow all the time. Nick pushed his ancient cycle as he walked at Helen's side. As he manipulated the five-barred gate which yielded entrance to the first field, he said laconically, "ground's thunderin' hard, Helen—but it might be worse, I suppose, from our point of view. It *might* be liquid mud. Most of the autumn it usually is."

"I came prepared, Nick. I've been in these parts before. Shod myself becomingly—so harbour no anxiety on my account."

"From some points of view," continued Nick, "we twain have the worst walk of the three. Certainly the one a good-class and discriminating Polar bear would have elevated his paw for! Ugh—what a wind to whistle round the ear-tips. Now—you cover the left-hand side of the path and I'll watch the right."

"I chose this route specially," said Helen quietly. Nick was genuinely surprised at the remark.

"You did? And why may I ask?"

"Because I think if poor old Medlicott *has* come to grief in any way—this is most likely the neighbourhood in which he'll be."

Nick turned his bike-handles and cocked his head over in his companion's direction. "Do I hear the 'Yard' talking? Please expound, my dear Holmes."

"Well—isn't it rather obvious? Think of what happened after lunch this afternoon. The girls—including yours truly—walked to Swanley Bottom and back. *We* saw nothing of Mr. Medlicott. Another party went along to the Comfit's place, through Montfichet Woods and round by the old mill. *They* saw nothing of him. They're both facts—not conjecture. I needn't say any more, need I?"

"It depends. I see the line of your reasoning, of course, but we don't know for certain *when* Medlicott went out, do we? *That* point seems to me to be a very vital factor. All the same—I'll hand it to you, Helen. Your argument's sound enough. The balance of probability is well on your side, I admit." He caught at her sleeve. "Turn left a little here, Helen. There's a rough field-path. We're within a short distance of the gate into the second field. Hard by the pond."

Helen looked ahead into the darkness. Nick, considerately, gave her a flash from the torch to help her. After she had taken a few more steps she could see the gate which divided the two fields of which Nick had just spoken. The snow was lying fairly thickly here.

"Where's the pond exactly?" she asked. "I don't want to go slap into it. A bit too cold for my liking."

"O.K. I'll guide you when we get to it. Here's the gate I spoke of. And I think we can safely say there's no sign of Medlicott in Field Number One. He'd have been bound in the afternoon to have kept to the path that we took. That was clear—you agree?"

Helen Repton nodded. "I saw nothing at all to excite any suspicion—and I watched everywhere carefully."

Nick pulled up the big wooden latch of the heavy gate that led to the second field and then brought back the gate itself for her to pass through.

"Wait on the other side, until I've shut the gate again," he said. "I expect you're aware that it's a crime to leave gates open in the country."

Within a few seconds he joined her in the second field. "Now keep by me, Helen. Pretty close. The pond's just to the left here. I'll flash the torch on to it."

Nick Wynyard suited the action to the word and as he did so, both he and Helen Repton uttered an exclamation.

"What's that?"

There was a dark shape lying near the edge of the pond. Helen started to run towards it and Nick Wynyard followed her.

6

When they came to the body, their worst fears became stark reality. Walter Medlicott lay there in front of them. He lay with his head in water and thin ice, on his face, but with his feet and legs well clear. His hands were gloved, but his hat had fallen off his head to lie near the edge of the pond. Nick bent down to look at him more closely. Then he glanced up at Helen.

"He's dead, poor chap. I'm certain of that. And I should say he's been dead some time. Though what the heck he's doing with his mouth in the water like that, I'm hanged if I know. See what I mean?"

He demonstrated to her the attitude in which Medlicott was lying. The afternoon sun had melted the ice to a degree of thinness and the water showed plainly round the edges of the pond.

"I should think," said Helen slowly, "that he must have had a seizure of some kind. But even then"—she knitted her brows—"I can't quite understand why he should have dragged himself to the water like this. No"—she shook her head at him decisively—"there's something here that, as far as I can see, doesn't make sense."

Nick made no reply. She glanced at him sharply. "What is it, Nick? You're—"

"I'm all right. But two in a day has rather knocked the stuffing out of me. It's rather more than I can stand. My father—and now this. It's made me all—sorry, partner—carry on, Helen."

As he spoke he noticed that she had turned Medlicott's body over on to its back and was staring at it with a curious look in her eyes.

"Look, Nick," she said—and her voice held fear—"don't you think his head and neck look strange? They look—as though they've been injured in some way. Look! Don't you agree?"

Nick peered down at the dead man. "Yes," he said, "I see what you mean. I think you're right. You didn't notice it when he was lying on his face. Which makes it infinitely more puzzling than ever."

He straightened himself and stood up. "Well—what do we do, comrade? No use us jabbering to each other out here. That won't get us anywhere. Shall I ride back or would you rather I stayed here? It won't be particularly pleasant for you—to be left alone."

"You go on the bike, Nick. I don't mind staying here. I shall be all right. You know the way better than I do and you'll be a good deal quicker, naturally. When you get there, and have fixed up the transport, ring for a Doctor at once. Tell him as much as we know. But no more. I mean—don't elaborate." She stopped and then continued: "You know what I'm thinking, don't you, Nick?"

"No—perhaps I don't. What?"

"Well—I'm not too sure that it won't be a matter for the Police."

He stared at her and then saw the implication. "Good God, Helen—you don't think *that*, surely?"

"I'm afraid I do, Nick," she replied quietly. "And I'm not sure we shouldn't leave the body here. Just as it is. Still—we'll chance that."

CHAPTER IV

1

HALF an hour after the body of Mr. Medlicott had been conveyed back to High Fitchet, Doctor Beddington had announced that the cause of death was a broken neck. The solicitor had not died from exposure—he had suffered a fatal injury. Though how this injury had been sustained, there was not the slightest evidence to show. In addition to the fracture of the vertebrae there was also a strange wound running from the area of the right temple, almost to the lobe of the right ear. It resembled in some ways a deep gash from a knife—or perhaps a deep scratch would be a more precise description. Doctor Beddington was quite frank about it all. He had both Nick and Quentin Wynyard with him when he announced the result of his findings.

"You must report this to the police," he said, "there's really no alternative."

"I take it from that remark, you suspect foul play," said Nick remembering the words of Helen Repton when he and she had found the body by the pond.

Doctor Beddington shrugged his shoulders. "Let me say—that I'm not satisfied, Sir Nicholas—and leave it at that. Will you 'phone? I should suggest Colbury rather than Montfichet. I think that's the better idea."

"All right," replied Nick, turning on his heel, "needs must I suppose—bearing in mind what you say."

By this time the other search-parties had returned to the house.

2

Shortly after eight o'clock, Sergeant Arnold arrived from Colbury accompanied by a uniformed constable. Nick and Quentin received him in the billiard-room. A board had been placed on the top of the table and Medlicott's body placed across the board. Between them, the brothers gave the Sergeant the full story of what had occurred, from the time that the body of Sir John Wynyard had been discovered by the maid Carter, almost exactly twelve hours previously.

The Sergeant had recourse to his note-book on several occasions and made copious notes.

"There are two matters, sir, which I should like attended to before we proceed any farther. One—I should like to 'phone the Divisional Surgeon, Doctor Buck—and the other—I regret insisting on this—I can't allow any of your guests to go away from here, certainly not for the time being."

"That's all right. They're all here, as a matter of fact. None of them intended to leave until to-morrow at the earliest and you can 'phone at once for your official doctor. There's a 'phone in the main hall."

Arnold, a broad-shouldered, florid-faced, stout man, motioned to the constable. "Get Dr. Buck over here at once, Gifford. Tell him I'm here and the matter's urgent."

"Very good, Sergeant."

Constable Gifford departed to find the hall telephone and deliver his message. Arnold went over and looked at the body.

"Nothing been touched, I suppose?" he asked.

"Nothing," replied Nick; "all Miss Repton and I did after we found him was to lift the body into a car and bring it straight back into here."

"Better if you'd left it where you found it," said Arnold rather curtly.

"Perhaps it would," returned Nick with spirit, "but don't forget it was dark *and* we didn't know for certain how the man had died. Neither Miss Repton nor I have professional medical knowledge. He might have had a sudden illness for all we knew. He hadn't a placard on his chest with 'I've been murdered—don't touch me' on it, in big letters."

Arnold grunted at Nick's defensive explanation and made no attempt to follow up his previous remark. Gifford came in at that moment. He addressed himself to Sergeant Arnold.

"Dr. Buck'll be here, Sergeant, as soon as he can make it. I told him the matter was extremely urgent."

Quentin made his first contribution for some little time. "Despite everything that's been already said I still want convincing that it's anything more than an accident of some kind."

"We shall soon know—or know *more*," declared the Sergeant. His tone was even curter than ever.

3

Dr. Buck, in the worst of tempers (he had just been about to settle down for a few hours in the bosom of his family), was quick to corroborate Dr. Beddington's opinion.

"Broken neck! And couldn't have done it himself. That's obvious to a blind man. Had a heavy blow of some kind, I should say. Probably from behind. Undoubtedly attacked by somebody—this wound on the face proves that—if any further proof were needed. Which it's not!" He turned and addressed the Sergeant. "Well—there's nothing more for me to do, I'm afraid. You've heard what I said. I'll leave the rest of the arrangements to you, Sergeant. Good night, gentlemen. I'm sorry you've landed into such a spot of bother."

Dr. Buck bustled out. Sergeant Arnold went over to the body again.

"Er—my guests, Sergeant," said Nick who had remained in the room, broaching the subject again, "and those remarks you made a short time ago—surely you don't think any of them has anything to do with this? A man found dead in a field—almost a mile from the house—a man who went out for a walk—unaccompanied—seems to me the idea's preposterous."

"That's as may be, sir," replied Arnold doggedly; "I don't know! *You* don't know! And until we find out a good bit more—well—I should like you to accept my ruling. It may be necessary for me to interview *all* the people in the house. Servants included. And now, if you don't mind, I should like to have a closer look at things."

The Divisional-Surgeon had removed Medlicott's overcoat, gloves, under-jacket, collar and tie. "First of all," said the Sergeant, "I'd like to take a dekko at the gentleman's pockets. After all—the idea *may* have been highway robbery."

"Very probably was, I should think," said Nick good-humouredly.

"Let's start with the overcoat." Sergeant Arnold pushed his fist into Medlicott's right-hand overcoat pocket and took out a handful of loose coins. "One shilling and fivepence halfpenny," he said pompously; "a sixpence, seven pennies and a threepenny piece and three ha'pennies. Don't look like robbery, sir."

"No—it's a big sum—I agree—for a thief to miss. Bad slip-up on his part."

Arnold was impervious to the shaft. He thrust his hand into the overcoat left-hand pocket. "Piece of paper," he commented; "feels a bit peculiar." He took it out and then opened his eyes wide at what he saw. "Here—take a dekko at this, sir. Something funny about this. I thought I was right from the beginning. There's a lot more in this case than meets the eye. This isn't an ordinary murder."

He moved one of the dead man's legs a little and spread the paper out on the board which covered the billiard-table. Nick looked at it with some eagerness. The sergeant's remarks had most certainly excited his curiosity. The words he read were as follows:

"Hand over the diamond—or else! Mr. Levi."

"Know the name, Mr. Wynyard?"

Nick shook his head.

"Suggests nothing to you?"

"No more than a pawnbroker."

"H'mph," grunted Sergeant Arnold.

But there was more to the communication than the mere words to stimulate his attention and his curiosity. Each of the words of the message had been cut from print of some kind and then been stuck on to an ordinary sheet of note-paper. The print looked to Nick like that of a newspaper.

"Damned peculiar, Sergeant," commented Nick. "I'll take back some of what I said. I think you're on to something. There *is* something extraordinary about the affair. You were right. Though what the heck it can all mean—well, I give it up."

"Let's have a look at his other pockets," said Sergeant Arnold. "May find something else." There was grim determination in his voice now. "Gold watch in top left-hand waistcoat-pocket. Still going. Nail file. Box of Swan vestas. No cigarettes or cigarette-case. Handkerchief. Small key-ring with three keys. Fountain-pen. Pouch containing tobacco—didn't smoke fags, apparently. Wallet in breast-pocket of coat. Let's see what that contains. A man usually keeps most of his important stuff in this sort of thing. At least that's been my experience."

Arnold opened the wallet. "Hallo—no money here! All gone. Bound to have had a note or two in his possession, I should have thought. Been pinched, probably. Now what about these papers? Hullo—I don't like the look of this. No—sir, I do not. Come over here, sir, will you?"

Arnold laid the leather wallet on the board at the side of the sheet of note-paper. "Take a dekko."

Nick looked at the contents of the wallet.

"See what I mean?" Arnold reiterated his point with a stab of his forefinger.

"You mean," queried Nick Wynyard, "that they appear to be in a certain amount of . . . shall we say . . . disorder?"

"Disorder!" almost snorted the Colbury sergeant; "I'll say—why, they're all higgledy-piggledy. Look at 'em, sir. It's as plain as a pikestaff what's happened. This wallet's been searched for something and the papers have been shoved back all anyhow." Arnold proceeded to demonstration. "Look here, Sir Nicholas. Envelopes with nothing in them. The contents have undoubtedly been taken out and not replaced. Some of the envelopes were lying what you'd call lengthways—others quite the reverse. No order or method at all. Just confusion everywhere.

"Look at this radio licence, for instance. Originally it had obviously been in the wallet—folded up. It's been unfolded by somebody to examine what it was, of course, and the person who unfolded it didn't trouble to fold it up in its original creases again. Just pushed it in anyhow. No—this wallet's been subjected to a pretty thorough search for something. No doubt about that. And obviously that something was the diamond that the murdered man had been ordered to hand over. That's how it goes. I think that point's pretty clear."

Arnold pursed his lips. Nick smiled inwardly. No doubt, he thought, Arnold could feel upon his shoulders the original mantle of M. Dupin.

"Is there anything of importance in the wallet?" he inquired meekly.

Arnold shook his head as he sorted out the contents. "No-o—I don't think so. Not what you'd call important. Mostly business letters. The radio licence I spoke of just now. Book of stamps, a few still left in it. One-two-three receipts for bills that have been recently paid. Identity card . . . nothing else much."

Arnold looked up suddenly. "Oh—there's one thing I've thought of. Perhaps you can help me, Sir Nicholas. Did the dead man—this Mr. Medlicott—wear a diamond ring, do you know?"

Nick thought over the question. "Well—perhaps I'm not too good at noticing matters of that kind. But I don't think so. I can't remember ever having seen him with one. During the last few days, that is. But you could ask some of the others. They might know. Try Miss Grenville—she might know."

Arnold looked up sharply. "Oh—and why should I ask her more than anybody else?"

More of the great detective stuff—evidently! Nick replied in dulcet tones "For two very good reasons—neither of them in the least degree sinister, I assure you. One—she sat next to him at all meals here— and two—she travelled down from town with him on Christmas Eve. They caught the same train."

But Arnold, undaunted by what he had heard, came again. "Oh— what's the association then, or relationship between them?"

Nick's tones became more dulcet. "Sorry, Sergeant. There's nothing to shy at. The late Mr. Medlicott and Miss Grenville merely found themselves occupying the same compartment from Liverpool Street."

Arnold grunted. But there was a distinct hint of dissatisfaction in the grunt and it was clear to Nick that the Sergeant was far from satisfied by the explanation that had been given to him and was already considering the possibility of clapping the bracelets on Elisabeth Grenville.

'Fatuous ass,' Nick thought to himself; 'how I'd love to plant a hefty kick right up your official pants.'

"Well," said Sergeant Arnold, changing the subject, "I'll see my man again and arrange for the removal of the body. I shall leave the questioning of the various people until the morning. It's late now and it's dark. Too dark for you to take me to the pond where you picked him up. That'll have to wait till the morning as well. But expect me over soon after breakfast to-morrow morning."

"O.K., Sergeant. If that suits you, it'll suit me. You know your own business best."

Nick left the billiard-room with the intention of finding his mother. As he went into the hall, he caught sight of Gooch, the chauffeur. The latter looked as though he were waiting for somebody. When Gooch spotted Nick Wynyard he went up to him.

"I'm sorry to bother you, Sir Nicholas—"

Nick winced inwardly at the mode of address from one of his late father's servants.

"—but could I have a word with you in private? It's urgent, sir."

"Well, Gooch, I'm afraid you can't at the moment. Won't it wait? I expect you've heard by now of the awful trouble we're in and, frankly, I've just about as much on my plate at the moment as I can stand. Whatever it is—can't it wait till the morning?"

"Well, sir—it's very important. There are no two ways about that. It concerns your dead father, sir—and in a manner of speaking, Mr. Medlicott, too—but I'll leave it till to-morrow morning, sir, if you wish it to be like that."

"Thanks, Gooch—if you will. I'd prefer it that way. I'll send for you. At the moment, as you can probably guess, there are things I simply *must* do at once."

"Very good, sir. I understand. To-morrow morning, then."

Gooch touched his forehead and made off. Nick watched him. He was of similar build to Nick, and as Nick watched his retreating figure he saw another vague, shadowy figure cross Gooch's path. But he paid scant attention to this, for he was thinking of what the chauffeur had said to him.

"Seemed worried—Gooch! Wonder what he's heard. Don't suppose he likes my suggestion of keeping him waiting. He'll have to get over that. I wonder if he heard the Guvnor tell Medlicott anything when they met on Christmas Eve. Anyhow, I'll listen to him later."

He crossed the lounge to look for his mother.

At eight o'clock on the following morning the body of John Gooch was found lying over the near front wheel of the large car in the main garage. From certain discoloured signs round his neck it was clear that death had been caused by strangulation. In the pocket of his overalls was found a printed message from Mr. Levi, similar in purport to that found on Medlicott.

CHAPTER V

1

THE Chief Constable of the County, realizing the deficiencies of the resources under his control and having interviewed both Sergeant Arnold and his inspector, Inspector Burrows, both of Colbury, showed the admirable temper of his discretion and wisely requested the immediate assistance of Scotland Yard. The Commissioner, Sir Austin Kemble, handed the case over to Chief-Detective-Inspector Andrew MacMorran, and the latter passed the word along to a certain gentleman by the name of Anthony Lotherington Bathurst, who, as it happened, already knew something about the High Fitchet murders through the agency of Helen Repton. For the reason that that lady had 'phoned to Anthony on the afternoon of the day that Gooch's body had been found in the garage, and given him the salient facts of the case.

"My dear Helen," Anthony had said to her over the telephone after he had listened to her story, "must you have crime with your Christmas Pudding and mix murder with your mince-pies?" He had listened carefully, however, to Helen Repton's story and when he had entrained for High Fitchet on the following morning in the company of Andrew MacMorran, he was able to give the latter a reasonably accurate picture of the various incidents that had occurred. Helen Repton met them on Colbury station platform.

"I've wangled a week's special leave," she confided, "so I'll be able to get in your way quite a lot. I hope you'll look pleased about it."

"Can't you give us some *good* news?" complained the Inspector, looking at his watch. "Half-past eleven! Just time for a coffee and—say—half an hour's chat. I asked for the police-car for twelve o'clock."

He indicated the station buffet. Anthony knew that resistance on his part would be useless, so he shrugged his shoulders at Helen behind MacMorran's back and they trooped in to face the worst. MacMorran ordered three cups of hot filth and drank from his while Anthony did telling work with a crude instrument made something in the shape of a spoon.

"I've given the Inspector a rough résumé of the affair as far as I know it, Helen," he said; "fill in the picture for him, will you?"

Helen Repton told MacMorran all that she knew and with attention to detail. Anthony listened with the keenest interest. When she had finished, MacMorran nodded two or three times, as though he were running over the various points in his mind while he had them comparatively fresh. Anthony turned to him.

"Any question, Andrew?"

"No. Not at the moment. I think I've got a fairly clear picture. You?"

"Yes. I'd like to ask Miss Repton one or two things. O.K.?"

"O.K. As long as you're not too long," added the Inspector.

"Tell me when I'm to stop."

"Right-o. Just before twelve. Go ahead."

"First of all, Helen," said Anthony, "Medlicott! Was he in the party as a guest—or on . . . say . . . a professional visit? Have you any clear idea as to that?"

"Presumably—as a guest. Not that I'd know for certain. But I've heard no suggestion to the contrary."

"Good. That's one point. Now—you and young Wynyard found him dead by the edge of a pond. At night. In the dark. I understand all about that. Now when the local police went over that ground—on the following morning I think you said—did they find anything that you and Wynyard weren't able to see?"

"Yes. I've made notes of that both for you and Inspector MacMorran. You shall have them when we get to the house. They found Medlicott's pipe—broken. It had some tobacco still in the bowl. It was found by the gate which leads into the field where the pond is."

"Interesting," commented MacMorran, "very interesting. *And* important."

"Anything else?" asked Anthony.

"Yes. Now how can I best describe it?" Helen puckered her brows. "It had been snowing during that morning. But the sun came out after lunch and some of the snow—where there was any to-ing and fro-ing to speak of—got melted. Out in the fields, though, most of it remained. And I believe that the local police came to the conclusion that there had been a struggle of some kind because the snow, in certain places, was all 'kicked up'. But the peculiar part about it was that this snow disturbance is in the *first* field, that is to say on the way to the gate that opens on to the field with the pond."

"Also interesting," remarked Anthony.

"It'll want looking at," declared MacMorran. "I can see that." He glanced at his watch. "Hurry up, you two, if you've got any more questions to ask and answer before we start moving. Time's getting short."

Anthony rubbed the ridge of his jaw with his fingers. "One more question, Helen, before we give way to this impatient beast who's swallowed his morning poison with such sangfroid—and a question of quite another colour. You're in a different position from the Inspector and me. You've been on the stage all the time. Sir John Wynyard has died, and his solicitor and his chauffeur have been subsequently eliminated. You've seen all the people here. I'm going to be very blunt. Suspect anybody? And it's not an idle question. I ask you because you already know how much I value your reactions."

Helen shook her head with strong emphasis. "Not a soul, Mr. Bathurst. And that's an absolute fact. I'm completely bewildered."

She stopped and Anthony saw from the look that showed on her face that a certain thought had come to her and was possessing her.

"What are you thinking of, Helen?" he asked her.

"One thing, Mr. Bathurst, and one thing only—I feel that Gooch, the chauffeur, was murdered by mistake."

Anthony looked grave. "By mistake? Go on from there, will you?"

"I believe he was mistaken for Nicholas Wynyard," replied Helen Repton.

2

MacMorran touched her on the arm. "We'll discuss that further in the car," he said. "You must have strong reason for thinking as you do. Come along. I can hear it striking twelve."

The police-car was ready and waiting for them in the station yard.

"Tell me, Helen," said Anthony as they started off, "I don't quite get this. Wasn't Gooch found dead in the garage?"

"Yes, I know. But there are one or two facts with regard to that which you ought to know. According to the doctor, Gooch was killed about six o'clock in the morning. Now both Nick and Quentin Wynyard say that Gooch was *never* at work in the garage as early as that. That's point number one. Whereas Nick himself *was*—occasionally."

"Why?" interjected Anthony quickly.

"Well—the explanation of that is this. When Nick came down from the 'Varsity in July, the Wynyards had no chauffeur. Couldn't get one for love or money. You know how difficult labour was. The previous man they had contracted T.B. and had to go into a sanatorium. So Nick, being more or less of a mechanical frame of mind, made the best of it and took over the job of keeping the cars in order, and he fairly frequently got up early, put on a suit of overalls and tinkered about in the garage before breakfast. Since Gooch was engaged, of course, he hasn't had to do it. Gooch was wearing overalls when he was killed." Anthony shook his head.

"But it was light—at any rate, not black-dark—and the murderer could see the man he was attacking, surely? I take it there'd be artificial light of some kind?"

Helen followed Anthony's example and shook her head. "Not if Gooch had been crouched over a car-wheel—say—and had his back to the murderer. Even with the electric light on. That's how it occurs to me. It's not impossible, is it?"

Anthony considered the point from other aspects. "Are the two men at all alike, Miss Repton?" asked MacMorran; "that's the point, surely, which should clinch the matter?"

"Not *unlike*," returned Helen. "They're of much the same height, of similar build, and their hair and complexion are pretty well the same colour. Of course, you wouldn't mistake the one for the other, if you saw their faces properly—I'm ready to admit that. But still—it's a theory—and I can't help feeling that I'm right."

Anthony put another question to her. "Gooch! How long has he been in the service of the Wynyards? Any idea?"

"I couldn't say exactly when they engaged him—but I know they haven't had him *very* long. He wasn't there in July, so it can't be more than a matter of three or four months."

"I see. How far to go now, Helen?"

Helen Repton looked out of the window. "Only a few minutes. You'll be able to see the house before long."

Anthony turned to the professional at his side. "What first, Andrew?"

"I thought of having a wor-r-d or two with the local Inspector chap—Burrows I fancy his name is—and then I thought we'd take a quick look-see at this field-pond where Medlicott was picked up. I feel that I'd like to go along there first. The Medlicott end seems to me to present more possibilities than the Gooch end. At the moment. What do you think yourself?"

Anthony shook his head again. "Apart from the facts, Andrew, my mind's a complete blank. I don't mind openly confessing it. The whole business seems haywire to me. Suggests a homicidal maniac running loose as much as anything. What a friend of mine once described as 'a religious sadist'—whatever that may be."

The car turned a corner and began to slow up. Anthony looked out and had his first sight of High Fitchet. It was a fine old mansion, built, he saw, on Tudor lines.

"By the way, Helen," he said as they prepared to alight, "when's the funeral of Sir John Wynyard?"

"It's fixed for Monday morning, at Montfichet church. The Wynyards have been buried there for some generations. Since the time of Sir Christopher."

"And the inquests?"

"Haven't heard. But there's one more thing I can tell you. By a rather strange sort of coincidence neither Mr. Medlicott nor poor Gooch had any near relatives. At least, so we gather. Medlicott was a bachelor and Gooch, apparently, an orphan."

"There's Inspector Burrows, I should say," said MacMorran with a gesture; "he promised to meet me here. In the doorway—see him? The big fellow."

He walked round to the driver of the car and spoke. "Don't go, driver. I shall probably want you again—in a matter of a few minutes, I expect."

"Very good, sir," replied the driver. "I'll turn the car round and be all ready for you."

3

Chief Det.-Inspector MacMorran, Inspector Burrows from Colbury, Anthony Bathurst and Helen Repton came in the car to the gate which opened on to the first field which Helen and Nick Wynyard had entered on the night of their search for the missing Medlicott.

"Leave the car here," said MacMorran, "we'll walk the rest. Take us the way you came, Miss Repton, will you?"

Helen nodded. The thaw had done all its work by now. All traces of snow had gone and the top of the grass was wet and slippery.

"Nick and I came through this gate. We took this same path. It's well defined, as you can see. I was on the left—he on the right. Nick was wheeling a bicycle on the grass at the side of the path. Just about where Inspector Burrows is walking now. That's as the lay-out was."

"Another question, Miss Repton." From MacMorran.

"When you split up into your three search-parties, which is what I understand roughly occurred, whose suggestion was it that you and Sir Nicholas should come this way?"

"Mine, Inspector. I thought that this was where we should find Mr. Medlicott—if he were to be found. For the reason that the two other routes which the other search-parties took had been used by members of the house-party during that afternoon."

"That is so," interjected Burrows. "I've checked up on that."

He was a big, beefy fellow, heavy and muscular with a deep voice and a trimly-kept dark moustache. Anthony put his weight in the sixteen-stone category.

They walked through the first field and came to within about a dozen yards of the second gate. Burrows said: "Now would you mind stopping just here? And step on to the grass, everybody, from the path. I want to explain something. That's it!"

MacMorran joined him on the right of the path and Helen and Anthony stood on the left-hand side. Burrows demonstrated.

"The snow had come down pretty thick that morning and although the afternoon sun had got to work on a lot of it, it hadn't touched it much round by this gate. But along the middle here"—Burrows pointed to the field-path—"it looked as though the snow generally had all been kicked up. For a distance of about twenty-five yards. The impression that I got when I saw it the next day was of a couple of fellows wrestling in it. This 'disturbed' track—as I'll call it—stopped about seven or eight yards from the gate itself."

Anthony turned to Helen. "When you salvaged the body, Miss Repton, from the edge of the pond, it was carried, of course, to a car waiting, say, where ours is waiting now? Yes?"

"Yes, Mr. Bathurst. As you say."

"Oh yes," continued Inspector Burrows, "we were able to form a fairly clear idea of most that had happened. We were able to build up the evidence of what Sir Nicholas Wynyard and Miss Repton here had told us they had done. The car-tyres left their impression near the first gate. Here and there were the prints of Mr. Wynyard's bicycle—beg pardon, Sir Nicholas's—and here and there we managed to pick up both Miss Repton's and Sir Nicholas's when they walked up."

"Did you trace Medlicott himself at all?" asked MacMorran. "Yes. Even that. But not many of his. It's more open and exposed in the field there than it is close to the gate, but we found three or four footprints that were undoubtedly his."

"Where did you find the pipe, Inspector?"

"Over there, Mr. Bathurst." Burrows pointed to a spot to the left of the gate.

"This side of the gate?"

"No. On the other side."

"Many people use this path?" asked MacMorran.

"I shouldn't think so," replied Burrows alter a slight pause. "A few, perhaps, on ordinary days and perhaps more at weekends—but taking into consideration that it was holiday time when the murder took place and seeing the sort of weather it was on that particular afternoon—I should say that those who were out here had it pretty much to themselves. They could have walked a mile and not met a soul."

"Now take us along to the pond," said MacMorran. "Right," replied Burrows. He swung the gate back to give them passage. "Now, Miss Repton, I'll hand over to you—you can tell your London friends what you found here."

Anthony recognized both the tone and the implication and decided to husband the memory. Helen re-capitulated the story that she had previously recounted to Anthony over the telephone. Then she went to the edge of the pond and demonstrated the exact position, and posture, in which Medlicott's body had been lying.

"Hat off and gloves on? That right?" asked MacMorran.

"Quite right, sir."

"And as was subsequently ascertained—a broken neck?"

"That's right, sir."

"What's the distance, Inspector Burrows," inquired Anthony, "from the pond to the gate?"

"Exactly fifteen yards, Mr. Bathurst."

"Any foot-tracks left between the gate and pond when you reached the scene?"

"No. You can see it's rough-ridged ground. It was too hard—too frozen—to take anything like satisfactory impressions."

"Thank you, Inspector."

MacMorran walked to the edge of the pond and looked at the water. "Where exactly was the dead man's hat, Miss Repton?"

Helen pointed. "There! Not more than three feet from the body."

"I see." MacMorran walked back to the others. "O.K., Inspector Burrows. That's the bundle as far as I'm concerned. I've seen all I want to see here for the time being. And remembering, too, the time that has elapsed since the body was found." He turned to Anthony. "Does that go for you, Mr. Bathurst?"

"That goes for me, Andrew," replied Anthony cheerfully. "But I expect I shall come again."

4

They returned to the waiting car. "I think a quick spot of lunch, Inspector, and then I'd like to see the garage where Gooch was killed and also the two bodies."

MacMorran settled himself. "Very good, chief," replied Burrows curtly.

"Miss Repton," Anthony leant over towards Helen Repton, "there was a wound, I think, on Medlicott's face? Am I right?"

Before he could answer, Inspector Burrows intervened. "I can help you there. Because I've paid a good deal of attention to that wound, I can assure you. It had been inflicted in a downward direction. It started near the right-hand temple and extended downwards. Went down the cheek and finished up underneath a lobe of the right ear. It was more of a laceration than anything else. A sort of deep scratch. But you can see it for yourself later on."

"A finger-nail?" suggested MacMorran.

"No," said Burrows. "Not in my opinion. Too deep, I should say, for an ordinary finger-nail scratch. More like, say, a scratch inflicted by . . . well . . . something like a pair of nail-scissors."

"Thank you, Inspector," said Anthony, "and I'd like to say how much I appreciate the care you've given to your answer. You've helped me considerably."

Burrows received the compliment with a set expression on his face.

"All the brains aren't in London—although most people seem to think so," he remarked.

"Good Lord—no!" said Anthony cheerfully.

Burrows turned and addressed MacMorran. "Will you interrogate all the people in the house? Is that your intention?"

"I think I'd like a few words with them. You know, Inspector, I like to *see* a person. It means so much more to you. A mere name, you know, doesn't convey a lot. But I shan't keep any of them overlong—unless—of course! You can let me glance over your own notes—if you'd be so good. I'd like to look them over before I start."

"You're welcome," said Burrows.

"Yes," continued MacMorran. "I think I'll make that my programme. After a spot of lunch, the garage, Gooch's body, Medlicott's body and then just a few words with the guests and perhaps with one or two of the staff. Oh—and the family—naturally. Mustn't leave them out."

"I see," said Burrows.

"And then," went on MacMorran, "perhaps a quick look round Medlicott's room and Gooch's room. I take it the chauffeur lived in the house?"

"Yes. He had a room in the servants' quarters. I don't think you'll find anything. I've been over all that ground pretty thoroughly."

"Good," said MacMorran, rubbing his hands, "and now I'm wondering what there'll be for lunch."

The local Inspector shot him a quick glance and then turned his head away. "You can't expect much," he replied, "in a house of sorrow."

"I don't," replied MacMorran blandly, "that's the reason why I was wondering."

5

The same four people stood in the garage. Burrows was slightly in front of the other three.

"Gooch was found lying over that wheel," demonstrated Burrows. "Doubled up."

"Who found him?" asked Anthony.

"A young gentleman named Stansfield. A Mr. Guy Stansfield. One of the guests staying in the house."

"What was *he* doing in the garage at that time of the morning?"

"He came—so he says—for a spanner. His car—or rather his father's—is in the small garage. He was intending to give it an overhaul. The small garage is about a hundred yards away from here." Burrows paused and then went on again. "Gooch was in a suit of overalls and had evidently been tinkering about with the car there. This was found in his right-hand pocket. You'll see it's marked 'Number Two'."

Burrows passed a creased sheet of notepaper to MacMorran. "Ah," remarked the latter, "so this is the second Levi message? I've been waiting to see this."

"Well," said Burrows, "and now that you have seen it?" MacMorran looked at him. "What's your point, Inspector?"

"Merely this," returned Burrows with a chuckle, "that I'll bet you aren't one whit the wiser."

MacMorran frowned at the sally. "Operative word—no doubt—is 'diamond'," he said eventually—and then—"this has been cut from newsprint."

"Quite so," said Burrows evenly.

MacMorran handed the sheet of note-paper to Anthony Bathurst. "Something in your special line, Mr. Bathurst."

"Thanks. Oh—yes—newsprint all right. *Daily Telegraph*."

"I agree," said MacMorran.

"And I," supplemented Burrows. "Must have needed patience," he added, "wading through the columns of the *Telegraph* twice to find the actual words he wanted."

"No," countered Anthony, "not *so* bad! Nothing like so tedious as you seem to imagine."

"How come?" responded Burrows with a rather supercilious turn of the head. "Afraid I don't get that."

"Any 'Rugger' report of fair length would supply in moderately close context five of the eight words—if not six."

"Five?" queried Burrows.

"I think five," Anthony came back. "'Hand'—'over'—'the'—'or'—'Mr.' Certainly those five. The sixth word I meant was 'else'. Not so certain perhaps as the other five—but quite a probable starter. Why—don't you find yourself in agreement with me, Inspector?"

"Hardly. How about your 'Mr.'?"

"Referee," replied Anthony laconically; "in the line directly beneath the names of the two fifteens. For example—'Referee—Mr. C. H. Gadney'. Surely, that's the normal lay-out?"

Burrows was a trifle disconcerted at Anthony's quick reply. He coughed. "May be."

"That leaves us with only Inspector MacMorran's operative word 'diamond' and 'Levi'. 'Diamond', I should say, can be found in most advertisement columns, I suggest, in respect of saleable commodities. Which fact again relieves our friend, the 'cutter-out', of anything in the nature of a tedious search for the words of his message. 'Levi' is our sole remainder. I agree—not so easy. In fact, nothing like so easy."

He peered at the word itself as it appeared pasted or gummed on to the sheet of notepaper.

"On second thoughts, gentlemen, I am not so sure that the third son of Jacob with whom we're so closely concerned *did* have his origin in the columns of the *Daily Telegraph*. That's mere surmise, however; it can be put to the test later."

Anthony smiled and gave the sheet of paper back to MacMorran. Burrows then produced the similar sheet which Sergeant Arnold of Colbury had taken from the overcoat pocket of Medlicott.

"Herewith," said Burrows, "the original of the species. Exhibit Medlicott. And as far as my ancient eyes are concerned the two pieces of paper are entirely similar to each other. Correct me, of course, if I'm wrong. I'm always open to learn."

MacMorran took the Medlicott message. Anthony drooped an eyelid in the direction of Helen Repton. Helen recognized it, and was thankful. MacMorran examined the message that had been found on Medlicott.

"Seems the same to me," was his one comment. "I agree with you, Inspector Burrows." He relayed it to Anthony.

"H'm," murmured the last-named. "*Telegraph* again all right, No doubt about that. Dear me—to what base uses! And I still harbour my original doubt with regard to the genesis of the 'Levi'. Definitely not the *Telegraph* in my humble judgment. Hullo, I'm competing with Inspector Burrows here, in the Humility Stakes. Mustn't let him think we're rivals."

His eyes twinkled as once again he passed the printed communication back to his professional colleague. Burrows shrugged his shoulders and turned again towards MacMorran.

"Mortuary?" he said curtly. "Or do you wish to—"

"Suits me," replied MacMorran, "mortuary! You needn't come, Miss Repton. You can remain here. We'll pick you up again here on our return. How long will it take us, Inspector Burrows?"

"Should be back," returned Burrows, looking at his watch, "in, say, forty minutes. Three-quarters of an hour at the outside."

"Very good, sir," said Helen Repton.

"I'll hunt up our driver again," declared Burrows, "and have the car brought round to the back for you."

"Thank you," responded MacMorran drily, "that'll be extremely nice of you."

6

The mortuary at Colbury was of modern type and had been zealously kept up-to-date by the intelligent and progressive administration of the County Borough responsible therefor. Thanks to the presence of Inspector Burrows in the party, but little time went to waste on introductions and preliminaries, and within a comparatively few minutes after entrance the three men concerned were looking at the dead body of John Gooch, recently employed as chauffeur by the late Sir John Wynyard.

"Quite a youngster," said Burrows as the sliding slab was pulled towards them. "Death by strangulation. Autopsy by Doctor Buck yesterday morning."

He pointed to the dead man's throat and neck. The blue-black discoloration was still evident.

"Rope," said Anthony; "I'm satisfied. I just wanted to make sure it wasn't a case of the murderer using bare hands. And the actual piece of rope, I've no doubt, will be found to be still in the Wynyard garage."

"Not a bad-looking kid," said Burrows; "been in the R.A.F. Cut above the average—you can see that. Came back to something—didn't he? Well, well—we never know."

MacMorran had been stroking his chin as he looked at the corpse. "What beats me," he said, "is motive."

"And me," retorted Burrows harshly, "you aren't the only one, Chief—so don't get too worried about it."

"It certainly is a puzzle," supplemented Anthony, "as to the connection between Sir John Wynyard's solicitor and Sir John Wynyard's chauffeur. And a dead Sir John, don't forget, in each instance. If we take your operative word 'diamond' as a step towards our motive explanation, Andrew, we find that although it may fit, perhaps, Medlicott, it certainly misses the mark with this poor devil, Gooch."

"Unless," cut in Burrows. His tone held just a soupçon of superiority.

"Unless what, Inspector?" asked Anthony equably.

"Unless Gooch took the diamond off Medlicott. You hadn't thought of that one, had you?" He smiled with something like satisfaction.

"Sorry, Inspector," said Anthony, "no can do! It leaks terribly. You're asking me to believe that Gooch served the 'Levi' on Medlicott and then 'X' followed suit and planted another 'Levi' on Gooch. Surely that would be too much of a coincidence?"

"I don't see your point at all," replied Burrows, "and once again you're omitting to consider what I think is a strong possibility. One that you simply must *not* shut your eyes to. Think again, man."

Anthony smiled. "Sorry—but you'll have to tell me. Sorry I'm so dense."

"Why, that Gooch and 'X' were in collusion. Working the job together. With a fifty-fifty cut each, in whatever the profits amounted to. Then came the old, old story. The thieves fell out. They had a row. Something blew up. Result—'X' outed Gooch and served him with the same medicine as they'd dished out to Medlicott. Anyhow, that's my story—and until you produce a better one I'm sticking to it." Burrows squared his shoulders.

"Right-o, Inspector. You may be correct, of course. But *I* don't think you are." He emphasized the words and then added: "It's that question of motive—you know."

In the meantime, MacMorran had walked over to look at the dead body of Walter Medlicott. He beckoned to the other two to come over.

"Thought we might kill two birds—er—er—h'm—look at the other poor chap while we're here."

"Broken neck." Burrows was curt again. "An injury . . . er . . . something like . . . er . . . that produced by judicial hanging."

Anthony became interested in what Burrows had just said. "Ah—friend Pierrepoint—eh? Ketch, Billington, Ellis and Co. And Gooch has died from the rope, too. But in not quite the same way. Now that's strange. Well—well. I wonder!" He turned to Burrows again. "Tell me, Inspector—the question has a *little* bearing on our recent difference of opinion—alibis! What sort of alibi did friend Gooch have for the murder of Medlicott? You must know—otherwise you wouldn't be suspecting him?"

Burrows shook his head and ignored the thrust contained in the last sentence. "Sorry. To repeat your words of a few moments ago—'no can do'. Gooch was never interrogated. There was scarcely time. When Arnold—that's my sergeant who was called here in the first instance to look at Medlicott—and I arrived on the morning after Medlicott's death, Gooch had already been killed. But I'll say this. Sir Nicholas Wynyard vouches for *some* of Gooch's time with regard to the murder of Medlicott. To be precise—the earlier portion of the afternoon. But, you observe, not the whole of it. On that account I can't give Gooch a clean sheet. No, I venture to say that when it's all added up and balanced, you won't find my version of the affair very far wrong. I flatter myself I can see through fog as well as most people."

"Gooch was killed," said Anthony deliberately, "because he knew something. That's where I differ from you, Inspector. But *what* he knew—I'm dashed if I know."

"We don't differ on that," replied Burrows obstinately. "I go a shade further than you do—that's all. I say that not only did he *know* something but he also *had* something. And that something is this diamond that's come into the picture. That's what they were cutting throats over."

"O.K." said MacMorran, "we'll be getting back to High Fitchet. No point in chin-wagging here for an hour. And on the way, Inspector, may I just glance over your notes in the car."

"As I said—certainly. And I'm pretty confident you won't want to interview *everybody*."

As he spoke, Inspector Burrows led the way back to the car. He was feeling distinctly better—there was no inferiority complex about him!

CHAPTER VII

1

MACMORRAN studiously examined the notes made previously by Inspector Burrows and his henchman, Sergeant Arnold. He saw, first of all, that Helen Repton was able to give entirely satisfactory alibis for Elisabeth Grenville, Ann Waverley, Virginia Proud and Clarice Irving. They had all been together on the walk to Swanley Bottom.

The second party which had travelled abroad on the afternoon of Medlicott's murder had consisted of Percival Comfit and his wife, Myra Lillywhite, Charles and May Stansfield and Henry Poulton, Catherine's husband. Each of the two parties had gone out "soon after lunch". (Burrows had timed it round about 2.30 p.m.) and returned round about "half-past four". Medlicott's death, as nearly as the medical evidence could place it, had occurred "between three and four o'clock". Thus MacMorran read the notes and passed their essentials on to Anthony. Which meant that unless something was radically wrong somewhere, eleven members of the house-party could be immediately eliminated from the area of suspicion.

"I'll see all the others," announced MacMorran firmly as the car reached High Fitchet again. "I've been long enough at this game to know that nothing's so informative as personal contact. No matter what else you may do. Yes, I'll have a word with all the others."

Burrows leant over to open the door of the car. "There's one thing, Chief, I feel obliged to point out. And that's this—that an alibi for the Medlicott murder might well be possessed by the person that murdered Gooch."

MacMorran smiled. "Here—here—what's that? I thought you suspected Gooch himself. Didn't you get that impression, Mr. Bathurst?"

"I did," replied Anthony, "but I think all the same that we've got to hand it to the Inspector. He doesn't miss much."

Burrows returned MacMorran's smile as they got out. He was feeling even better than ever.

2

MacMorran, who had made himself and his colleague known to the Wynyards before lunch, was very affable all the time. He saw the members of the family first—beginning naturally, with Lady Wynyard herself. He was sympathy itself. This interview was soon over. She could throw no light whatever on either murder. Coming so soon after the tragic death of her husband, she found it difficult even to think clearly and it all seemed to her like a horrible dream—unreal.

On the afternoon of Medlicott's death she had stayed indoors and occupied herself with various household tasks. Just to take her mind off things. Several people *must* have seen her. Two questions. The first from MacMorran.

"Did she know *anything* about a diamond or anybody named Levi?"

Lady Wynyard replied that she had diamonds of her own—some very valuable—but none could be called "the diamond" as far as she knew, and none was missing. She had no one diamond that stood out in any way from all the others. The name Levi was unknown to her—except, of course, in the passages of Holy Scripture. She seemed to remember that she had met it there somewhere. The second question came from Anthony.

"Was there any special significance, did she know, attached to Mr. Medlicott's invitation to High Fitchet for Christmas?" There could be no doubt that Lady Wynyard showed a certain hesitancy before she answered.

"Not—as far as I know," were the exact words of her reply. She spoke slowly. Anthony waited for her to amplify her answer. She had given him the impression that she was going to but subsequently, evidently, she had thought again and decided not to. He attacked again, therefore.

"You are just . . . a little doubtful . . . Lady Wynyard?"

"No. I wouldn't say that. But my husband was entirely responsible for Mr. Medlicott's invitation. That's all I know about it. He came and told me that he had invited him. And it was a belated invitation."

"How belated, Lady Wynyard?"

"The Saturday prior to Christmas Eve."

"And Sir John gave you no indication as to why he had extended this rather sudden invitation to Mr. Medlicott?"

"None at all, Mr. Bathurst. It was not my habit to question my husband's actions in any way. And, of course, he and Walter Medlicott were very old friends. Right from boyhood."

"Thank you, Lady Wynyard."

Anthony nodded to MacMorran. The interview terminated. Miss Wynyard was the next of the family on MacMorran's list.

"Enter the venerable battle-axe," thought Anthony at his first glance of her. She had, as Catherine had told Elisabeth Grenville, a forbidding exterior, most prominent in which was an aggressive high-bridged nose.

"I know nothing whatever, my dear policeman, and I'm old-fashioned enough to tell you to your face that I strongly resent being questioned by you or by any of your underlings."

MacMorran purred to her that he came to her merely suppliant. An earnest solicitor for her help and assistance.

"Stuff and nonsense," was the uncompromising reply, "you're grilling me. I'm not a congenital idiot. I was indoors all the afternoon—my sister-in-law will confirm that—and I'm an old woman. My arms aren't strong enough to wield a blunt instrument."

"A blunt instrument." MacMorran expressed surprise. "I wasn't aware that any—"

"Poppycock, my man! Everybody who isn't shot, stabbed or poisoned is killed by a blunt instrument. That's an absolute certainty. You know that as well as I do—so don't pretend to me, you don't.

I *loathe* hypocrisy—even in a policeman. The blunt instrument is with us from the cradle to the grave—like that Beveridge fellow's pink paper was supposed to be."

Aunt Amy twitched her combative nostrils at MacMorran and scored heavily on points all through the round.

"Another thing," she said fiercely. "I shouldn't go for an afternoon walk across the fields with a man! Not even with a man I knew like Mr. Medlicott. I happen to have been brought up properly and to know what decent conduct is. And not for any lack of opportunity, Mr. Policeman, in my early days. Oh, no, don't you think that. That was *far* from the case. I may be a survival—I may be a 'has-been'—but I'm certainly not a 'never-wasser'."

Aunt Amy was piling up the points. MacMorran let her go eventually, and as Anthony (appealed to) acquiesced immediately, they came to Nick Wynyard. Nick looked tired and anxious. Anthony could see that he had been through a tough time. He answered various questions from MacMorran with regard to the finding of Medlicott's body but could furnish no real information with regard to Levi or to any diamond that Medlicott might have had in his possession. When MacMorran tackled him with regard to his own alibi, he looked up and said something rather surprising.

"The murder of Gooch, my chauffeur, has come rather awkwardly for me I'm afraid—from that point of view. Because after lunch that afternoon—until I should say about half-past three—I was helping Gooch in the garage. The big car had been giving trouble for some days—it was the carburettor we discovered eventually—and we put it right that afternoon. If it hadn't been for that job, I should have gone out with the girls over to Swanley Bottom. You see," he added by way of explanation, "for some time before we engaged Gooch we had been without a chauffeur and I've learned to mess about with the cars quite a lot. And of course it's down my street, because I'm mechanical, and I rather like it." Nick smiled.

"I see," said MacMorran. He looked at the notes. "After half-past three, Sir Nicholas. That was the time you said, I think, that you stopped. What happened then?"

"Happened? Oh—I see what you mean. You mean after we finished the job. I went up to my room to clean up, naturally. I was in a pretty filthy mess. I don't know what Gooch did. Probably, much the same, I should imagine. But I had a bath, dressed and came down to tea. I had been in the lounge, I should think, about twenty minutes when the girls came back from their walk. They got in about a quarter of an hour before the Comfit party did."

MacMorran nodded to Anthony. The latter tried Nick Wynyard on the same lines as he had his mother. Concerning the Medlicott invitation.

"I don't think," said Nick, "that you need attach too much importance to that. You must always bear in mind that my father and Medlicott were very close friends. In addition to their business relationship. And Medlicott was a bachelor, don't forget. My father probably rang him up on an ordinary matter of business, then said casually 'what are you doing for Christmas, Walter?' Medlicott said 'nothing in particular', and the Guv'nor clinched it with 'well then, why not come and spend it with us. Because you'll be very welcome.' That's my opinion what occurred."

Anthony nodded. "Thank you, Sir Nicholas. I take your point."

Nick turned to MacMorran. "But before we part, Inspector, there *is* something which I feel I should tell you. Something further."

"About Medlicott?" queried MacMorran.

"No—Gooch. And this is something which I *do* regard as significant. I don't know how you'll react to it when you've heard what it is."

"Let's have it, Sir Nicholas—then we can judge."

"It happened," began Nick, "on the evening that Sergeant Arnold came here. After we'd sent for him—when Miss Repton and I found poor old Medlicott. When the Sergeant had finished his investigation and told me he was through for the time being, I came downstairs from the billiard-room to have a word with my mother and saw Gooch standing in the hall. He wasn't doing anything in particular. He was just standing there. He was in his uniform and he gave me the impression that he had either been sent for or was waiting there to see somebody. The latter idea turned out to be the correct one. Because he came straight up to me and asked me if he could have a word with me in private. That was the phrase he used—'in private'. Well, I was very busy and tired and pretty well 'all in'; there was my father's death and all the inevitable complications arising therefrom and then had come the Medlicott trouble on top—and to speak bluntly, I put him off. Told him that whatever it was, it must wait and that I'd send for him in the morning. Well, he eventually accepted the suggestion but pointed out that the matter was important as it concerned both my father and Medlicott. Anyhow he didn't press it and that was that."

"I should have thought," said MacMorran, "that you would have listened to him then and there. In view of what he said. As it was to do with your father and Medlicott."

Nick nodded. "I should have. I know that now. And I blame myself for the delay. But it's easy to be wise after the event. And frankly—I was tired—I was worried—I considered that in all probability Gooch was exaggerating the importance of some trivial incident he had heard or witnessed between perhaps my father and Mr. Medlicott and I didn't want any more trouble that night. The morning could take care of itself."

The bitterness in Nick's voice showed conclusively how he regretted his action and the shrug of his shoulders denoted likewise. Anthony, however, had listened with a strong feeling of satisfaction. Here was something which fitted. Gooch had been killed because he knew too much.

"I'd like to ask Sir Nicholas a question" he said to MacMorran. MacMorran gestured his consent.

"How long had Gooch been in your employment, Sir Nicholas?"

"Not quite three months. He came along early in October. As I informed you just now, we were without a chauffeur for some time."

"Was he a local man?"

"I couldn't say for certain—but I should say not."

"How did he come to you—through the local Ministry of Labour?"

"No. Not directly. In answer to an advertisement. He had been in the Air Force and been discharged. The Labour Exchange people here didn't demur when the matter was put to them."

"Did you engage him personally?"

"Oh no. I had nothing whatever to do with it. My father did all that. Always did."

"Was the man satisfactory?"

"Absolutely. I've never heard a complaint against him. We always considered ourselves very lucky to get him."

"When the search-parties went out to look for Medlicott, did Gooch go? I rather think, from memory of what I've heard, that he did. Yes?"

"Yes. Gooch went."

"With which party? Just confirm the idea that I have, Sir Nicholas, will you please?"

"With my brother—Quentin. In the direction of Swanley Bottom."

"Thank you. That was what I thought." Anthony sat back and nodded to MacMorran.

"Perhaps your brother would be good enough to come in, Sir Nicholas," said Inspector MacMorran. "And thanks for your help."

3

Anthony was interested to see the physical dissimilarities between Quentin Wynyard and his elder brother. His fair, slim slenderness rather took Anthony by surprise as he hadn't particularly noticed Quentin Wynyard when they had had their hasty lunch.

"Artistic temperament," thought Anthony to himself, "whatever that may mean. Nervy, highly-strung."

MacMorran, if possible, exuded more cordiality than ever. And Quentin for once belied his looks and seemed almost absurdly at ease under the Inspector's questions. Also—like Nick—his most important contribution came towards the end of the interview. MacMorran shepherded him through what he knew and plied him with the normal questions—and the results were entirely negative. His own alibi? Quentin remained unperturbed. He had written three letters in his room to three friends of his—informing them of his father's terribly sudden death and of the funeral arrangements—and had then walked down to the Post-office to post them. Which Post-office? Well, not the Post-office exactly—the pillar-box on the Colbury Road. About a quarter of a mile's walk. He usually referred to the pillar-box as the Post-office. It was the nearest posting-place to them and the one they almost always used. No, that was not in the direction which Medlicott had taken. He himself had returned to the house about four o'clock.

Anthony watched him closely all through the interview. And it was just on the moment when MacMorran appeared to be deciding that he wouldn't need Quentin's services any more for the time being, that Quentin held up his hat as it were and produced his rabbit. And a rather remarkable specimen it was, too!

"There is one thing," he said, just a little diffidently, perhaps, "that I feel I ought to let you know about."

"Yes, Mr. Wynyard?" prompted MacMorran.

"It may or may not be important," Quentin went on, "and that will be for you to judge, but it's annoyed me considerably."

"What is it, Mr. Wynyard? Let's have it."

"It's this. During the afternoon that . . . er . . . we've been talking about . . . my camera was stolen. It was a beautiful camera, and apart from the . . . er . . . pecuniary loss, I shall find it most difficult to replace."

Anthony's interest was stimulated. He waited eagerly for MacMorran's next question.

"Are you positive, Mr. Wynyard, that the theft took place on that particular afternoon?"

"Absolutely positive." Quentin was emphatic.

"Will you tell me *why* you feel so certain about it?"

"Only too pleased, believe me." The indignation in Quentin's voice was most noticeable. "I'm a keen photographer. *Very* keen. Have been since I was a kid. I brought my camera downstairs that morning in the hope of getting a photograph of a real snow-scene in England. The weather seemed absolutely made for it. All round here about midday looked like a slice of another country. And the light for the time of the year was marvellously good. So I decided to wait until just after lunch when the sun might even be stronger. I left my camera on a table in the hall. It was there when we sat down to lunch. I know that because I saw it . . . saw it several times. But when I went to pick it up after lunch—it had gone. There wasn't a sign of it anywhere. I enquired of several people and looked everywhere for it, but nobody seemed to know anything about it at all." Quentin approximated sulkiness.

"And it hasn't shown up since?"

"It has *not*," replied Quentin Wynyard curtly.

"You've looked for it, I take it? Made a search?"

"You bet! Been everywhere—except, of course, in people's bedrooms. Must draw the line somewhere."

"H'm," said MacMorran, "strange business." He lit a cigarette, emitted smoke and then waved away the smoke from his face with his hands.

"A question, Mr. Wynyard, if I may." The speaker was Anthony. Quentin turned to him. "Were there any undeveloped plates in the camera?"

Quentin hesitated before answering. "I'm not sure. I'm trying to think."

Anthony let him wait. "Yes," said Quentin after a period of reflection, "there was—one."

"What was the photograph?"

"I took it about ten days ago, I should think, and I hadn't had time to develop it. It was of my father and Nick standing leaning up against the car. I took it one sunny morning, just outside the house here. It's the last photo of my father ever taken—probably. Although I hadn't thought of that till you reminded me."

"Who knew of its existence, besides the people in it and yourself?"

"Oh, all the family, I should say. Catherine and Henry—that's my sister and brother-in-law, they were here at the time. And Aunt Amy. And some of the servants, I should think. There was no secret about it."

"Tell me, Mr. Wynyard, was Gooch in the photograph?"

"Gooch? Oh—yes! He was sitting at the driving-wheel."

"Thank you, Mr. Wynyard." Anthony gestured to MacMorran. "That's all from me, Inspector, thank you."

"Perhaps, Mr. Wynyard," said MacMorran, "as you go out, you'd be good enough to ask Mrs. Poulton to come in. I hope I shan't have to keep her very long."

"Very good, Inspector," replied Quentin.

Anthony watched him as he made his way out. Quentin Wynyard's face was grim and set. "I should hate to do him an injustice," thought Anthony to himself, "but as I see things he almost seems to feel the loss of his camera more than the loss of his father. Or doesn't he?"

4

Catherine Poulton arrested Anthony's attention the moment she entered the room. The loss of her father, and the two tragedies which had followed it, had naturally left their mark on her face, but Anthony saw at once that here was a beautiful specimen of an English girl.

Without, of course, being aware of it, he thought on the lines of the late Mr. Medlicott's conversation with Elisabeth Grenville on their train journey. That Catherine and Quentin were like each other and that Nick Wynyard was the odd one of the three. Catherine replied to all MacMorran's questions with candour and composure. And really, she was quite unable, she insisted, to give him any help. She had stayed in after lunch on the fatal afternoon—for the only reason that she just hadn't felt like going out. After what had happened that morning all she wanted was to be alone.

"But your husband, Mrs. Poulton—did go out? With some of the ladies? That's so, isn't it?"

Catherine's clear and friendly eyes opened wide at the remark. "Well—why not? I'm afraid I don't understand. What is your point? Will you please make it clear?"

MacMorran showed signs of embarrassment. "Oh . . . er . . . nothing, Mrs. Poulton. I felt that I might mention the fact." He withdrew in disorder and passed rapidly to another matter. He asked her a question which Anthony couldn't recall him having asked any of the others and Anthony found himself wondering why MacMorran had asked it.

"Did you happen to see the late Mr. Medlicott after lunch—anywhere in the house? I ask you that because you . . . er . . . say that you stayed in the house yourself."

To Anthony's surprise, MacMorran's shot registered a bull.

"Yes," replied Catherine Poulton, "I did."

"Where was that, Mrs. Poulton?"

"It wasn't exactly *in* the house. I expect you'd like me to be exact. It was in the drive, just where it curves round, about half-way to the garage. I should say the time was about a quarter-past two."

"Was he dressed for out-of-doors?"

"Oh yes. As far as I could see he was wearing overcoat, hat and gloves."

"What was he doing? Waiting for somebody?"

Catherine shook her head. "No. As a matter of fact he was talking."

MacMorran leant forward towards her with some eagerness. He began to feel he had got somewhere at last. "Ah! Who was talking to him?"

"He was engaged in conversation with two people. Mr. Isaacs and Gooch."

Anthony noticed Inspector Burrows nod to himself with a suggestion of complacent satisfaction. Then Anthony remembered. Burrows had probably already heard this from Catherine when he and Sergeant Arnold had made the initial inquiries after the death of Medlicott. Before MacMorran could jump in again, however, Catherine had gone on.

"But I can't tell you any more, Inspector. I saw what I saw from one of my bedroom windows. It wasn't very long after lunch. And I came downstairs immediately afterwards."

"Perhaps you can, Mrs. Poulton. At any rate—we'll see. Were the other two men—Mr. Isaacs and Gooch—dressed as though *they* intended going out?"

"Gooch had on a suit of overalls—I couldn't say with regard to Mr. Isaacs. I really didn't take sufficient notice."

Anthony shook his head after MacMorran glanced towards him, and as he did so Catherine had her last say.

"No doubt Mr. Isaacs can tell you himself, Inspector—if you care to ask him."

"I expect he'll be able to, Mrs. Poulton," returned MacMorran cordially. "And thank you very much for what you've told us."

5

MacMorran subsequently interviewed Guy Stansfield, Alfred Lillywhite, Gregory Copplestone, Ebenezer Isaacs and Percival Comfit in that precise order. It was not his intention to trouble about Mrs. Copplestone unless anything transpired from the series of interviews which might appear, on the surface at least, to render such a procedure desirable or necessary.

The interview with Guy Stansfield proved as barren as most of its predecessors. He, too, had stayed indoors on the afternoon of Medlicott's death. He had not accompanied his father and mother to the house of the Comfits because, frankly, he hadn't been feeling too fit. And he had never been *too* fond of walking. A car now . . . or yacht . . . was a different matter. Bit of a hangover too, in all probability, from the night before. How had he occupied his time before tea? Oh—he had dodged about a bit—fooled around generally—listened to the radio—read a bit—really nothing in particular. The afternoon had been on the empty side and more than once he had found himself wishing that he *had* felt more energetic and gone out. Specially as nearly all the girls had. There was really very little indeed he could tell the Inspector. Much as he would have liked to.

Anthony had listened carefully as MacMorran had put his questions. He thought that from all appearances, young Stansfield seemed a decent enough chap. Bit weak-chinned, perhaps. *And* a trifle nervous. Yes—nervous certainly, on more carefully-gathered impressions.

"One question, Mr. Stansfield," said Anthony, "I believe you were the person who found Gooch, the chauffeur, dead in the garage?"

"Er . . . yes . . . that is so."

"What time would that be?"

"As I crossed to the garage, I remember hearing a clock strike eight in the distance. A church clock, I should say, from the sound of it."

"Tell me what happened, if you would be so good, Mr. Stansfield."

"Well, I'd been in the smaller garage to have a squint at Dad's car. The morning before it had got frozen up and I wanted to keep an eye on it. I just messed about with it for a bit and I found I wanted a bigger spanner than any we had brought with us. So I thought I'd drift along to the big garage and see if I could borrow one from the chauffeur. I thought he might be there. Of course I had no real idea whether he would be or not. Well, I found the poor blighter dead over the wheel."

"You knew he was dead—at once?"

"Oh—no—" Guy Stansfield's eyes flickered a little unsteadily for the moment—"I sang out to him, you see, as I entered. I thought from his position that he was at work on the car. Anyone would have thought the same. When he didn't answer—I went up to him. I could see he was dead then, all right. Well, it didn't take me long to see it. So I just left him where he was, went back to the house and informed Sir Nicholas Wynyard. Thought it was the best *and* proper procedure."

"There was no disorder in the garage? No sign, say, of anything in the nature of a struggle?"

"Oh no! Nothing of that kind whatever."

"Was it reasonably light in the garage?"

"Oh yes. You could see all right."

Anthony thought that Guy Stansfield seemed relieved at the turn the questioning had taken. But he could grasp at nothing upon which to embroider any theory, and a few seconds later the young man was dismissed.

Alfred Lillywhite was a horse of another colour altogether. He seemed bathed in an oleaginous perspiration which in some way appeared to be produced by a non-stop activity of complete self-satisfaction. He knew Walter Medlicott well. Had known him for years. Any close friend of the late Sir John Wynyard over any length of time, as he had had the honour to be, *must* have known Walter Medlicott! But he could throw no light on the man's death. None whatever. As for 'diamonds' and this 'Levi' business—well, he was in timber himself—a very different proposition. He and Sir John Wynyard had been fellow directors for more years than he cared to remember. How had he spent the afternoon? Asleep, my dear sir! In his bedroom. Did the Inspector know a better way of spending an afternoon in December? After a good meal? If so, he, Alfred Lillywhite would like to hear of it. He was always open for excellent and profitable suggestions. Always had been—perhaps that partly accounted for the success he had made of life.

He folded his podgy hands on his paunch complacently and looked round the room like a man who had just concluded a most gratifying bargain. His small, pale-blue eyes glinted as they travelled from the contemplation of one face to another. When he retired, Anthony, who had had no questions to ask him, noticed that Burrows was looking distinctly worried over something. Something, evidently, which a little later on forced him to the examination of his note-book.

The local Inspector was still turning over the pages rather feverishly when the door opened to admit Gregory Copplestone.

6

Anthony saw a brown-bearded man enter. A man, too, who looked definitely out of place in the surroundings in which he found himself. What was it about him that caused this impression? He was certainly un-English looking. Also, his face was worn and showed unmistakable traces of tiredness.

His hands arrested one's attention, too. Almost as much as his beard and that strange, almost haunted look in his eyes. They were podgy, it's true, but not in the way that the hands of Alfred Lillywhite were. Copplestone's were strong-podgy, whereas Lillywhite's were flabby-podgy. And besides strength, they had a most extraordinary restlessness. The fingers were seldom still for more than a few seconds at a time. They wavered and vacillated, caressed, cajoled and then suddenly became predatory and, after that, minatory. Anthony listened for the accent when Gregory Copplestone first spoke.

"I shall be relieved, gentlemen," he said with a curious, superior-like pomposity, "when I can depart from this abode of sorrow—this house of Death. In three days, Death has struck thrice at the assembled company. Who knows what a fourth and fifth day have in store for those who stay here?"

"Er . . . quite . . ." said MacMorran, "and do please sit down, Dr. Copplestone . . . and I'm sure that whatever your feelings may be, you'll do your best to help me."

Copplestone sat down with a curious little jerky half-bow to the Inspector.

"I am sorry—but I am *not* able to help you, in any way whatever. I am simply—my wife and I rather—the friends of Lady Wynyard. And we are here at her invitation. I am a musician. Before that I was a musician. And after that I shall be a musician. I am not, was not and shall not be anything else. If I were anything else—I should not be a musician."

Copplestone folded his arms and brooded darkly at MacMorran.

"Lady Wynyard," he continued, after MacMorran had come up for the third time, "was charming enough to invite my wife and myself to High Fitchet for Christmas. She flattered me by showing a very great interest in my work. We came. We are still here. We would now like to make our departure. Beyond that, I can tell you nothing."

By this time, MacMorran had been able to effect a partial recovery, and Anthony to remember that he had heard of Copplestone in some remote way. What was it? Something to do with music, no doubt. Hadn't the man hinted, rather, that he had some slight connection with the art? Of course he had.

"I see," said MacMorran rather gallantly, "but perhaps you will be able to assist me in *one* direction."

Copplestone stared at him blankly. MacMorran took another step.

"Did you happen to see the dead man at all on that afternoon?"

Anthony saw the pit which MacMorran had dug for himself yawning at the Inspector's feet.

"Which dead man?" trumpeted Copplestone, "which dead man of three?"

'You're a little too clever,' thought Anthony.

"I'm sorry. My carelessness. Medlicott."

"Medlicott," repeated Copplestone, "what had I to do with Medlicott? Medlicott was a man of the law. I am a musician. Is there any affinity between the two? Frankly, I know of none."

Copplestone shrugged his shoulders as though the matter had reached finality. But MacMorran had met people of this type before. He was not to be put off by 'blah'.

"That may be so. But it doesn't answer the question as it was put. I take it you did *not* see Medlicott? Is that your answer?"

"It is," returned Copplestone shortly. "I imagined that I'd made it clear."

"Thank you. And now would you be good enough to help me again? How did you spend the afternoon?"

"I haven't the slightest idea. I'm not a man who dockets his time. I did nothing of paramount importance—therefore I have forgotten it. I make a point of never cluttering up my mind with the memories of trivial things which don't in the least matter. In all probability I listened to some music of my own making. But merely *pour passer le temps* and therefore of no importance. You must remember that the circumstances of the house were abnormal. Yes—I did! I played the piano first to myself and then to my wife—in the music-room. I remember now. Very softly and extremely quietly. I have little doubt that anybody else who was privileged to hear it was delighted."

Anthony waited to see what MacMorran would try next. On the whole, perhaps, and bearing in mind the idiosyncrasies of the man facing him, the Inspector adopted the wisest course. Even though it may have been coincidental with the line of least resistance. He decided to terminate the interview. If he wanted anything more from the awkward Dr. Copplestone, he would wait until another day before he attempted to obtain it. There now remained but Isaacs and Comfit, in the former of whom Anthony couldn't help feeling considerable interest. In view of what Catherine Poulton had recently told them, Isaacs was the man who *might* have more information with regard to Medlicott's movements on the afternoon of his death than anyone else in the house.

So when Isaacs came in—a few moments later—Anthony at once subjected him to a searching scrutiny.

"Sit down, please, Mr. Isaacs," said MacMorran.

7

As Elizabeth Grenville had thought on Christmas Eve, so did Anthony think now. Ebenezer Isaacs immediately suggested a tall and much more robust Benjamin Disraeli, one-time Earl of Beaconsfield. He was spare, it is true, but he looked strong and healthy. He was a Jew—there was no doubt about that. His eyes and his nose gave the greatest evidences of that. The eyes were dark-set and restless, and the nose prominent and cast in the mould of Judah. Anthony judged his age to be either in the late fifties or the early sixties. Probably the latter.

After MacMorran had made his opening passes, Anthony was surprised when Isaacs first spoke.

"Brother," he said, "you have your duty to do. Say no more. I have full understanding of it. It's a very strange world and instead of us all sitting down to enjoy a nice little hamper from say, Fortnum and Mason's, or even Barham and Marriage's, and opening a bottle of the real stuff so that we could all be convivial together—here we are doing our best to lay a murderer by the heels. Verily a case of life being mixed up with death, as my old friend Solomon Dinn of the International Bankers' Federation would say."

Isaacs crossed his legs where he sat and looked benignant. MacM-orran agreed with the expressed sentiments. This man, although unusual, was more his line of country, he felt, than Dr. Copplestone had been.

"And, brother," went on Isaacs, "I'm sorry—more sorry than I can possibly say—that I can't help you much. The late Sir John Wynyard and I had certain business ties. If the grim reaper had not intervened, we should probably have had more. I'm a bachelor. Sir John invited me here to spend Christmas with him. I accepted. I was glad to accept. Little knowing, of course, what the outcome of it all would be. But you never know how Life is going to serve you. You never know what lies tucked ahead—just round the corner. You never know how men and women are going to act. And, brother, if you ask me, it's just as well. Look at this, for example. I cut it out of the paper yesterday. It seemed to me to be really beautiful. As a breath of Spring or the music of the nightingale. What a tribute—and above all—how unexpected a tribute! Something right away from what I'm sure you'll permit me to refer to—as 'the book of form'."

Isaacs rolled his eyes and fished in his waistcoat pocket to produce a cutting from a newspaper. He handed it gravely to the Scotland Yard Inspector.

"It warms your heart, brother. It does really. Read it, and when you've read it, pass it round to these other gentlemen. They have hearts—let them be warmed as well as your own."

MacMorran took the cutting and read it. It was worded as follows:

"Dissenters Receive Unexpected Windfall. By the death of Samuel Levy, bookmaker (better known in racing circles as Malcolm Cameron Ltd.), the Nonconformist sect known as 'The Brethren', whose place of worship is situated in Lower Pendleton Road, Manchester, become entitled to a bequest of £5000. We are informed on unimpeachable authority that the late Mr. Levy's first wife, who pre-deceased him by over twenty years, was a member of this religious community—hence doubtless, the primary reason behind the late Mr. Levy's most generous gift."

MacMorran passed it to Inspector Burrows, who looked at it casually and relayed the cutting to Anthony. When he read it, Anthony began to wonder, and then to wonder still more, but he pocketed the cutting in order that he might listen to the subsequent verbal exchanges between MacMorran and Ebenezer Isaacs.

"Fantastic?" continued the latter, in relation to the cutting, doubtless, "perhaps! And yet—the epitome of benevolence! The fusion of two worlds. Consider it in all its implications. Two worlds lying far apart from each other and yet suddenly brought together by a charitable action. And a charitable action that had its origin in a good woman's love. So shines a good deed, brother, in a naughty world."

Isaac's dark eyes roved round the room. "Very interesting indeed," commented MacMorran, "and, as you say, well away from . . . the . . . er . . . beaten track. But to get back to our job—or rather to my job."

"Of course, Inspector. Please pardon the digression. I was to blame. It was thoughtless of me. But I was carried away. It's a weakness of mine. But there you are. 'One touch of nature makes the whole world kin.' Proceed, brother, if you please, and consider me entirely at your service."

MacMorran cleared his throat for action. "I've been endeavouring to trace, as far as possible, Medlicott's movements on the afternoon of his death. Now you, Mr. Isaacs, remained in the house that afternoon. You weren't a member of either of the parties that went out walking in the sunshine. Neither was the dead man. Now did you happen to see anything of him? In—or, say, about the house?"

Isaacs shook his head. "No. He and I had little in common. 'And one of them which was a lawyer.' But . . . er . . . enough of that. The answer is 'no'."

MacMorran's hand went up to his chin and rubbed it thoughtfully. "You're certain of that?"

"Oh—yes. I think so. But why—do you doubt me? Surely not? I wouldn't like to think that for the world."

"Well, one of the people we've had a brief chat with thought it was you talking to Medlicott, near the garage-doors, or in the drive, perhaps, soon after lunch was over on that particular day. Soon after two o'clock, say."

A warm and embracing smile flooded the face of Ebenezer Isaacs. "Brother, you are right! My apologies for having misled you. It was purely unintentional on my part. I *did* speak: to our poor friend who has passed over. I remember now. Now, how did I come to forget

that? My mind, I suppose—too full! Too full to concentrate properly. Snowed under, brother, snowed under! Yes—that must be the
explanation. Could I trespass on your kindness, brother, for a cigarette? Just one little smoke?" MacMorran frowned, but a Scottish
cigarette found its way into a Hebrew hand. Anthony was beginning
to enjoy the duel. Isaacs lit the cigarette.

"Thank you. That's very charming of you. I didn't happen to have
a cigarette in my pocket. I don't always carry them and I suddenly
felt an overwhelming desire for one."

"I'm glad you've remembered about Medlicott," went on MacM-
orran, "because it confirms what we already have. Now a further
question, Mr. Isaacs. Was he going out when he spoke to you?"

"I really couldn't tell you. That is, to say for certain. But I've an
idea that he rather hinted at it. As a matter of fact he was talking to
Gooch, the chauffeur, when I came upon them. Really—what a sinister coincidence! Medlicott and Gooch together. It hadn't occurred to
me before. Those two poor souls. So soon to cross the Styx—each of
them. To cross it almost hand in hand. Sad—very sad."

"Did Medlicott seem—er—normal?" MacMorran tried again. "Yes.
I think so. But I was with him for too short a time, you see, to answer
you with anything approaching certainty. He and Gooch had been
talking. Yes—that was it. When I came up to them—they stopped.
What did I say to them, now? Oh—a commonplace remark with
regard to the quality of Sir John Wynyard's lawn. It's all beginning
to come back to me. No more than that. The lawn! 'Some nocturnal
blackness mothy and warm, when the hedgehog travels furtively over
the lawn.' As far as I can remember, Medlicott laughed and agreed
with whatever it was that I had said. Just before I turned back into
the house for a spell of reading before tea."

Isaacs drew smoke into his lungs.

"He was in good spirits, then?"

"Definitely," replied Isaacs. He seemed to hesitate a trifle as he
spoke. "Let me amend that. The little more and how much. And shades
of meaning are *so* important! *Les nuances!* Let me say rather that
Medlicott wasn't in *bad* spirits, or even in *low* spirits—whatever it
may be you care to call them. I make that emendation deliberately—
because Medlicott was a quietish man—the lawyer both at home and

abroad. Not exactly dry as dust—I couldn't bring that accusation against him—but getting on that way, you know."

This time he exhaled tobacco smoke from his nose. MacMorran went off in another direction.

"What did Gooch, the chauffeur, do after you had spoken to Medlicott? Did you happen to notice?"

"Ah! Gooch! That other poor soul. I think he walked away and left Medlicott standing there. And I think, too, that he was just a little annoyed at my interrupting the conversation. He did *just* convey that impression. Which was, of course, brother, the very last thing in the world that I would have wished to do. My remark concerning Sir John's lawn had been made entirely on the spur of the moment."

MacMorran made a note and looked across at Anthony. "Only one question, Mr. Isaacs," said the latter, "and that's in relation to your newspaper cutting. Which I agree with you is most unusually interesting. Of what sort a man was this bookmaker, Samuel Levy?"

Anthony held up the piece of newspaper. For the first time, perhaps, during the interview, Ebenezer Isaacs looked just a little perturbed. But the dark eyes found a smile from somewhere and turned it on to the questioner.

"Surely the newspaper paragraph tells us what you are asking, young man? A man of open heart, of charitable mind, of an entirely benevolent disposition. One who would positively revel in doing good. Is there any room in your heart for doubt?"

Anthony returned smile for smile. "That is agreed between us. But *apart* from the qualities which the newspaper depicts. That was what I meant by my question. Was he dark, fair, tall, short?—did he like oysters?—was he a total abstainer?"

"Brother, I understand." Isaacs became himself again and beamed on Anthony. "How admirably you do put things. But alas I cannot tell you. Perhaps I didn't make it clear to you in the first instance. I should have done. It was a sin of omission on my part. The man was a complete stranger to me." His smile became bland.

"Thank you, Mr. Isaacs," returned Anthony. "I'm sorry to have troubled you, but I had the idea that he might have been a friend of yours."

This incident closed the interview with Isaacs and paved the way for the entrance of the well-known novelist, Percival Comfit.

8

It would have been impossible to find more fitting adjectives to describe him than those used by Catherine Poulton to Elisabeth Grenville upon the latter's arrival at High Fitchet. He certainly looked languid and he equally certainly looked drooping. And neither a sunflower nor a lily in either of his hands would have seemed at all out of place. Either in Piccadilly or elsewhere. He sank gracefully into the chair which MacMorran indicated to him and looked at his finger-nails with the air of somebody examining a rare object at a distance. But effete though he looked, he was astute enough to sit reasonably quiet and to let MacMorran do most of the talking. After the usual preliminaries had been negotiated, MacMorran came to the main point.

"You were out, sir, I've been given to understand, on the afternoon of the death of Mr. Medlicott with several of the guests who are staying here. That is so, isn't it?"

Comfit dropped his head in acquiescence.

"Now, sir," continued MacMorran, "will you be good enough to tell me the names of the people who accompanied you."

"It will be an effort," came the drawling reply, "a prodigious effort—but I'll do my best for you."

Percival Comfit closed his eyes and sat motionless. There came quite a lengthy pause. Anthony had the idea, for a moment or so, that the novelist had fallen off to sleep. The idea was wrong, however, for suddenly Comfit, still with his eyes closed, began to speak.

"My wife—Cynthia Delaunay Restarick Comfit, Henry Poulton, I'm certain he was there with us, because I have a distinct remembrance of seeing one of his shoe-laces undone and on another occasion, his nose running—Mr. and Mrs. Stansbridge—my apologies—Stansfield—I knew a man named Stansbridge once and I'm always inclined to confuse the two names—and one other. Now who was that other? Was it a man or a woman? I must think. These differences have always bothered me. Ah—I've got it—a woman—Mrs. Lillywhite."

MacMorran checked the names with those on his list. "Thank you, Mr. Comfit. I'm much obliged to you. And they were in your company all the time you were out?"

Again Comfit dropped an affirmative head.

"You walked through the woods, I believe? Round to Montfichet Mill?"

"How right you are, Inspector," replied Percival Comfit. "And you saw nothing of Mr. Medlicott on your travels?"

"Assuredly not. From all that I've heard since, that unfortunate man had gone in another direction. It is most unlikely that any of my party *could* have seen him. Things which are equal to the same thing are equal to one another."

"Thank you," said MacMorran. "I agree with you, of course. But it's necessary for me to check up, you know, as closely as I can."

He looked at Anthony, but this time the latter had no questions to ask and signified as much with a quick shake of the head. Percival Comfit, therefore, favoured them with a courtly bow and made a dignified and eminently graceful exit from the room.

"That," said MacMorran, rather wearily, "is the bundle."

CHAPTER VII

1

WHEN Inspector Burrows had gone, MacMorran and Anthony compared notes. Anthony knew, sometime before the various interviews terminated, that his professional colleague was all at sea. He knew Andrew MacMorran well enough to be reasonably sure of that. Because he made the judgment from several external signs and portents too obviously present to be overlooked. Which is not to say that he himself was feeling very much better placed. But he had a clear idea of what each person who had been interviewed had said, and when he came to sort the various stories out in his leisure he felt confident that something of value to him would eventually emerge from one, if not more, of them.

"Well?" said MacMorran, "and what did you think of that collection? Saucy lot, weren't they? About as satisfying as two penn'orth of cold gin."

Anthony went on from there. "The main feature—the *worst* feature perhaps—is that the alibis generally are so much on the nebulous and shadowy side. 'In my room.' 'Posted some letters.' 'Read all the afternoon.' 'Messed about generally.'" Anthony stopped as though something of importance had suddenly occurred to him.

MacMorran took up the parable where Anthony had left it. "Played the bloody organ! But quietly and soulfully! People who listened to me would have loved it. Oh yes and oh yes. Personally I can't see a glimmer of light." He subsided gloomily.

"I can see two," said Anthony, "but I'm ready to admit at once that either of them may go out at any moment. And at the lightest puff of wind."

"You can? What are they?"

"The several indications that Gooch knew something which Medlicott had also known, and that strange tribute to the deceased Samuel Levy which came to us from a brother artist. Which also was either highly significant or merely extremely clever."

"Well?" said MacMorran rubbing his chin again, "while I agree with all you say, what did any one of them *bring* to us? Now I ask you! The only piece of news we picked up was that Medlicott, Gooch and Isaacs were together in the garden somewhere just before Medlicott seems to have gone out for his last walk. Now what brought 'em together? You'll tell me that Isaacs says his share consisted of praising the lawn. My answer to that's—hooey! More likely they were discussing this blessed diamond that somebody seems very interested in. That's the only solution I can come to." MacMorran grew gloomy again.

"There's another point though, Andrew," remarked Anthony, slowly and thoughtfully, "to which I'd call your attention."

"Which is?"

"Don't lose sight of the fact that Medlicott and Gooch were murdered *after* the death of Sir John Wynyard."

MacMorran looked and said, "Well—what is there in that?"

Anthony grinned. "I don't know. I wish I did. But there *might* be something in it. It *might* help in some circumstances to solve what is, after all, our greatest difficulty and our biggest problem."

"Being?" queried the Yard Inspector.

"Motive, Andrew! Motive! Which, at the moment, to me, as I'll frankly confess, is a distinctly large-sized stumbling-block. Because I just don't get it."

"What about this diamond?"

"Which diamond?"

MacMorran stared at him. Anthony came to repetition. "I mean it, Andrew. *Which* diamond? Nobody in the whole crowd yields even a glimmer of admission that he or she knows the first thing of any diamond. Cut the guests out, if you like, as being outside the family circle and interests, and concentrate all your artillery on the Wynyards themselves. The entire Wynyard family. Nick, his mother, his aunt, his brother, his sister, and there's still not a breath of this 'ere precious stone, Andrew. Is there or was there? Of course—I'll admit there's one weakness—we didn't tackle the son-in-law."

"He was out in the walking party through the woods. He's 'alibied' all right."

"In the Comfit-box—eh? I wonder—how much we can really rely on the statements of a man like Percival Comfit?"

"Well—if we admit that—where are we? We're just high and dry. Unless we take *somebody's* word we might just as well start all over again." More MacMorran gloom.

"Yes, and that's a quite likely possibility, Andrew—as I see things. But we'll hope not. And we won't scream before we're hurt. Anyhow, I propose we get back to the 'Red Lion' at Montfichet and see what's on the menu for dinner this evening. I'm just beginning to get the first warnings of an appetite. If you've a better suggestion than that, Andrew, I'm open to hear it."

MacMorran hadn't.

2

After a reasonably good dinner at the 'Red Lion' and several drinks in the Bar parlour to follow, Anthony decided to retire to his room, comparatively early. He had in mind one of his habitual exercises in what he always described to himself as "concentrated and intensive thought". The problem which confronted MacMorran and himself, comprising as it did, two murders, was so complicated and so entangled that he felt he must evolve some measure of order out of it, and at the earliest moment, if he were to have any hope of achieving anything like a satisfactory result. He sat down in his room, therefore, produced fountain-pen and paper and compiled two lists. The first he called "Family Circle". The second he entitled "Guests". He drew them thus.

FAMILY CIRCLE (LIST ONE).

Name.	Position as to "Medlicott Alibi".	If alibi supported, —terms of support, comments, etc.
1. Nick Wynyard.	Garage with Gooch during early part of afternoon. Then "cleaned up".	None. But unlikely, on face of it, to have murdered Gooch who could have confirmed the alibi.
2. Lady Wynyard.	Indoors all the afternoon — presumably household tasks.	No actual confirmation. Can no doubt be obtained. *Inconclusive.*
3. Miss Amy Wynyard.	As previous person (approximately).	Similar remarks apply as to Number Two.
4. Catherine Poulton.	Indoors — in her room (saw Gooch, Isaacs and Medlicott).	Unsupported. Inconclusive.

FAMILY CIRCLE (LIST ONE)—*continued.*

Name.	Position as to "Medlicott Alibi".	If alibi supported —terms of support, comments, etc.
5. Quentin Wynyard.	Writing letters in his room—then to pillar-box to post them (opposite direction to the way Medlicott went).	Unsupported. Inconclusive. ? Loss of Camera during the fateful afternoon.
6. Henry Poulton.	Not interviewed but vouched for by Comfit as a member of his walking party (Montfichet Woods).	? Would Comfit have missed him if he had suddenly detached himself from the party (comment—doubtful).
7. Helen Repton.	Movements sponsored by several girls —all members of Swanley Bottom walking party. Not interviewed.	No detailed check-up of this party yet made.
8. John Gooch.	Garage with Nick Wynyard early afternoon. ? Afterwards.	Man himself since murdered.

GUESTS (LIST TWO).

Name.	"Medlicott Alibi."	If alibi supported —terms of support, and comments, etc.
9. Percival Comfit.	Montfichet Woods walking party.	As Number 6 (list One). ? Could Comfit have left his party.
10. Cynthia Comfit (wife of above).	As above.	As above.
11. Ebenezer Isaacs.	Indoors reading, but with Medlicott and Gooch early afternoon.	First part as yet unsupported.

GUESTS (LIST TWO)—*continued.*

Name.	"*Medlicott Alibi*".	*If alibi supported —terms of support, and comments, etc.*
12. Alfred Lillywhite.	Indoors—asleep in bedroom.	No support—inconclusive.
13. Myra Lillywhite.	With Comfit walking party.	As Number 6 (list One).
14. Charles Stansfield.	As above.	As above.
15. May Stansfield.	As above.	As above.
16. Guy Stansfield.	Indoors — Radio — loose end generally.	Not yet checked.
17. Ann Waverley. 18. Virginia Proud. 19. Clarice Irving. 20. Elisabeth Grenville.	*See* Helen Repton. Swanley Bottom walking party.	As Number 7 (list One).
21. Gregory Copplestone.	Indoors—"Music hath Charms" (perhaps).	No support as yet and inconclusive.
22. Lydia Copplestone.	Not interviewed. According to husband—part of the time in music-room.	As above.

When he had completed his task, Anthony looked at his two lists with feelings akin to dismay. He realized, perhaps, for the first time, how flimsy were the threads in his hands. He went through the two lists a second time and then grimaced to himself at their almost entirely unsatisfactory nature.

'Nothing for it,' he said to himself, 'I'll now make a list of 'Possibles' as against 'Almost Impossibles'. I don't particularly care for the classifications, but they'll pass for the time being.' He examined the two lists again and decided that his best plan would be to deal with the "eliminations" first. It was a more simple task, he argued, to eliminate the "seemingly impossibles" than to nominate the "possibles"—for after all, any "possible" from his point of view should have attached thereto just a soupçon of "probable".

After a considerable exercise in intensive thought he resolved on the following list of eliminations. Helen Repton (this from his knowledge of her was the one certainty in the field), Cynthia Comfit, Myra Lillywhite, May Stansfield, and the four girls who had been in Helen Repton's company in the walk to Swanley Bottom. He counted them. Eight. With Gooch eliminated by the Dread Reaper—nine. Nine from twenty-two left thirteen. Appropriate number, murmured Anthony to himself.

"I'll now divide," he said to himself, "that thirteen into two more groups. 'Plus Possibles' and 'Minus Possibles'. And again I'll do the eliminating part of the act as a start-off."

Eventually his "Minus Possibles" list read as follows. In each instance, Anthony added his reason for the elimination. Nick Wynyard (because of the Gooch alibi and the chauffeur's subsequent murder), Lady Wynyard (highly improbable murderess), Catherine Poulton (doesn't look like a killer), and Lydia Copplestone (if either of the Copplestone's is guilty, the husband is much the more likely person). Four! Nine left now. He read the names of the "suspect" nine over to himself again. At many of them, he paused and shook his head doubtfully. He felt far from satisfied at the result of his efforts.

He put the lists on the dressing-table and walked over to the window of his bedroom. "Motive," he said aloud. "How can I expect to move, until I am clearer in my mind with regard to motive? Until I have some really definite views on that, I am doing no more than grope my way in the dark. Surely there's something there somewhere that is waiting for me to recognize it and grasp its value and significance? There must be. An action, something said, something hinted at or something deliberately masking something else? Isaacs? He talks with Gooch and Medlicott not long before the last-named was killed, and then deliberately throws Samuel Levy on to the table.

"Copplestone, afraid of something unless I'm hopelessly mistaken, makes music to soothe his soul. Lillywhite sleeps while his wife goes walking. Quentin Wynyard reports that his camera was stolen, psychologically at the right (or wrong) moment. And two newspaper cuttings which feature a diamond and Mr. Levi. Concerning neither of which and whom, 'nobody don't know nothink'."

Anthony smiled at his own whimsicality. But that was all he did. Nothing came to him from any of the matters which he turned over in his mind, to lighten his darkness or to give him a finger-post which indicated the destination of solution. Ah well—he would sleep on it! There were at least four main lines of enquiry which attracted him and it would be singular indeed, he thought, if they all proved barren and unprofitable. It was in this frame of mind, therefore, that Anthony Bathurst went to bed; entirely unaware of the startling complication which the next few days were destined to bring forth.

CHAPTER VIII

1

NEITHER Anthony nor Chief-Inspector MacMorran went to High Fitchet again until after the funeral of Sir John Wynyard. In the meantime, on MacMorran's instructions, Inspector Burrows had asked for and obtained from the Coroner adjournments in the case of both inquests. But late in the afternoon of the day of the funeral, Anthony took MacMorran with him to the house. For one thing he wanted to have a few words with Elisabeth Grenville, as it had been conveyed to him by somebody, *en passant*, that Elisabeth had travelled from town with Medlicott on the Christmas Eve before the house-party.

But upon the arrival of Anthony and the Scotland Yard inspector, they were met with a piece of startling news. The first member of the Wynyard family to greet them was Quentin. Anthony noticed at once that his face was pale and drawn. Then Anthony remembered that the funeral of Sir John had taken place that morning which probably accounted for Quentin's dark-ringed eyes and the pallor in his cheeks. Since the day that Anthony and MacMorran had first come to High Fitchet, the inspector had given permission for certain of the guests to be allowed to return home, if they so wished, with the stipulation that Inspector Burrows be informed before they departed, as to what address would find each one available in the immediate future, should the Police desire to establish further contact with any of them.

Quentin turned rather impulsively to Anthony when they met and said jerkily, "I'm glad you chaps have come. Something pretty terrible's turned up since your last appearance. Er . . . my mother would like to have a word with you at once—if it isn't too inconvenient."

Anthony's eyes met MacMorran's questioningly and the latter nodded.

"Certainly," said the "Yard" Inspector, "we shall be pleased to see Lady Wynyard at once."

Anthony then noticed something else—that Quentin Wynyard's hands were trembling violently. But he seemed to pull himself together with an effort and took Anthony and MacMorran along to the library.

"Come in here, will you, please?" he said.

'Voice also unsteady,' commented Anthony inwardly. Inside the room were Lady Wynyard and Nick. And the same shock which had evidently laid its hand on Quentin had also taken toll of his mother and elder brother. Lady Wynyard was seated in a big straight-backed chair and Nick Wynyard was standing at her side. Lady Wynyard's face was pale and strained. Sir Nicholas's was grim and set.

"Good afternoon, gentlemen," said the lady. "I'm gratified that you're here. I have some rather dreadful news for you." Nick, as his mother spoke, made a quick, impetuous gesture, but his mother waved it away.

"No, Nick. It *is* dreadful. You're trying to comfort me by saying that it makes no difference. That isn't so. To me it makes all the difference in the world." Lady Wynyard choked back an unmistakable sob.

2

Sir Nicholas Wynyard said quietly, "Sit down, gentlemen, will you, please? My mother has something of importance to tell you. I think that when you've heard it you'll be of my opinion and able to comfort her as I have tried to do. The only thing is that I hope you'll be more successful than I've been." He turned to Lady Wynyard. "Now—Mother."

"My trouble is, gentlemen," began Lady Wynyard, "that I'm afraid my husband was murdered. That he didn't die from natural causes, as we all supposed."

Anthony said nothing. When, however, MacMorran was on the point of intervention, Lady Wynyard stopped him at once.

"I'm not speaking idly. There is reason for my belief." Turning to her elder son, she said quietly, "Show them, will you, please, Nick?"

Quentin, who had been standing in a far corner of the room, came forward and sat between the Wynyards and Anthony, MacMorran being on the extreme edge of the circle.

"This," said Sir Nicholas Wynyard gravely, "was found this morning in the pocket of my father's dressing-gown. The dressing-gown, you must understand, which he was wearing when he was found dead."

He handed a piece of paper to Inspector MacMorran. The latter's face registered surprise when he saw what it was that Sir Nicholas Wynyard had given him. Anthony took one quick glance at it over MacMorran's shoulder and knew at once that his speedily-conceived guess was an accurate one. It was, he felt certain, the third (or the first) communication from Mr. Levi.

"Who found this?" asked MacMorran.

"I did," replied Lady Wynyard. "I felt this morning that I could at last bear to put some of my late husband's clothes away. The dressing-gown of which Sir Nicholas has spoken was the last garment my husband wore. He put it on that night or morning, when he got up and went down to his writing-room. Why—God alone knows! I don't! A corner of the garment had been burned by the electric fire. Naturally, as I was putting the clothes away, I felt in the pockets. That paper, with a handkerchief, was in the right-hand pocket. When I read it, I nearly collapsed at the shock."

MacMorran said nothing. He handed over the note to Anthony. It was couched in exactly similar terms to those which had been found on Gooch and Medlicott.

Hand over the diamond—or else! Mr. Levi.

While Anthony was examining it, Nick Wynyard spoke. "I've told my mother, gentlemen, that Doctor Beddington was certain my father died a natural death. That this message may have been the indirect cause, I agree. Caused his heart to fail. But that my father died before the murderer could carry out his threat—I'm absolutely positive."

He paused, to go on again almost immediately. "Mother's also worried over another aspect of the matter. She's been most exercised in her mind as to whether she should have given orders for the postponement of the funeral. So that a P.M. could have been held."

"I am," declared Lady Wynyard, emphatically, "bearing in mind the new circumstances which have arisen through the finding of that beastly paper."

Anthony waited for MacMorran to answer. He was interested to see how his professional colleague would handle the situation in its present development.

"Well," said MacMorran to Lady Wynyard, "I don't think, my lady, that you need worry yourself unduly. I shall have to interview this Doctor Beddington, naturally, in view of this . . . er . . . most recent . . . er . . . incident. But, on the whole, from all I've heard, I'm inclined to agree with Sir Nicholas Wynyard's opinion—that the receipt of the Levi message acted as a shock to your late husband and affected his heart. Had there been any evidence or suggestion of foul play, surely we are justified in thinking that Doctor Beddington would have noticed it."

'Good for you, Andrew,' thought Anthony; 'couldn't have been better.'

"I am relieved, Inspector," replied Lady Wynyard, "although not *entirely* satisfied. Sometimes it requires sharper eyes than a local G.P.'s to observe what after all may be minute signs of foul play. Still"—she shrugged her shoulders—"I've put the matter in your hands and you must do what you think best."

MacMorran said, "You may rely on that, my lady," and then as a sort of afterthought he swung round and addressed Quentin Wynyard. "Any news of your lost camera?"

"None, Inspector. It's vanished completely. The whole thing's an absolute mystery to me."

"Very peculiar," returned MacMorran. "I agree. And you've searched everywhere?"

"Everywhere. Not only all over the house, but outside as well. Not a smell of it anywhere."

"Have you looked for it in the garage, Mr. Wynyard?" asked Anthony.

A look of startled surprise flashed into Quentin Wynyard's eyes as Anthony shot the question at him.

"I have. I said everywhere. I meant to include places like the garage in that comprehensive statement. No—the camera's gone—been spirited off the face of the earth."

"Stolen—if you ask me," said Nick Wynyard, drily, "a human agency's a much more likely proposition."

"H'm," returned Anthony, "as you say—a mystery." MacMorran rose from his seat. "Well, your ladyship—if you'll be good enough to excuse me—and Mr. Bathurst—and leave matters to us generally?"

Lady Wynyard nodded. "And set your mind at rest," added MacMorran, "with regard to that other matter. Don't distress yourself. I'll see it through for you. In the meantime, Mr. Bathurst and I were going to have a look round. By the way, has Inspector Burrows been along to-day?"

Nick Wynyard answered. "Haven't seen him, Inspector. As a matter of fact, I haven't seen Burrows since he made all the arrangements with regard to those of our guests who wanted to get away."

"I see. Thank you, Sir Nicholas. Which of your guests are still here?" inquired Anthony.

"Seven," replied Nick. "The Lillywhites, the Copplestones, Ebenezer Isaacs—and two of the girls—Miss Grenville and Helen Repton. Those two are stopping at Catherine's request—my sister. The others will all probably leave us to-morrow, sometime."

"Thank you, Sir Nicholas," replied Anthony, "the Inspector and I'll be getting along then."

3

Elisabeth Grenville had stayed on for a few days for two reasons. Firstly, Catherine Poulton had begged her to, and secondly Helen Repton had added her wishes to Catherine's.

"You'll be company for me, my dear, as well as for Catherine. So do see the week out—if it's not putting you out too terribly."

At first, Elisabeth had demurred but eventually, under the dual assault, she had given way to the joint entreaty. She felt that in some small way she was repaying the kindness of Catherine's original invitation by staying on when Catherine wanted her. She had stayed in the house after the cortège had moved slowly off to Montfichet churchyard, and after watching it make its sombre way down the curved drive she had looked for Helen Repton. But Helen was not showing at that particular moment, so Elisabeth decided to go up to her room and sit there until the funeral service was over and the mourners had returned.

There were at least two letters she felt she ought to write, and when these were finished she could put in a spot of advance packing against that day at the end of the week when she herself would be returning to town. Elisabeth found a writing-pad, rummaged in her bag for her fountain-pen, put the pad on her knees and wrote the two letters which she had regarded as urgent. When they were tucked away in their respective envelopes and the said envelopes duly fastened down and stamped, Elisabeth looked round for one or two comparatively easy packing jobs which she could very well do now instead of leaving them to the end of the week. Several things speedily suggested themselves and Elisabeth set to work.

As she bent to her task, her thoughts reverted to Christmas Eve and her first meeting with Mr. Medlicott. To think that a few days could bring about so much that was ghastly and terrible! Sir John Wynyard—then poor Mr. Medlicott—and then that rather nice-looking chauffeur. But her thoughts were mainly centred on Medlicott—due no doubt to the fact of that journey in the train with him. How they had talked and what they had talked about! And then Elisabeth remembered how he had borrowed one of her books. Which, of course, Fate had prevented him from returning. And it was a book that she had no wish to lose. She wondered if it were still in his room. She knew his room, because one evening as they had been going down to dinner she had seen him coming out of it. It was on the floor below. Perhaps she might be able to get it now, if she went and tried!

With Elisabeth, a thought was usually coincidental with the relevant deed, so without further ado she got off her knees by the side of her suitcase and tripped quietly downstairs. She went straight to the room which she knew had been Mr. Medlicott's and tried the handle. She had had a fleeting wild idea that the Inspector of Police from Colbury might have had it sealed up or something—but the handle yielded to Elisabeth's turning and she went in. To her relief the room was empty, so Elisabeth took a quick glance round the room to see if there were any sign of the book that she was seeking.

Her search was rewarded almost instantly, for there was her book, the *Summa* of St. Thomas Aquinas, lying in the very front of the dressing-table.

So Elisabeth moved quietly towards her book, feeling just a little delighted that she had remembered it, and turned again towards the door of the room to make her way out. As she did so, she saw to her amazement the handle of the door slowly turning and her heart went to her mouth. Elisabeth stood there with her book under her arm and wondered what on earth she would do if it were the police and what they would do, too, seeing that she would be caught in Mr. Medlicott's room, *in flagrante delicto*. Of course—she had a perfectly good explanation—but would it sound so good when she was offering it to the Police? Then, to her increased astonishment, the door opened and who should come in but Miss Wynyard—or Aunt Amy, as Elisabeth had come to call her.

4

"Good gracious, Elisabeth," said Aunt Amy, "and what on earth are you doing in here?"

"Oh, Aunt Amy," replied Elisabeth, "you did give me a fright. I wondered who on earth (oh dear—that's almost what she said to me) it could be! I was terrified that it might be the Police. When I saw it was you—"

"You haven't told me," Miss Wynyard reminded her.

"Why I'm here? I came for a book I lent poor Mr. Medlicott—the night before he was killed, I think it was. This is it."

Elisabeth produced her book from under her arm and held it under the Wynyard nose. "He saw me reading it, you see, in the train," Elizabeth continued, "and said then how much he'd like to borrow it from me if I didn't mind lending it to him. That's the explanation."

"But what made you come and get it now of all times, my dear?"

"I was just throwing some things into my case and I happened to think of it. So I thought I'd just pop down here while nobody was about and see if I could find it. I was lucky. I did. Here it is."

Elisabeth almost giggled nervously as she finished her full explanation. "I've told you why I'm here," she said to herself tremulously, "but you haven't breathed a word to me as to why *you're* here. And if you don't tell me before I clear out, I'll make it my business to ask you, you old so-and-so."

"H'm," grunted Aunt Amy, "lucky to find it here, if you ask me. Expect the Police have been poking their noses round in most of the nooks and crannies. Trust them—if they get half a chance. Revel in it. Wonder one of them didn't walk off with your precious book. Wouldn't put it past them—officious humbugs."

Aunt Amy emitted a noise something like a snort. Elisabeth stood her ground and watched her closely.

"You still haven't told me," she kept saying to herself.

But Miss Wynyard was looking at her watch. "They ought to be back now," she said captiously, "in fact they ought to have been back before this. All through that fool of a Vicar, I suppose. Bleating in the pulpit for half an hour about my brother's virtues, and the labourer's task being o'er. Lot he knows about him! Or anything else come to that! But the man simply must talk! Thinks people like listening to him. Somebody should take him on one side one day and tell him what a crashing bore he is. Maybe it'll have to be me. Ah well—the job could be in worse hands." Aunt Amy held up her hand as though she were listening to something. "Fancy I can hear the cars," she said, "at the end of the drive. You and I had better make ourselves scarce, young lady. Run upstairs and put that book in your case."

"I suppose I'd better," said Elisabeth, "before the others come in." She passed Aunt Amy on her way to the door. Then she turned and asked with honeyed sweetness, "Were you looking for something, Aunt Amy? Is that why you came in here?"

"Yes, I was," replied Aunt Amy. "My nephew Quentin has lost his camera and it struck me a few minutes ago, that it might possibly be up here. Now you pop along while I just have a quick look round."

As Elisabeth ran upstairs, she murmured to herself, "Now—I wonder."

5

Later on that same afternoon, Elisabeth and Helen Repton were with Nick, Catherine and Quentin in the lounge, when Anthony Bathurst strolled in. Helen immediately transformed the official into the social.

Anthony sat down with a smile saying, "That's very nice of you— but what I really wanted was a quiet word with Miss Grenville."

"Shall we all go?" said Helen.

"No. Not at all. There's nothing particularly secret about it. But I find myself just a little more than ordinarily interested in Miss Grenville."

"Who wouldn't be?" said Nick both gallantly and pointedly.

"Should I be enormously flattered?" asked Elisabeth.

"Miss Grenville," said Anthony seriously, "I never flatter people. Although I sometimes allow myself to pay them a compliment."

Elisabeth smoothed her dress over her knees. "Well? And after all that—do I start or do you?"

"I start on you, Miss Grenville." Anthony smiled again as he spoke and all three girls recognized the attractiveness that lurked in the grave, grey eyes.

"Don't let me think the handcuffs are there and that I can't see them," said Elisabeth, "and please don't tell me to come clean. Because if you do, I shall immediately fear the worst."

"I promise," said Anthony, "also—no handcuffs. Yet! There's no knowing, of course, what the future holds." Another smile. Anthony went on. "What I wanted a word with you about, Miss Grenville, was your train journey on Christmas Eve with the late Mr. Medlicott. I'm told that you travelled down here with him?"

"That's quite true. I did. From Liverpool Street to Colbury and then by car here from Colbury station."

"By design? By arrangement?"

"Good gracious—no. He happened to get in the compartment where I was sitting. At the very last moment. If the train hadn't been late, he wouldn't have caught it. And then you wouldn't have been questioning me now," she added mischievously.

"In that case, Miss Grenville, I'm glad he caught it."

As he spoke, Anthony caught Helen's eye and she smiled back at him.

"Thank you, Mr. Bathurst," responded Elisabeth demurely.

"Getting quite a friendly party," interjected Quentin, "we may even yet finish up with musical chairs."

Anthony thought there was a slight edge on Quentin's voice; and if he had asked her, Helen Repton would have been in agreement with him.

"I see," said Anthony to Elisabeth, "it was just a chance meeting. Well now—you had excellent opportunities of observing him—how did he seem on the way down?"

"He seemed," said Elisabeth slowly and obviously picking her words, "to be just what he was. A solicitor, on *very* friendly terms with a client with whom he was looking forward to spending Christmas. He was interesting, and he behaved to me perfectly charmingly all the way down. *But—*"

Elisabeth stopped abruptly. Everybody in the room sensed the importance of the pause and there came a dead silence. Anthony didn't prompt her. He waited for her to continue in her own way.

"I'm afraid I shan't be very clear now. I may find it difficult to make you understand. But, as Nick and Catherine and Quentin know, when Mr. Medlicott and I got to Colbury, there was no transport waiting for us. You see, our train was late owing to the fog and of course things got a bit muddled this end. So Mr. Medlicott 'phoned here. I think he said that Quentin answered him."

She looked across at Quentin for corroboration. Quentin signalled violently that she was correct.

"Well, Quentin sent a car to Colbury Station for us and Mr. Medlicott and I got into it and we started off. As the car moved away I thought I heard men talking and one of them call out something. I looked across at Mr. Medlicott who was sitting opposite to me and spoke to him. He didn't answer." Elisabeth paused again. "I looked at him a second time. He looked absolutely ghastly. He was simply staring out of the window like a man who'd just suffered a terrible shock. When I spoke to him again, he seemed to make an attempt to pull himself together and he answered me. But his face looked really awful. And when we arrived here and got out of the car, his hands were trembling like a leaf. *And,*" concluded Elisabeth emphatically, "he was never quite the same man again. I mean by that, the same man who got into my compartment at Liverpool Street on Christmas Eve."

The silence that had pervaded the room when Elisabeth had reached the pith of her story prevailed for some time after she had finished. Anthony thought over Elisabeth's statement for some little time. When he looked up he said to her, "The car that was sent came from this house? You said that, didn't you, Miss Grenville?"

"Yes," said Elisabeth. "That's right," interposed Quentin. "I answered Mr. Medlicott's 'phone-call and I at once gave orders for a car to go to Colbury station. I can endorse Miss Grenville's statement all along the line—about the 'phone and the car, I mean."

"Who was the driver?" queried Anthony.

"Gooch," replied Quentin, "naturally. He was on the premises and I told him to buzz along."

"Ah," said Anthony significantly, "Gooch! I think that we may be getting somewhere."

He turned back to Elisabeth. "Are you able to assert, Miss Grenville, with any degree of certainty, that Medlicott exhibited this condition of anxiety when he saw Gooch? Please think carefully before you answer."

Elisabeth sat with her hands folded primly in her lap. After a time, she began to speak. "If it were Gooch that upset him, I don't think it showed itself when he first saw Gooch. It seemed to me to happen afterwards. After somebody had called out something. But there's this to remember. It was very dark and foggy when Gooch drove up to the station with the car. I mean—it wasn't easy to recognize anybody. Have I made myself clear?"

Anthony took some time before he answered her. "Yes," he replied eventually. "I think you have. And I've been considering at least three definite possibilities. Medlicott may have recognized Gooch for somebody he knew. He may have seen somebody else whom he thought he knew. He may have thought he heard a voice which was familiar to him. I shall have to think it over and try to do some sorting out."

As he spoke, Anthony noticed a new look dart into Elisabeth Grenville's face. Directly he saw it, he knew that another reminiscence had come to her. He waited.

"Do you know," said Elizabeth slowly, "I am a perfect idiot. I've just thought of something. And why I haven't thought of it before, goodness alone knows! I must be going daft in my old age."

"I'm all attention, Miss Grenville," prompted Anthony.

"I don't know *what* you'll think of me," went on Elisabeth, "but I've just remembered something which *may* be frightfully important. In relation, I mean, to what Mr. Bathurst has just said. There was a man on the train with Mr. Medlicott and me, who was a guest here for Christmas as we were. I saw him pass down the corridor during the journey and recognized him again when I was introduced to him."

'Isaacs,' thought Anthony, 'a hundred to one on Ebenezer Isaacs.'

"Who was that, Elisabeth?" called out Nick Wynyard.

"Doctor Copplestone," replied Elisabeth quietly. "And—what's more—Mr. Medlicott recognized him."

"Sure of that?"

"Pretty sure. He almost admitted it."

"How do you know that?"

"I taxed him at the time about having seen a ghost."

"Why? Was he upset in the train, then, when he saw Copplestone?"

"No. Not really. I wouldn't say *'upset'*. I was semi-joking when I talked about the ghost. No—nothing like as upset as he was outside Colbury station when the car came. And now I can tell you something else," continued Elisabeth excitedly, "it couldn't have been Dr. Copplestone who upset Mr. Medlicott at the station, because I saw him drive off in front of Mr. Medlicott and me."

"In front of?" queried Anthony.

"Before."

"You mean from the point of view of time?"

"Yes, Mr. Bathurst."

"Sure of that?"

"Yes—absolutely sure of that. I saw him distinctly."

"I'm sorry, Miss Grenville, if I appear exacting. But you say distinctly. What about the conditions? The fog and the darkness?"

"Well, I agree with all you say, but I did see him well enough to recognize him as the man I had seen previously in the corridor of the train."

"May I speak?" suddenly and rather surprisingly said Quentin Wynyard.

"Certainly," replied Anthony.

"I think I can clear all this up for you. And in doing so confirm entirely what Elisabeth has just told you."

"Good man," responded Anthony, "and please remember that I welcome anything in the nature of information."

"Well," continued Quentin, "it all happened like this. Gooch was instructed by me to meet the train by which we knew Elisabeth was travelling. Old Medlicott should have arrived earlier, but didn't. One of the local men had the job of meeting him, but as Medlicott didn't turn up at the proper time, the firm 'phoned and told me. I knew then that Medlicott would come on Elisabeth's train and our big car would be able to bring along the two of them. But again, the second train was very late. *And* the Copplestones and Lillywhite were on it. They evidently spotted Gooch before Medlicott and Elisabeth did, told him they were for High Fitchet and drove off up here. Then Medlicott 'phoned and I sent Gooch back for him and Elisabeth. Which, I think, confirms Elisabeth's story in that particular respect."

Elisabeth Grenville beamed at him—the sapphires at their best and most attractive. "Thank you, Quentin. That does prove to a large extent what I said."

She turned to Anthony. "You do feel satisfied now, Mr. Bathurst, don't you?"

Anthony smiled at her. "Yes, Miss Grenville. I think that gives me quite a clear picture of what occurred at the station. Although, of course, I don't know yet what it was that frightened Mr. Medlicott. *And* if you'll all pardon my seeming insistence—one more question. I fancy that I must put it to Mr. Wynyard—he'll probably be best able to answer it. Mr. Lillywhite, you say, shared the car with Dr. and Mrs. Copplestone. Where, then, was Mrs. Lillywhite?"

"No trouble there," answered Quentin, "she had travelled down earlier in the day. Caught one of the morning trains from town. Lillywhite himself couldn't come with her—he had some important business to transact in the city. At least—that's what I've been given to understand."

"So Mrs. Lillywhite was actually in the house when her husband arrived with the Copplestones? I can take that as absolute?"

"That's so," said Quentin, "and both my brother and sister can corroborate that. I've no doubt they will, if you ask them."

Before Anthony could reply, both Nick and Catherine had added their confirmations of what Quentin had stated.

"Good," declared Anthony. "Well then, all that's pretty well cleared up. I'm glad I came in when I did." He looked at his wrist-watch. "I don't think that at the moment I need worry you any more. So I'll ask you to excuse me. There are one or two other little jobs I want to do before it gets too dark. Many thanks, everybody."

Anthony waved to the assembled company and made his exit.

6

He hadn't gone very far when he ran into MacMorran. The latter buttonholed him at once.

"I've just been on the 'phone," he said, "to this Doctor Beddington. Luckily for us he happened to be at home—afternoon surgery or something. I told him I wanted to see him rather urgently so I've arranged to go along there now. Will you come along with me?"

Anthony thought over MacMorran's question. As it had been put to him, he wasn't quite certain whether it was a question or a request. He decided to treat it as the former.

"I don't think I will, Andrew, if it's all the same to you. I've got an idea which I'd like to put in the colander and see what happens to it. Call here on your way back, will you, and pick me up. You won't be with Beddington overlong, I take it?"

"No. Shouldn't be. Unless I run into some other damned complication. All right then—I'll pick you up again here on my way back."

"Thanks, Andrew. And I'll tell you what you can do for me before you go. Leave me those three messages from our elusive friend 'Mr. Levi', will you? The idea that's tickling my brain is to do with him."

MacMorran took out his pocket-book and handed Anthony the three slips for which he had asked. "There you are—and good hunting!"

"The wish is reciprocated, Andrew," returned Anthony.

7

Anthony saw MacMorran off the premises and then made his way to the garage. He chose the garage for the principal reason that he desired seclusion and he thought that his chance of getting it there would be fairly sound. In this idea he was right, so he popped in and made another examination of the three messages which had come to three dead men in the name of "Mr. Levi".

As far as he could see, each word had been cut *en bloc* from newsprint and then stuck on to the notepaper by means of an adhesive substance—in all probability, ordinary stationer's gum.

"Daily Telegraph," said Anthony to himself. "I still think what I thought before."

He looked at the three slips again and made careful comparisons. "And still I harbour doubts about the 'Levi'. Although it *may* have been taken from one of the advertisement columns. One of the small type advertisement columns for choice. The other words, I'm pretty certain, are all off the *'Telegraph* lines'." He grinned to himself at the phrase he had used. "Now for my little test. And *bonne chance!*"

He came out of the garage, closed the doors behind him, and walked round, across the curved and gravelled drive, towards the kitchens. As he had hoped, when he had started off on the expedition it wasn't long before he ran into one of the kitchen staff. It was the housemaid—that was Anthony's guess. He had seen her before, in and about the house, once or twice, and she had seen him. On this occasion, she favoured him with a smile to which Anthony suitably responded.

"Looks intelligent," he thought. "I might do worse than tackle her."

He stopped and walked towards her. Carter, for it was she, smiled at him again. It was a warm, friendly smile. Certainly not one of those smiles that might have meant anything and in all probability, something.

"Good afternoon," said Anthony, "I wonder whether you could help me in a little matter?"

"I'm sure I'll try, sir, if I can. What was it you were wanting?"

"Can you tell me if your late master took in a local paper?"

"Oh yes. I can answer that. He did. We always 'ave the *Colbury Chronicle.* That gives all the Montfichet news, sir. And the news for all the outlying villages."

"I thought it might. Good. Now do you think you could lay your hands on a copy for me?"

"This week's, sir?" came the rather eager question.

"No," replied Anthony slowly, "the copy I wanted would be the one for about three weeks ago. Let me see now." He affected to be making a mental calculation. "It would be for about the 12th of December. Would it be possible to find it—or has it been destroyed."

Carter screwed up her face thoughtfully. "It might be here—and it might not. You see—it's like this. When the family finish with the papers, they go into one of the salvage-boxes. But sometimes, some of the papers have to be used for lighting the fires. I could look for you though, sir," concluded Carter hopefully.

"I see," replied Anthony. "I was afraid that something like that might happen. But tell me, how often are the papers cleared to this salvage-box as you call it?"

"Every week-end, sir. Usually on the Sunday morning. I do it. It's one of my regular jobs. What do you call it? Routine?" Carter giggled a little.

Anthony nodded. "That's good. That does give me a chance. Now, do you think you could show me where this salvage-box is?"

"I'll do that with pleasure, sir. Would you please come this way?"

Carter indicated the direction by turning to the left. Anthony followed her at once. She led him to an out-house, tucked away at the far end of the kitchen-garden.

"There," said Carter, "there's the box where I put the newspapers when they're done with. Shall I look through them for you, sir?"

"No—don't you bother. Thank you all the same. I've taken up too much of your time as it is. With your permission I'll have a look through them myself."

"Right you are, sir," agreed Carter, "then I'll leave you to it. Come and tell me when you're finished—if you don't mind, sir."

Carter darted off and Anthony turned to his task with pleasure. As far as he was concerned, the encounter couldn't have gone off better. He began to turn over the varied assortment of newspapers and discarded magazines.

Observer, Sunday Times, Sport and Country, Country Life, The Listener, Colbury Chronicle, Radio Times, Times, Daily Mail—ah—good—*Daily Telegraph* at last. That's all right, then. The *Telegraph* was delivered daily to the house. Now how many copies could he find here? It wasn't going to be conclusive, of course, because of the fire-lighting factor. All the same, he might find evidence which would at least *fit* his pattern. He would concentrate on the copies of the *Telegraph* which he *was* able to find. December 29th—one. No more for some time. Then December 28th and December 27th together—one underneath the other. No issue, of course, for either Christmas Day or Boxing Day. Papers not published. A gap now. A long gap. Ah—*Telegraph* again. December 24th. Then December 22, 21, and 20. Three in a row. Then the copies for December 18 and 19. That for December 17 seemed to be missing from the heap. Anthony's heart responded suitably to the incident. What else was he going to discover?

He continued the search until he reached the bottom of the bundle. Then he collected all the copies of the *Telegraph* which he had managed to rake up and began to assemble them in chronological order. He found that they dated back to the middle of November. And allowing for Sundays and the two Christmas holidays, there were three missing—two Mondays and a Wednesday. "Yes," said Anthony to himself, "suits me admirably. Rugger reports regularly on the Mondays, and the missing Wednesday issue was for the day following the 'Varsity match at Twickenham. Yes—I'm like the Scotch dipsomaniac threatened with the choice of blindness or total abstinence. I've seen all I want to see."

Anthony tidied up the papers, replaced them in the salvage-box with the various *Telegraph* copies in well-scattered distribution and went back to the kitchen to see if he could contact the maid again. When he looked in the door, she was making up the fire.

"O.K.," he said, "I managed to find that copy of the local paper all right. And many thanks for all the help you gave me." He slipped a currency note into her hand, "Buy yourself a new hat."

Carter remonstrated but Anthony would have none of it. "For the New Year," he asserted, "and I'll promise to come and see how nice you look in it."

Anthony walked back in the direction of the garage. "Next to finding the copies with the actual words cut out of them—I couldn't have done better," he argued. "Narrows my circle pretty devastatingly, too. Seems to me to leave in Miss Amy Wynyard, Quentin Wynyard, Poulton, the son-in-law, Comfit and Lillywhite. Which means that from my nine which I had remaining as 'Plus Possibles', I must now delete Gregory Copplestone, Stansfield, *père et fils*, and Ebenezer Isaacs. For the eminently sound reason that they aren't likely to have known where to find those three copies of the *Daily Telegraph*. Not a certainty by any means—but the odds are that way. On the other hand, Comfit, as a near neighbour, and Lilly-white, as an extremely old acquaintance, can't be dealt with in that way. They *may* have been aware of some of the Wynyard domestic arrangements. But I'm afraid," went on Anthony, "that my new 'five' must be increased to eight, by the obvious addition of Nick, Catherine and Lady Wynyard herself—three who *must* now re-enter the area of suspicion. So the sum total of all that," concluded Anthony, "is that my nine becomes five and then my five comes back to eight. An elimination of one only. The details of which boil down to the fact that the three Wynyards—to my mind an entirely unlikely three—take the place of Dr. Copplestone, the two male Stansfields and Ebenezer Isaacs. Not so good at a summing-up," deliberated Anthony. "Don't like my new list anything like as much as I liked my previous one. I lose Isaacs, young Stansfield and Copplestone, all of whom seemed to possess definite possibilities. Anyhow—it can't be helped if that's the way it goes. And now for my next move." Anthony went back to the house. His objective on this occasion was the bedroom which had been occupied by the murdered Mr. Medlicott.

8

He had previously inquired of Inspector Burrows as to which room had been Medlicott's and having been told, had made a note of the floor and the actual position. So Anthony made his way upstairs, just as Elisabeth Grenville had made her way down, and quietly entered the late Mr. Medlicott's temporary bedroom.

Strangely enough—and had he been asked, he couldn't have answered exactly why—Anthony had the idea that Mr. Medlicott might have possessed a copy of the Holy Bible. At any rate, he felt pretty positive that there must have been a copy about in the house somewhere. When he entered the room, he stood just inside the door and looked round. Disappointment engulfed him. The room, save for the normal furnishing, was bare of everything which might reasonably have belonged to Medlicott.

Anthony had been informed, of course, of the various articles which had been taken from his pockets by Sergeant Arnold at the initial examination, but he had hoped that certain other belongings might have remained and be still in the bedroom. He walked to the wardrobe and looked inside. It was empty.

He went across to the dressing-table. There were seven drawers here, three on the right-hand side, three on the left, and a large one in the middle. They all yielded the same result as had attended him at the wardrobe. They were all empty and it appeared that clean lining-paper had already been put in them. But just as he was about to close the top drawer on the left-hand side, Anthony fancied that he could see something screwed up in one of the far corners. He extended his hand and felt to see whether his idea had been correct. His fingers closed on something—it was a piece of screwed-up paper. It felt like paper which had been hastily scrumpled up and pushed to the back of the drawer.

Anthony pulled it out of the drawer and smoothed it out. It was an envelope, the flap of which was torn. He turned it over and saw, to his surprise, that it had been addressed. In ink. And the name of the addressee was Miss Elisabeth Grenville! That was all. There was no more—just the three words of the name only.

Anthony stood there with the creased envelope in his hand and wondered. It had been addressed to Elisabeth Grenville, but had Elisabeth Grenville ever received it? As far as he could see there was no guarantee of this. Whatever the envelope had contained when it had been fastened, had been removed, but he had no certainty that it had been taken out by the actual person for whom it had been intended. Problem! Anthony scratched his cheek as he pondered. Again—problem number two! Who had written it? Medlicott? The chances were distinctly that way, he considered. Anthony felt worried. There was some stealthy, treacherous work going on at High Fitchet—nothing could be more obvious. Anyhow he was making some sort of progress. That in itself was all to the good.

He pushed the screwed-up envelope into his pocket and took another look at the room. There was no sign of a Bible anywhere.

There was no sign of a book of any kind. So Anthony rather reluctantly came out of the room and closed the door quietly behind him.

For a few seconds he stood on the threshold, thinking. This envelope matter would have to be handled very warily. The first point he would have to establish was with regard to the handwriting. Primarily, whether it were Medlicott's or not. If it were Medlicott's and he had addressed a message of some sort to Elisabeth Grenville, why hadn't the lady made publication thereof? Curious that! If it were another person's handwriting, a similar query at once took shape. On the other hand, had the letter been *intercepted* by a third person? If so, the chances were that that third person was the murderer. Another thing! What had Medlicott to write to Elisabeth Grenville about? A girl whom he had known a few days only?

Anthony went downstairs again—a prey to conflicting thoughts and emotions. The case had taken, he thought, an exceedingly nasty turn and he felt that before it was finished with, both he and Andrew MacMorran would encounter deep waters.

CHAPTER IX

1

ANTHONY strolled back to the lounge in the hope that the group of people whom he had left there would still be available. He found the same people there with the exception, however, of Quentin Wynyard.

"Come in, Mr. Bathurst," said Catherine cordially, "you've timed your entry well. Tea will be ready in a very few minutes."

"That's very charming of you," returned Anthony. "But I don't know that I shall be justified in accepting your hospitality. I haven't really finished yet. Still—it's very kind of you."

"Sit down," said Catherine, "you shall be honoured and sit between Helen and Elisabeth."

"Before I capitulate," went on Anthony, "and surrender myself to the three attractions you promise me, may I ask a question?"

"What is it?" almost chorused Nick and Catherine.

"Could anybody find me a copy of the Bible?"

Catherine put down the pouffe which she had been placing in position and stared at Anthony in astonishment. "What on earth do you want a Bible for at this time of the day? Oh—I'm sorry—I'm afraid that's very rude of me."

Before Anthony could answer, the door opened and a man came in. He was tall and thin—and his hair was almost of the past. Anthony put him as being in the middle fifties. His legs were 'spindley' and he seemed to experience a certain difficulty with regard to picking them up properly when he walked. A cigarette hung from the corner of his mouth, but his eyes were on the kindly side and were, perhaps, the one redeeming feature of his face.

"Oh, come along, Henry," said Catherine, "I can't think why you seem to make a point almost, of always being late."

Poulton grinned at her and Anthony saw, with something of a shock, that there was greediness in the grin.

"Sorry, my dear," said Henry Poulton, "but I didn't realize how late it was."

"This is my husband, Mr. Bathurst." Catherine introduced them. "I don't *think* you've met."

Anthony knew the implication which the remark contained at once. Recognition by him had been immediate. He and Poulton nodded to each other. A maid brought tea and the usual accessories and Catherine began to pour out.

Anthony spoke with studied meekness. "You haven't forgotten my request, I hope? If you'll forgive my persistence."

Nick turned and answered, "You're serious?"

"Quite," replied Anthony.

Helen Repton was watching the exchanges as closely as she dared within the confines of courtesy. Nick spoke again.

"You really want a Bible now?"

"I shan't exactly expire if I don't get one, but I would like to have a look at one, if it's not putting you to too much inconvenience."

Then, to Anthony, a most surprising thing happened. The intervention came from Helen, and again Anthony took the full implication directly she had spoken.

"There *is* a Bible here, Nick."

He looked at her almost enquiringly. "You remember," added Helen Repton quietly.

"Of course," returned Nick Wynyard, "my father!"

Anthony was now listening with both ears open. What revelation was on the way now? Nick turned to him.

"I should explain, I suppose. Helen has just reminded us of something. When my father was found dead that morning in his writing-room, there was a Bible open in front of him on his writing-table. I'll see if I can find it for you."

Nick slipped out of the room. The plot thickens, thought Anthony, and I begin to think that I'm really on to something. He looked across at Catherine.

"I had no idea of that, of course, when I asked for a Bible in the first place."

Catherine dispensed tea. Anthony suitably thanked her. "Far be it from me," he said gravely, "to open old wounds. Nothing could be further from my desire. But does anybody remember at what page Sir John's Bible was open?"

There was a silence as Anthony put the question. He saw Catherine shake her head. And neither Nick nor Quentin was present. But salvation came from an unexpected quarter. The bearer of it was Henry Poulton.

"I can answer that, Bathurst," he said quietly. "I went into the writing-room shortly after my father-in-law was found dead and I happened to notice not only the Bible itself, but also at where it had been opened." He paused.

"Where?" said Anthony.

"It was open," replied Poulton, "at 'The Psalms'—but I can't remember any more than that. So please don't ask me."

"The Psalms—eh," remarked Anthony, "I am more than ordinarily indebted to you."

As he finished speaking, Nick returned. He shook his head as he entered. "Sorry," he said, "I can't find it anywhere. Somebody must have moved it. I'll ask Mother later. I don't particularly want to bother her now."

"I understand," conceded Anthony. And then to himself, "Has the Bible gone the way of the camera? Strange!"

He drank his tea and replaced the cup and saucer on the wagon. The Psalms—eh? The Psalms of David. "Don't bother Lady Wynyard, Sir Nicholas," he said, "I can turn up the passage I wanted some other time. And many thanks for the good intention."

Quentin came in. Nick called to him at the moment of his entry. "I say, Quentin, any idea where Dad's Bible has got to? Bathurst wanted it for a reference, but I've looked nearly everywhere for it. Can't put my hand on it."

Quentin shook his head blankly. "Haven't the foggiest. You know the last time I saw it. Have you asked Mother?"

"No. Not yet. She wants to be left alone."

Quentin nodded. A maid knocked at the door.

"Mr. MacMorran," she announced, "is waiting for Mr. Bathurst."

2

Anthony got in the car and seated himself next to MacMorran. He said, "Did you see Beddington?"

MacMorran said, "I did. And I'm feeling very satisfied. I don't think there's any complication going to arise in that direction. I don't think there'll be anything for us to worry about."

"Good. What did he say?"

"That Sir John Wynyard died an absolutely natural death. Heart failure. Brought on by shock of some kind. Beddington says he'd take his medical reputation to the stake on it. Furthermore, he says he's pretty certain that a P.M. would have disclosed signs of incipient angina. So that's that. Pleased?"

"Certainly not displeased, Andrew."

"What have you been doing yourself?"

Anthony put some of his cards on the table. MacMorran whistled when he heard of his colleague's discoveries in the matter of the missing *Telegraphs*.

"Good work! And I agree with you—it narrows the circle considerably."

Anthony told him of the envelope addressed to Elisabeth Grenville. "Wants handling very carefully, Andrew," he added, "and I'll confess that I haven't made up my mind yet as to the best way to tackle it. I'll discuss it with you again."

They came to the 'Red Lion' at Montfichet. As they alighted, MacMorran chose to be disconcerting.

"Motive," he said, "what was the motive? I'm hanged if *I* know."

"And I'm hanged if I know, either, Andrew. But to-morrow, laddie, is also a day."

3

Anthony and MacMorran went again to High Fitchet on the following morning. On the way, Anthony was unusually quiet and decidedly uncommunicative. He was pondering over many things generally and over one thing in particular. Suddenly he leant over towards MacMorran.

"There's a little book-shop on the corner of the Montfichet Road where it turns off for Canoldon. I want to stop there for a moment. I'll tell the driver, Andrew."

The driver, duly instructed, stopped at the little shop. Anthony alighted from the car and went in. As he had thought, by reason of earlier impressions, the shop stocked many publications of the Religious Tract Society. He asked for a copy of the Bible, was quickly served and walked back to the car with his purchase.

"What have you got there?" asked MacMorran, "infallible systems?"

Anthony showed him. "What's the idea?" demanded the Inspector.

"A little research, Andrew. I grieve to say that I find I can't trust my memory."

"Research for what?"

"Well, the name of Levi isn't unfamiliar to you, is it?"

MacMorran opened his eyes. "I see. One of your hunches?"

"Not sure yet, Andrew. At the moment I'm afraid I'm only groping. But if I grope long enough, I may get hold of something." Anthony opened the Bible. "The Psalms of David," he said to himself, "and if my memory's worth anything, I'm down the wrong street. Genesis, Exodus, Numbers, Deuteronomy, Kings and Chronicles—yes. Almost a certainty in all those—but I *don't* think in the Psalms."

He found the Psalms and began to work rapidly through them. He had a quick eye and was a rapid reader and the operation he was engaged on didn't take too long. He was almost through—with his theory still holding water—when he encountered a shock. The shock was administered by the twentieth verse of the one hundred and thirty-fifth psalm. The relevant words of the Psalm were "Bless Levi, O House of Levi". Or what interested Anthony even more—the word "Levi" found twice within a phrase of only six words.

He closed the book. They were very nearly at High Fitchet. Anthony thought again—hard. He was unable to recall any other passages in Holy Scripture where the word "Levi" would occur twice anything like so quickly. Strange! All of it. And Sir John Wynyard, when he was found dead, had a Bible open on the table in front of him. Open at the Psalms of David. It was precisely at that moment that Anthony began to see his first ray of real light. Of course! Sir John Wynyard was dead!

4

"I'd like a look at the late Sir John Wynyard's writing-room, Andrew. The room where he was found dead. The first in the line of the High Fitchet tragedies."

MacMorran couldn't fail to notice the emphasis which Anthony gave to his last sentence. "Now, I told you what Dr. Beddington said. Death from natural causes. So please don't start that hare again."

"Hares or no hares," replied Anthony imperturbably. "I see no reason to alter what I just said or even the way I said it. And you know what you can do with your Beddington."

Nick and Quentin Wynyard met them in the hall and MacMorran told them what they wanted. The two brothers took them along to the writing-room. Anthony walked towards the table.

"Tell me, Sir Nicholas," he said, "of everything you found here with your father's body."

"Carter, one of the maids, was the first to discover that my father was dead. She at once fetched me. I came straight in here with her. Now I'll try to reconstruct the scene as I saw it and with the details as I saw them." Nick Wynyard paused for a moment in an effort of visualization. "My father's body was sort of sprawled across the table. One of his shoulders seemed to be a little twisted as though he had tried to turn round in some way. To call for assistance, perhaps, when he felt himself coming over ill. It was his right shoulder. The electric fire in there was on. Father turned it on himself—no doubt. A corner of his dressing-gown had been burned and the outside of his left leg was rather badly scorched and blistered. The girdle of his dressing-gown was tied. On the writing-table at the side of his outstretched arms was an opened Bible—which you know all about—father's pen—his fountain-pen—and two or three sheets of our private note-paper. On which, mind you, he had written nothing. He was seized, evidently, before he was able to make a start." Nick stopped. On his face was sadness. He had cherished a tremendous affection for his father. "I think," he went on, "that I've told you everything I can remember."

"Thank you, Sir Nicholas," said Anthony. "You have given me what I wanted. A clear picture of what you saw that morning when you entered the room." He went even nearer to the writing-table. "I suppose you've had no luck with regard to that Bible of your father's?"

"I haven't," said Nick. He looked at Quentin. "Have you run across it anywhere, Quentin? Since yesterday afternoon?" Quentin Wynyard shook his head. "No—I haven't made an exhaustive search. But I asked Mother and Aunt Amy if they knew anything about it. I didn't get anywhere. All Mother could say was that the last place she saw it was in here."

"Thank you," said Anthony again. His thoughts rioted as he stood there. What had been the impelling force which had made the late Sir John Wynyard leave his bed in the early hours of the morning, come downstairs to his writing-room while the house slept, make preparations for the act of writing, open his Bible—and die in his chair? If he could find the answer to that question, he felt that the kernel of the entire problem would be in his hands.

MacMorran came and stood at the writing-table with him. All the usual articles which one is accustomed to find on a writing-table of this kind were there. Desk-calendar, large square pad of blotting paper inset in a leather holder, pen-tray with pens and pencils, piece of eraser, various boxes containing, no doubt, different varieties of stationery, scissors, paper-fasteners, eyelet punch, pins, sealing-wax and a bottle of adhesive paste. Anthony pointed out the array to his professional colleague.

"It's all there, Andrew," he remarked, "the full bundle. But you've doubtless noticed it as I have."

The Inspector grunted some sort of reply which Anthony didn't properly get. MacMorran turned and addressed Sir Nicholas Wynyard.

"Burrows 'phoned me this morning—just before Mr. Bathurst and I came out. He informs me that most of your guests have gone. I mean most of those who had stayed on."

"That is so, Inspector," said Nick, "only the two girls whom I mentioned to you are still with us. Miss Grenville and Miss Repton. Inspector Burrows, I understand, is quite satisfied with regard to the arrangements that he has made. Why? Was there any point which you—?"

"No," replied MacMorran. "I just wanted to confirm what Inspector Burrows told me," and then to Anthony, "is there anything else you want in here, Mr. Bathurst?"

"No. I don't think so, Inspector. I fancy I've satisfied myself as far as this room is concerned."

"Good. Thank you, Sir Nicholas. Thank you, Mr. Wynyard. And we won't trouble you any more for the moment."

Anthony and MacMorran left the two brothers in the writing-room. "Personally," said the Inspector, "I'm going to give all the rooms a thorough comb-out. I've got an idea. I may be lucky and pick up something. What about you?"

Anthony stood there outside High Fitchet in deep thought. "I think, Andrew," he said after some moments of consideration, "that I'll wander a little farther afield. See you later."

Anthony walked off and the Inspector watched his retreating figure.

5

Anthony walked to the fields. To the fields that led to Sturton Ridge. To the particular field with a pond, at the edge of which had been found the dead body of Mr. Medlicott. Dead from a broken neck! And with a strange wound running somewhere from the area of the right temple towards the lobe of the right ear. Like a deep scratch. *And*—according to Sergeant Arnold of the Colbury police—who had made the first examination of Medlicott's body, the dead man's private papers had been subjected to a rigorous search. So the murderer was looking for something, said Anthony to himself.

He came to the edge of the pond, turned his back to it, and viewed the surrounding country. The gate leading to the second field was now on Anthony's left. Not more than a few yards away. And, over the hedge, farther away to the left, still, Anthony could see the gate which gave entry to the first of the fields—the one near the road. He walked out of the second field into the first. For a few moments he stood at the gate with his arms leaning on the top bar. What was he thinking of as he stood there? There was a semi-elusive reminiscence somewhere. Oh—he knew—he had it! A field in Northamptonshire somewhere about the time he'd been playing for the O.U.D.S. In late autumn.

He left the gate, abandoning his picturesque attitude, took eight long paces, and then walked along the path of the first field for a distance of about twenty-five yards. For that was approximately the distance, according to Inspector Burrows, that the snow had been disturbed and kicked up generally. Anthony turned and paced it. Yes—it was a trifle under twenty-five yards—about two and a half yards longer than a cricket-pitch. "But why this field?" he asked himself, "seeing that the water is in the other one?"

Anthony went through the gate again and looked at the water of the pond. If the main struggle took place in the first field and continued for a distance of nearly twenty-five yards—there would still be this gate to negotiate, to say nothing of the eight yards where there had been no disturbance. It was then that an idea occurred to him. All really, because he had thought of a field in Northamptonshire which possessed a five-barred gate. But why? And then kill Gooch in the garage? To prevent Gooch from spilling the beans to Nick Wynyard? Or because—?

The former seemed to be the more likely proposition. He thought of the search-parties again. Quentin and Gooch had set out in the Swanley Bottom direction. The others had gone round by Montfichet Mill. It had been due almost entirely to Helen Repton's foresight and intelligence that she and Nick Wynyard had taken to the fields which led to Sturton Ridge. Would it be worth while dragging or draining the pond?

Anthony thought and then suddenly, remembering, became impatient with himself. Of course it wouldn't! Heavy odds against that probability. What was the matter with him? Going daft in his old age? He somewhat reluctantly turned his back on Mr. Medlicott's pond and retraced his steps towards High Fitchet. Although he considered he had made a certain amount of progress, he nevertheless felt a strong degree of annoyance. His mind wasn't clear. It was cluttered. And for his mind to be 'cluttered' was a condition which he loathed.

Thoughts tossed themselves about in his brain as he made the journey back to High Fitchet. Sir John Wynyard, Walter Medlicott and John Gooch. All of them had been alive this time last week. More ideas came to him and at least one which seemed to hold more than ordinary attraction. He thought of the crumpled envelope he carried in his pocket addressed to Elisabeth Grenville. He thought of the Bible on Sir John Wynyard's desk, open at the Psalms. He thought of Mr. Levi—and then like flashes, as it were, another revelation came to him. The Psalms! Wynyard in all probability hadn't known his Bible too well. And if he were right—Anthony rubbed his hands. He was beginning to get hold at last. A new theory had been born in his mind.

He walked into the house and straight into Elisabeth Grenville. One glance at her face told him that things were not well with her. Elisabeth saw him, seemed to heave a large-sized sigh of relief, and minus all ceremony placed her troubles in front of him immediately.

"Oh, Mr. Bathurst," she said, "I'm so glad to find you. While I've been out this morning, my bedroom's been absolutely ransacked! Everything has been turned out and turned over and left in hopeless confusion on the floor. A positively appalling mess. Whatever is going on in this house?"

Anthony said to her, "What's everything, Miss Grenville?"

"Well, I'd more or less packed my suitcase. Just with clothes and things. In readiness for my departure. They've all been turned out and thrown on to the floor."

6

Anthony saw the implication immediately. "Take me to your room, Miss Grenville," he said, "and show me what's happened. This is most interesting."

"I'm glad you think so," replied Elisabeth, "personally, I can think of many adjectives much more appropriate. Come along now—will you?"

Anthony raced upstairs in her wake. Elisabeth pushed open the door of the bedroom.

"There you are," she said with indignation, "just look at that! Did you ever see such an appalling mess in your life? I could cry to think that I've got to do that all over again—apart from the beastliness of it all."

Anthony looked at the confusion that reigned on the floor. It certainly presented an unholy mess. He walked past Elisabeth, closed the bedroom door and stood there with his back against it. He listened for some few seconds before he spoke. When he did say anything, he said very quietly, "What are they after, Miss Grenville? What have you got in your possession that they want so much?"

He watched her face carefully before she answered him. The only emotion that he was able to trace on it was astonishment. Before her answer came she shook her head.

"What do you mean, Mr. Bathurst? I really don't understand you."

"Surely I was plain?" he replied. "Could I have been more explicit?"

He repeated his two previous questions. This time her response was ready enough.

"Nothing! Absolutely nothing at all! What on earth could I have? I've never been here before in my life."

Anthony came away from the door. "Miss Grenville," he said, "please try to help me. Your help now may well be the turning-point towards the solution of all this recent dreadful business. Make sure, will you, please, that nothing of yours has been taken. Go through your things *now*. While I'm here with you."

Elisabeth nodded that she understood and knelt down by the heap of sartorial disorder on the floor. "I'll do my best," she said, "as far as I can."

She went through the things methodically, folding some and smoothing out others. Anthony let her do the work minus interruption. He stood between her and the door. When she had finished, Elisabeth looked up at him.

"As far as I can say, relying entirely on memory, there's been nothing stolen. I *think* that all my things are here."

"Thanks very much. That fact established then, I'll revise the terms of my questions. I now ask you, Miss Grenville, what do they *think* you've got—and *why* do they think it?"

Despite the amendment of the reference, however, the look of astonishment remained on Elisabeth's face.

"I'm still wondering what on earth you mean, Mr. Bathurst. Because I assure you with the greatest possible sincerity that I haven't the slightest idea what you're talking about."

The indignation which had been Elisabeth's when she brought Anthony upstairs seemed to be increasing. Anthony smiled.

"In the face of such a categorical denial, Miss Grenville, let me hasten to say that I believe you. But all the same, let's get this straight. Because you're in the very thick of this murder drama, whether you like it or not. Extremely willy-nilly."

"But how?" she gasped.

Anthony looked at her again and what he saw pleased him. He determined to take a chance. He found the envelope which had her name written on it. "What did this contain?" he asked her.

Again he watched her closely as she took the envelope.

"What's this?" she exclaimed incredulously, "and where did you get it from?"

But Anthony had no explanations for her yet awhile. On the other hand, he waited for her.

"Why is this addressed to me?" demanded Elisabeth.

"All I can tell you," said Anthony at last, "is that I picked that up in this house. Just as it is. I mean by my remark that it had already been opened. Actually it was much more creased up when I found it than it is now."

"I've never seen it before—I don't know what was in it—and why do interfering busybodies open my letters?" returned Elisabeth—all in one breath.

"Then," returned Anthony, "you know exactly as much as I do. So we're all square."

Elisabeth looked as though she were gathering breath for a second verbal onslaught.

"Take it easy, Miss Grenville," went on Anthony, "I'm not in this for a Happy New Year, believe me—and two men have died, you know."

Elisabeth's resentment melted like snow under sunshine.

"I'm so sorry—but this envelope rather got me on the raw. And coming on top of what had been done to my room, it rather put the lid on things. You tell *me*—what's it all mean and what's some of it about?"

"Sorry. No can do! I'm just as mystified as you are. Still, you can answer one question—or perhaps you can." He pointed again to the envelope. "Whose handwriting is that?"

Elisabeth laughed weakly. "And it was only 'perhaps' after all. I can't even tell you that. I don't know, and as far as I can tell, I've never seen it before." Elisabeth subsided.

"Pity. I had hoped you would be able to help me. And now I want to say something to you of the very highest importance." Elisabeth's eyes met Anthony's. She was impressed not only by what she saw, but also by the gravity of his tone.

"What is it, Mr. Bathurst?"

"I want you to regard what I've told you and shown you—in the matter of that envelope marked with your name—as a strict confidence. Please don't whisper it to a soul. I'm sorry to be so melo-dramatically insistent on the point, but it's vital. Please tell me that you understand."

"I do understand, Mr. Bathurst. And it shall be as you wish. You may rely on me implicitly."

"Many thanks, Miss Grenville. And one more thing before we float back to the others. Make light of this outrage to which your things have been subjected, if you're taxed with it. If nobody mentions it to you—keep silent about it. That's the best card we can play, I think. Whoever was responsible was interrupted in some way." He stopped as though he were trying to think of something. "Oh, and there's something else. Medlicott! You travelled down from London with him. I know we've had all that out before."

He smiled as he said this. Elisabeth smiled back. "Well, what were you going to say?"

"It's difficult to put into words. But I'm not asking the question idly, believe me. Did he exchange *any* confidence with you? No matter how trivial?"

"None at all, Mr. Bathurst."

"Nothing that by any stretch of imagination could be regarded as a confidence?"

"No. Nothing even by that standard."

The blank wall again, thought Anthony, and yet *something* must have occurred at *some* time or the other. What the heck could it have been?

He thanked Elisabeth again and turned to go. But he perceived that something was troubling her. "What is it, Miss Grenville?"

"Don't think I'm silly," she said impulsively, "but since this last business has happened"—she gestured towards the contents of her suitcases—"I've been the victim of some horrible thoughts." She paused.

"Go on," he said encouragingly.

"Well," she continued, "when I think of Sir John Wynyard and then poor Mr. Medlicott and then Gooch, the chauffeur—and now this—well, I'm beginning to get cold shivers." She faced him fairly and squarely. "Need I?" she asked.

Anthony hesitated. "Tell me the truth," she insisted. "I'd rather know than not know. Much rather. And if it's . . . er . . . sticky . . . I'll try not to be too frightened."

"You mean do I think that you're in any sort of personal danger?"

Elisabeth nodded bravely. "Exactly that, Mr. Bathurst."

"I think that it's quite feasible, Miss Grenville. But . . . take courage. Steps will be taken immediately for your protection. At the same time, don't go anywhere alone, and when you go to bed at night, see that your bedroom door is locked."

"Would it be better if I went home? I could easily invent an excuse of sorts. If it's as bad as you seem to think it is."

Anthony considered her suggestion. "How long have you promised to stay?"

"Till the end of the week. It was really for Catherine's sake. But I could easily—"

He cut in. "No. Stay on. Let the existing arrangements stand. As I said, I'll speak to Inspector MacMorran and you shall have adequate protection. And if you obey instructions, I don't think you'll have any cause to worry." He patted her on the shoulder. "Come on—downstairs—and chin up."

"O.K. Sergeant," responded Miss Grenville.

As they went downstairs she wondered if she should have told him of her encounter with Aunt Amy.

CHAPTER X

1

ANTHONY had immediate conference with MacMorran and Helen Repton. He informed them of what had happened to Elisabeth. MacMorran listened and nodded.

"Job for you, Helen. Lucky you're here. Look after the little lady with the blue eyes. As Mr. Bathurst says—from now onwards she's the apple of both your eyes."

Helen signified her understanding. "I think I can manage that," she said, "but all the same, I wish I could see a little daylight."

"And you're not alone in that r-respect," supplemented MacMorran, "for as far as I'm personally concerned, the case is as black to me to-day as when I first started to work on it."

"It's black, Andrew, I agree," contributed Anthony, "but it might be blacker. I think, perhaps, that one or two glimmers of light are beginning to show through. Just here and there. What's been happening this morning?"

"Burrows has had his men make a thorough search of the hedge that separates the two fields. On each side of the gate near Medlicott's pond."

"Oh, what was the idea?"

"Well, he came to me for my O.K. before he fixed things. I let him go ahead. He's got an idea that we may be lucky and pick up some sort of a clue there."

"Is the job over?"

"He's not back yet. Or at any rate, if he is, I haven't seen him."

"Well," said Anthony with a grin, "there's a camera missing and also a copy of the Bible which belonged to the late Sir John Wynyard.

If Burrows is lucky enough to find either of those, you might be good enough to let me know, Andrew. But I don't think he will—in a hedge."

As he spoke he caught sight of Quentin Wynyard. Anthony beckoned to him. Quentin came up, looking a little disgruntled. "Any sign of your missing camera, Mr. Wynyard?"

"No," replied Quentin shortly; "if you're so interested, why don't you chaps hunt for it?"

Anthony was in like a flash. "Why—do you consider it of such great importance?"

Quentin countered successfully. "Not at all, I had the idea you did. You've made so many enquiries about it."

Anthony knew that the round had gone against him. He essayed another thrust. "And the missing Bible, Mr. Wynyard? Has that turned up anywhere?"

"No. There's no sign of that either. There's another job for you. Probably the person who took the one, took the other."

"Mr. Wynyard," said Anthony, "you've presented me with an idea."

"Glad of that," riposted Quentin, as he turned away, "although I'm afraid it'll find itself a little on the lonely side." Helen Repton made no attempt to conceal her indignation. "What's biting him? The idea! Talking to you like that! Disgusting, I call it."

Anthony laughed gaily. "That's all right, Helen. I can take it. He put me down for the count twice. Good job the bell saved me." But his mood changed when he addressed MacMorran. "Andrew," he said, "I'm going to take a day off to-morrow. Fresh woods and pastures new. I'll be back on the following day."

"Oh—ay! And where will you be goin' to?"

"To the Midlands, Andrew. Aldersford. The home of the late Walter Medlicott."

"I've a mind to come with you," replied the Inspector.

"I know of nobody, Andrew, who would be more welcome."

"Gertcher," returned the Inspector.

2

When Anthony and MacMorran arrived in Aldersford, the old county town was celebrating market-day. And Anthony and MacMorran, served by an excellent train from Paddington, hit it at almost the busiest hour of the day.

As the late Mr. Medlicott had heard the clock of St. Clement's strike eleven on the day which had sealed his fate, Anthony and MacMorran heard it strike twelve a few minutes after they left the station *en route* for the offices of "Medlicott, Stogdon and Medlicott".

The streets of the quaint old town were thronged. Some of the farmers were beginning to move slowly off to the hostelries of their choice for lunch, but, generally speaking, the business of the day was still near its height and there was the usual scurrying, jostling crowd on the corner by the Midland Counties Bank, at the summit of Crabbe Hill. But few of the smaller lorries had started on their journeys to the more distant valleys, and cars, motor-vans, larger lorries and even in some instances, carts, still lingered in and near the market-place and their respective owners helped to fill the streets of Aldersford with a chattering and moving multitude. Knots of people were to be found near the fronts of the old-fashioned, low-browed shops, and other groups formed in awkwardly placed formations on the kerbs, in the gutters, and even in the roadway itself.

As Anthony and the 'Yard' Inspector made their way along the streets, the crowds moving towards the inns began to grow larger, and judging by their temper and general air of hilarity most of them, according to their fashion and the fashion of their forbears, intended to dine well and drink deep. For Aldersford lay in the heart of a county of plenty and the words 'restriction' and 'austerity' had small meaning for the majority of its inhabitants.

Anthony and MacMorran passed from Sheep Street, skirted the market-place and entered the High Street. The first thing to catch Anthony's eye was the quaint stone figure of the ancient Prince Julian, the conqueror of his day, and who now looked down serenely and benignantly on the turmoil of the High Street. As they passed St. Clements, the great clock raised its voice above the din and sounded the first quarter.

Anthony nudged MacMorran. "We'd better hurry up, Andrew, or we shall find our people have cleared off to lunch."

MacMorran nodded and the two men quickened their pace. They came to the 'Lion' and saw the light of the blazing fires shining through the windows. The same light that Medlicott had seen from his own windows on the twenty-second day of the previous month.

"The offices are somewhere round here, Andrew. Opposite the 'Lion', we were told. I suggest that we cross over."

They crossed. Directly they reached the pavement on the other side of the road, Anthony pointed to the welcome brass plate, almost in front of them. "Medlicott, Stogdon and Medlicott".

"Here we are, Andrew. Twenty-two minutes past twelve. And a good hope of landing our fish before he responds to the call of the inner man."

They entered and saw from the evidence in the doorway that the offices of "Medlicott, Stogdon and Medlicott" were situated on the first floor. Anthony motioned to MacMorran to precede him up the staircase. A youth answered their tap on a small window marked "Enquiries".

MacMorran pushed his professional card towards him. The youth picked it up. Anthony saw from his expression that he was suitably impressed.

"Just a moment, sir," and then, "I'll see if Mr. Adderley's free. Won't keep you a moment, sir."

The youth closed the window and disappeared with unusual alacrity. MacMorran turned and winked at Anthony.

"He'll tell his mother a yarn to-night. Unless the excitement proves too much for him."

They weren't kept waiting long. The window was slid open and the face of the youth reappeared in the aperture.

"Come this way, gentlemen—if you please."

He ushered them into a bare austere-looking room. A tall, thin, cadaverous-faced man sat at a desk. He rose as the office youth brought them in. The boy closed the door and made himself scarce.

"Good afternoon, gentlemen," said the tall man. He indicated two chairs, which obviously had just been placed by the side of his desk. "Sit down, will you, please."

MacMorran and Anthony sat in the two chairs. "I'd better introduce myself," went on the tall man. "I am Stephen Adderley, the late Mr. Medlicott's managing clerk. And you—?"

He paused. MacMorran supplied the details. "Chief Detective Inspector MacMorran. This gentleman is Mr. Anthony Bathurst." Adderley nodded. "Well . . . er . . . now that those little preliminaries are over, what can I do for you?"

"Well, Mr. Adderley," replied MacMorran, "I'm afraid our business really is with the remaining partners. Either . . . er . . . with the other Mr. Medlicott—or Mr. Stogdon. It's in connection, you see, with the circumstances of Mr. Walter Medlicott's death." Adderley shook his head and smiled a pitying sort of smile. "That, sir, is, I regret to say, impossible. The late Mr. Walter Medlicott was the sole surviving partner of the firm of 'Medlicott, Stogdon and Medlicott'. Mr. Stogdon died three years ago and Mr. Roger Medlicott, Mr. Walter's elder brother, predeceased him by nearly ten years. I really don't know what will become of us. I expect a neighbouring firm of solicitors will eventually amalgamate. There should be no difficulty. We had the cream of the Aldersford and district legal business."

This was a bit of a facer to MacMorran so Anthony decided to take a hand.

"In that case, then, Mr. Adderley, the position becomes very different, and you are no doubt the man whom we want to have a talk with. From our point of view, now, *you* become Medlicott, Stogdon and Medlicott."

Adderley made the semblance of a bow, but the effort was not easy and bordered perhaps on the grotesque.

'H'm,' thought Anthony, 'local boy makes good—eh?'

MacMorran came in here again. "Well, you've heard how Mr. Bathurst has put it, Mr. Adderley. In the circumstances you've outlined—we're prepared to talk to you. My colleague would like to ask you a few questions."

"Then I'll do my best to answer them. Although I'm afraid—" Adderley stopped abruptly. Anthony noticed the sharp cessation but ignored it. He addressed Adderley.

"Mr. Medlicott left Aldersford on Christmas Eve to travel to High Fitchet, the home of his friend and client, Sir John Wynyard, in order to spend Christmas with that gentleman and his family."

Adderley inclined his head. "That is so, Mr. Bathurst."

"Do you know if he had any *other* reason for going? Beyond the one that we may call the social one?"

"No. I do not. But let me explain. I was not in the late Mr. Medlicott's confidence to that extent. Mr. Medlicott was a solicitor of the old-fashioned type and extremely reticent with regard to all his business. I am not a partner, remember. I was simply the chief clerk."

"You are, then, unaware if he had any *special* business with Sir John Wynyard?"

"I am certainly unaware. But"—Adderley looked down at his finger-nails—"if my personal opinion is worth anything, I *think* that he had."

"That's interesting, Mr. Adderley. Most interesting. And will you please tell us why you hold that view?"

Adderley repeated the finger-nail business. "Gentleman," he said pompously, "I very rarely make any statement unless I am pretty sure of my ground. And I think I can assert without boastfulness that I have built up a reputation in Aldersford for . . . er . . . accuracy . . . and . . . er . . . reliability." He leant forward over his desk and looked at Anthony and MacMorran with extreme solemnity. "Gentlemen, the first indication that I had that Mr. Medlicott would be spending Christmas with Sir John Wynyard at High Fitchet was during the afternoon of the 22nd of December—that was the Saturday before Christmas."

"Do I take it," interjected MacMorran, "that there was anything unusual about that?"

"Unusual! I'll say there was." Adderley approached vehemence. "Whenever Mr. Medlicott went away, the arrangements were *always* left in my hands. Invariably! I would be informed days—more likely weeks—beforehand. I would look up his trains for him and generally see to all the details of the necessary transport. In short, gentlemen, it was my practice to take all those irksome little duties out of his own care and worry. On this occasion, however, I knew nothing. Nothing whatever—until about half-past three on that Saturday afternoon. He had given me instructions before midday not to leave the office until I had seen him again. So I stayed on. About half-past three he telephoned for me. I went in. He then informed me, gentlemen, that he was spending the Christmas holiday at High

Fitchet. With his old friend, Sir John Wynyard. And that he would return to business on the Monday after Christmas. That was the first and only intimation which I had concerning Mr. Medlicott going to High Fitchet."

Stephen Adderley stopped. But before either Anthony or MacMorran was able to put a question, he began again.

"There is also something else which I should like to bring to your notice. Somewhere about eleven o'clock on that Saturday morning, Mr. Medlicott spoke to me on the internal telephone. He instructed me to take in to him the box containing the Wynyard papers and a copy of the current 'A.B.C.' Naturally I did so. He then told me that on no account was he to be disturbed for an hour. No doubt, gentlemen, from the information that I have given you, you will be able to make the same deduction as I have. Namely, that Mr. Medlicott's journey to High Fitchet was *not* entirely due to social amenities."

Stephen Adderley sat back and pursed his lips. MacMorran looked at Anthony. The latter shook his head.

"You, Andrew," he said.

MacMorran nodded. "This . . . er . . . box . . . you mentioned, Mr. Adderley? I take it that it . . . er . . . contains the private papers to do with the Wynyard estate? The . . . er . . . Wynyard deed-box?"

"Precisely," said Adderley, prim-lipped.

"What happened to it? After Medlicott had finished with it?"

"It was replaced by Mr. Medlicott in our strong-room. It's in there now."

"Has it been opened since the death of Medlicott?"

"Unfortunately no, Inspector. Mr. Medlicott kept certain keys in his possession. They were never out of his possession. Where they are now I have no idea. But I presume that if they were not found on his person when he was found dead, they must be kept somewhere at his private house. I have already written to both Sir Nicholas and Lady Wynyard to that effect."

Adderley pursed his lips again.

"Where did Mr. Medlicott live?"

"About two miles out of Aldersford, Inspector. On the road to Magdalen Verney."

"The servants are there, I suppose?"

"I understand so. There's a maid and a cook-housekeeper."

MacMorran thought things over. After a time he came at Adderley with another question.

"You can assure me, Mr. Adderley, and I'm extremely serious in the matter, that you have no knowledge *whatever* of the business which took Mr. Medlicott to High Fitchet, or even of anything of importance which has recently transpired between him and Sir John Wynyard? Please consider my question most carefully before you answer me."

Adderley showed no hesitation. Or did he spend any time on consideration of MacMorran's question. On the other hand, he shook his head almost pontifically.

"I have no knowledge whatever, Inspector, of the kind you mention."

"Thank you, Mr. Adderley." He turned the matter over to Anthony. Anthony gestured his acceptance.

"One or two questions, Mr. Adderley, and these, I imagine, you'll find no difficulty in answering. You had no intimation, in this office, that Mr. Medlicott was concerned with any current Wynyard business, *before* that Saturday morning you told us about? That's the Saturday morning which immediately preceded Christmas?"

Stephen Adderley shook his head emphatically. "None at all, Mr. Bathurst. I can give you my word of honour that prior to that morning I hadn't heard the name of Wynyard mentioned in this office for some months at least."

"Thank you. That clears that. Now you stated just now that Mr. Medlicott sent for you and told you, *inter alia*, that you weren't to leave the office until he'd seen you again. I think, from memory, that they were the exact words you used. And that, acting in accordance with those instructions, you stayed in the office until about half-past three. Now the day was Saturday, Mr. Adderley. Isn't it your custom to close at midday on Saturdays?"

"No. Not altogether. Mr. Medlicott always stayed until about four o'clock. He was old-fashioned in many ways. Neither of us ever went *before* lunch. I used to pack up about two o'clock. Anywhere, say, between two and half-past."

"I see. A little unusual—these days."

"Perhaps," replied Adderley, "but doubtless the reasons would not be too difficult to find. I have said that Mr. Medlicott was old-fashioned. He was a bachelor, too, as you know. Which meant that he had no strong home interest—in fact, he had little interest of any kind in anything outside his professional work." Anthony nodded. "I agree. And also, if I may say so, a firm like yours, Mr. Adderley, is scarcely comparable with an ordinary commercial undertaking. The point is taken. Now another question. Have you ever heard Mr. Medlicott refer to anything in the nature of precious stones—or jewellery? Pearls say—diamonds—or anything of that kind?"

"No-o," answered Adderley, "I can't say that I have." Anthony pressed him at once. "You aren't altogether too sure?"

"Well, I was thinking of something which isn't quite on the lines you mentioned. There is just this. Lady Verney, of Magdalen Verney— that's a village a few miles from here—whose family had been clients for generations, died a few months ago and made a bequest to Mr. Medlicott of a very valuable diamond ring. A very valuable ring indeed. It had belonged to her late husband, Sir Cyril Verney. But that's all I can think of. If you hadn't mentioned the word 'diamonds', in all probability I shouldn't even have thought of that."

Anthony evinced interest. "Did Mr. Medlicott wear this ring, Mr. Adderley?"

"Do you mean—wear it habitually?"

"Well—yes."

"The answer's 'no', Mr. Bathurst. But I've seen him wearing it on special occasions. Not *very* often."

"Could you describe this ring, Mr. Adderley?"

Adderley almost smiled at the question. "I don't know that I'm much of a hand at that sort of thing. Whatever training I've had hasn't been in that direction. But it was, of course, a man's ring, gold with a really magnificent diamond in it. I've never actually handled it, but I have seen Mr. Medlicott wearing it on one or two occasions since the bequest was made to him. But I do happen to know this, gentlemen—the ring was worth a considerable sum of money."

"Thank you, Mr. Adderley—that information may be very useful to us. I'm certain that Chief Inspector MacMorran will agree with me. Now I've only two more questions to put to you. In the course of your professional association with Mr. Medlicott, have you ever come across a Mr. Levi?"

"Never," replied Adderley—without the slightest hesitation—"in this district of England, a name of that type would arrest the attention at once."

Anthony nodded. "The name conveys no association to you at all?"

Adderley's hatchet-face approximated geniality for the first time since the beginning of the interview. "No association whatever, beyond its normal one. And the only real one of which I can think on the spur of the moment is that I once saw a pawnbroker's shop in Birmingham which bore that name—I think the full name was Solomon Levi."

"Thank you again. Now my last question, Mr. Adderley. At least, as far as I know, it's my last. A man has died at High Fitchet, since Mr. Medlicott, by the name of Gooch. Christian name—John. John Gooch. He was employed as a chauffeur by the late Sir John Wynyard. And when I say died, there's little doubt, I'm afraid, that like Mr. Medlicott, the poor fellow was murdered. Is the name 'Gooch' familiar to you as being connected in any way with your late employer?"

Neither Anthony nor MacMorran was in any manner prepared for the answer which Adderley gave to this last question. He reached over the desk, found a paper-knife and began to balance it on one of his fingers.

"If I answer your question, Mr. Bathurst, strictly in the terms in which you asked it, my answer is again 'no'. To the best of my knowledge, Mr. Medlicott has never had any dealings, professional or otherwise, with any person of that name."

He paused. The pause was deliberate. It had been calculated—for effect. "Go on," said Anthony.

This time, Stephen Adderley permitted himself to smile. There was no doubt about it. "Well, what I was about to add, gentlemen, was this. *I* know a family by the name of Gooch. But I'm afraid there can be no possible connection with them and this unfortunate young man who's been murdered at High Fitchet." Anthony felt much as a drowning man may feel when he clutches an unexpected life-belt.

"Your Gooch family, Mr. Adderley. Where do they live?"

"In my own village, Mr. Bathurst. But a few miles from here. In the village of Magdalen Verney."

Anthony pushed back his chair and stood up.

3

At last, thought Anthony, the trail is leading somewhere.

"Tell me, Mr. Adderley," he said, "as much as you can concerning the Goochs of Magdalen Verney."

Adderley poured a frigid smile on what he evidently regarded as Anthony's misplaced eagerness.

"There isn't very much for me to tell, gentlemen. They have nothing to do with Mr. Medlicott. Or with Sir John Wynyard. Or with any of the Wynyard family. Or even with Lady Verney—if that's the direction your mind's travelling in. Gooch is the village blacksmith. His family have had the smithy there for many years."

"Is this Gooch at High Fitchet no relation? Are you sure of that?" Anthony put the questions quickly.

"I don't think he can be," replied Adderley slowly. "To the best of my knowledge and recollection, Jim Gooch, the smith at Magdalen Verney, has only two sons. And they both work at the forge with their father. Strangely enough, considering the nature of their work, neither was taken up for military service. The elder, Jim, same name as his father, is lame. Had a bad foot from birth. And the younger has had epileptic fits. So old Jim was able to keep them both. This fellow who's been killed at High Fitchet couldn't have been either of them."

This was disquieting news for Anthony and MacMorran.

"Have you seen Gooch, the smith at Magdalen Verney, since the news was published of the death of the Gooch at High Fitchet?"

Adderley shook his head. "I don't think I have, in the way you mean. That is to say, I haven't spoken to him. But I very rarely do speak to him. If I walk by the smithy, I can hear Jim and his two boys at work in there; and if he were standing outside the forge when I happened to go by, I'd pass the time of day with him, but that's about the extent of my contacts with him." Adderley stopped, but before either Anthony or MacMorran could say anything he had gone on again.

"But I can add this, gentlemen, if it will help you at all. There's been no talk in the village, as far as I'm aware, that the Gooch killed at High Fitchet was any relation or connection of old Jim's. And I *think*, if there had, it would have come to my ears."

"There hasn't—eh?" Anthony turned to MacMorran. "Doesn't seem so promising as it looked, does it, Andrew? And yet—something in my bones seems to tell me—" He broke off. "Is Jim Gooch a talkative man? A man likely to spread news amongst the villagers?"

Adderley was not too quick in replying. When he did find words for the answer, they came rather slowly and very deliberately.

"No. I shouldn't call him a gossip, by any means. Rather the other way—if anything. On the dour—taciturn side. And I can quite understand that if the news were bad—or in the nature of being discreditable in any way—old Jim Gooch would keep his mouth shut about it."

This, Anthony felt, sounded a great deal better. MacMorran threw theories away and became practical.

"This village of Magdalen Verney, Mr. Adderley—how do we get there from here?"

Adderley rose from his chair and walked to the windows which faced the warmth and comfort of the 'Lion'. He beckoned to the Inspector.

"You see that corner there? Just past the 'Lion'? There's a red low-decked bus runs from there every hour. Leaves at ten past each hour. It runs between Aldersford and Scimitar St. Mary. It passes through Magdalen Verney. Get off at the 'Green Dragon'. You ask the conductor—he'll see you're all right. Jim Gooch's smithy is about five minutes' walk from the 'Dragon'. You walk up the main street on the left—same side as the bus puts you down. It's just past the village hall."

"Thank you very much, then, Mr. Adderley," returned MacMorran, "for all the information you have given us."

Adderley spread out his hands deprecatingly. "I'm afraid it hasn't been very much. I feel, indeed, that I know so little. So little about anything—and everything. I'm just bewildered." He came to the door of the office to show them out. "I haven't been able yet, gentlemen, to work out what Mr. Medlicott's death is going to mean to me. Good-bye."

They shook hands.

4

"What do you make of it?" asked MacMorran when Anthony and he got outside.

"Don't know," said Anthony. "Get very little beyond a mere glimmer here and there. But I'll tell you what I do think's indicated. A spot of lunch at the 'Lion' before we catch the 2.10 bus to Scimitar St. Mary via Magdalen Verney. Can you put forward a sounder suggestion, Andrew?"

The Yard Inspector could not, so they acted on Anthony's proposal and lunched at the 'Lion', Aldersford. Anthony picked up the menu and gave it a quick glance.

"Not so bad, Andrew. Thought it mightn't be. Seein' as 'ow it's market day in these 'ere parts. Roast turkey, me lad."

"Unless we're too late," said MacMorran, the practical, looking at his watch.

The waitress who eventually came to serve them announced with a smile that their luck was in.

"We're pretty crowded," she said, "but not so crowded as on some market-days. So we've got a bit over to-day."

Over the lunch, which was excellent, Anthony made one point. "There's at least one thing, Andrew, I'd like to do. I feel that it may clear the air a trifle. It certainly will for me. See the telephone people with regard to a possible call on the Saturday morning before Christmas—the date would be December 22nd—either from Medlicott to Sir John Wynyard at High Fitchet or the reverse way—from Sir John at High Fitchet to Medlicott here. I would like to know whose fingers it was that started this particular ball rolling."

MacMorran nodded. "I had it in mind," he said dourly, "the same idea occurred to me when we were in Adderley's office. I don't know that it will tell us much, though," he added.

"Some morsels, Andrew," countered Anthony, "are valuable. And it's no use starting on a case unless you begin on it from the right angle."

"This one's got so many damned angles! And now we've collected, so it seems to me, at least two more."

"And what would they be, Andrew?" asked Anthony.

"I should have thought you knew them as well as I did. There's this valuable diamond ring which was left to Medlicott by this Lady Verney we've just heard about, and then there's this Gooch coincidence."

Anthony nodded. "I agree, Andrew. And which of the two would you regard as possessing the greater importance?"

"The diamond ring, undoubtedly. Bearing in mind what we already know in terms of Mr. Levi. Although personally, I don't think either of them will lead to the murderer."

Anthony crumbled bread as he listened to his professional colleague. As he made no reply, MacMorran came again.

"Well, you've heard what I have to say. What do you think yourself?"

"About the questions I asked you, do you mean?"

"That's right."

"Well, Andrew—I feel just a little more optimistic than you appear to do. As I said, when we came away from Adderley just now, I have got a glimmer here and there and now and then. And you know yourself how quickly a 'glimmer' can become a real light." He stopped—to drink from his tankard. "Personally I'm attracted by this new Gooch development. What you just called the Gooch *coincidence*. To me, the odds are that it's much more a *bona fide* connection than a chance coincidence. And that's what I'm banking on principally, Andrew, as I sit here eating this excellent poultry and drinking this admirable beer." He grinned at MacMorran.

"Meaning," said the latter, "that whichever way you look at it, life has its compensations—eh?"

"You've said it, Andrew." Anthony drained his tankard. "What were your impressions of Adderley?"

"I wasn't *too* impressed," replied the Yard Inspector; "my description of him is a 'would be'. He seemed to me to be trying all the time to create the impression in *our* minds that he was a much more important personage than we think he is. Did you get anything like that?"

"Something, perhaps. And I think, too, that there's a reason for it."

"How do you mean?"

"The death of Medlicott. In a way, this Stephen Adderley feels that he's become 'the firm'! From a position of subordination, he has now nobody in charge of him. Something like an N.C.O. when all his officers have been killed."

"That's the idea," confirmed MacMorran, with something like enthusiasm; "that's just about the impression I formed. Sums it up pretty well. What's the time?"

"Just on two, Andrew. I'll get the bill and we'll be moving."

5

There were several people waiting for the Scimitar St. Mary bus when Anthony and MacMorran arrived to take their places in the queue. But they were able to obtain seats and booked to the 'Green Dragon', Magdalen Verney.

"How long shall we be?" enquired Anthony of the conductor. "Forty minutes, sir."

"Thank you."

The country through which they passed was pleasing to the eye in almost every respect. The downland curved away in olive-green folds and here and there could still be discerned traces of rifts left by the recent snow. Eventually, the bus came to the 'Green Dragon' and Anthony and MacMorran alighted.

"Five minutes' walk up the left-hand side," said Anthony. They passed an ivied church, the vicarage adjoining, and a row of red-brick cottages, each with its own trimly-kept front garden. Then the village school, two large yellow cottages, the 'New Inn', the village hall, and came to the smithy of James Gooch.

The reddish glare of the forge could be seen as they approached it and the music of hammers on anvil came to their ears. "Clink . . . clink . . . clunk." Two men were at work in the forge—an elderly man and a younger man who limped at his job. He was dealing with a glowing plough coulter as Anthony and MacMorran came to the doorway of the smithy and the hammers were swinging with rhythm and regularity.

As Anthony and his companion stopped in the doorway, the elder man of the two workers came to him. He held a half-fullered shoe in a pair of tongs.

"Good afternoon, gentlemen," he said in a strong, resonant voice, "and what can I do for you?"

MacMorran stepped forward at the smith's challenge. "Good afternoon. I presume that I am addressing Mr. James Gooch?"

"My name," returned the smith—not without a certain surliness.

"There's my card," added the Inspector. "I'd like to have a word with you. Shall we step inside."

The smith took the card in his disengaged hand, read it and frowned. "Give over, Jim," he called out to the man who limped. The noise of the hammer ceased. "Come inside," said the smith, "though what Scotland Yard has to do with the likes of me, the good God above alone knows."

Anthony and MacMorran followed him into the forge. Gooch unclasped the tongs he was carrying and let the half-fullered shoe fall to the ground. Then he put down the tongs.

"Now, gentlemen," he declared, "let's have it out whatever it is. Jim—stand away there."

"I hope that we shan't take up too much of your time, Mr. Gooch," said MacMorran, "but we're making inquiries with regard to the death of a young man named John Gooch at High Fitchet, which took place a few days after Christmas. To be more precise, the *murder* of this young man. If it will help you at all, he was employed as a chauffeur by the late Sir John Wynyard."

Gooch stood immovable, his powerful hands pressed against the front of his leather apron.

"Well," he said stolidly, after a brief period of silence, "and what has all that to do with me?"

"The position's this, Mr. Gooch," continued MacMorran, "we are trying to trace any relatives that he may have had, and, in accordance with that, we have found our way here. Is it possible that he is a connection of yours, or of your family? Or are we entirely on the wrong track?"

Anthony saw Gooch glance in the direction of the recesses of the forge, as though he were trying to catch the eye of his son. But the man looked away again and eventually his eyes came back again to face MacMorran.

"What was the young fellow's Christian name?" he asked—the surliness still present in his voice-tone.

"I told you—John."

There came another period of silence—and then, somewhat to Anthony's surprise, the smith spoke.

"I reckon you've brought your pigs to the right market, Inspector. I won't deny it. From what you've just told me, I'd say he was my nephew."

"Your nephew—eh? Well, that's interesting to know."

"All the same," the smith went on, "I can tell you very little about him. He's the last of his own lot. My brother, Joe, he was older than I was—had another boy—Fred Gooch his name was—and they've all passed over. Joe, his wife, Fred, and now young John."

"When did you last see your nephew, Mr. Gooch?" asked Anthony.

"I'll tell you," said Gooch, still stolid and unbending, "I've clapped eyes on him but once within the last seven years. My brother Joe used to live in the village of Jewel Cross—that's between here and Scimitar St. Mary—and I didn't see a rare lot of either him or his family even in those days. And about seven years ago young John joined the Air Force. When the war come along, he went out East somewhere and I never clapped eyes on him again until early last autumn. He came in to see us—he'd just been demobbed. And that's the only time I've seen him in the last seven years."

Anthony watched Gooch's face as he divulged the information. He was in at once with further questions.

"When your nephew, John Gooch, came to see you in the autumn, was there anything special about the visit—or did he just drop in, as it were, to celebrate the fact that he had been discharged from the Air Force?"

Anthony did not miss the flicker that smouldered in the smith's eyes. When the answer to his question came, Anthony felt that the smith was not speaking with the readiness that he had shown before.

"He came here," said James Gooch, "because I asked him to. Let's leave it at that."

Anthony knew that he must walk warily. "I'm sure you won't mind adding to that statement, Mr. Gooch? Because we need all the help that we can get. And your nephew's been murdered, you know. Your kith and kin. Your own flesh and blood—almost."

The smith, for the first time, exhibited impatience. "My nephew's visit here had naught to do with his death. You may rest easy on that. But if you must know, I'll tell you why he came. My brother Joe died—almost a year ago. Last January. He had an accident on the farm where he was working. That left only young John. As Joe lay dying, he sent for me and asked me to do something for him. There was naught sensational about it. He gave me a letter for young John. To give to 'im when he did come home. Not to send to him, mind you. To *give* to him! To put into his hands. Joe gave me the address. So I wrote and told John to call here when he came back to the old country as I had something for him from Joe. He did call and I gave him Joe's letter. And you can make no murder out o' that."

Anthony glanced across at MacMorran. The latter nodded. Anthony knew the significance of the nod. The Inspector took over.

"Now a question from me, Mr. Gooch. When your nephew, John, came here to see you in accordance with the terms of your request to him and your brother's request to you, you say it was in the early autumn?"

"Ay. That's right. In the autumn it was. Roughly, I should say, about a matter of four months ago."

"Four months? That would make it round about September, then?"

The smith nodded. "Ay. September wouldn't be far out. Either September or October, I should say. One or the other."

"Good. That fixes that, then. Now when John was here, did he happen to tell you if he were in employment or not?"

"Can't recall that he did."

"Did he say anything that might have led you to believe that he was thinking of becoming a chauffeur?"

"No. Can't recollect anything of that kind."

MacMorran probed deeper. "He didn't say anything, for instance, to the effect that he was entering the employment of Sir John Wynyard at High Fitchet?"

"No. Never mentioned the name. Either of the man or the place. If he had 'a' done, I feel certain I should have remembered it." The surliness was coming back again.

"Thank you, Mr. Gooch," said MacMorran, "you've been very helpful to us."

"I've told you all I can," replied Gooch. "But it's not pleasin', any of it—not for a respectable family like ours has always been. A young fellow murdered like that, miles away from his home and from his own folks. Leaves a downright nasty taste in the mouth. Makes you want to keep quiet about it." Gooch spat on the floor of the forge.

"Well," admitted MacMorran, "that's one way of looking at it, I grant you. But I don't know that it's the right way. You mustn't forget this, Mr. Gooch. Any one of us may be the victim of a murderer any day in the week and that applies equally to any one of our family. You mustn't treat it as though your nephew has brought disgrace on the family. I'm sure you'll agree with me—if you look at things fairly and squarely."

"Maybe—maybe not. But I'm an old-fashioned man, Inspector, and my family's always been one to hold its head high and keep away from the Police. And I like to think that we keep our name out of the papers."

MacMorran held out his hand. The smith wiped his on his leather apron and took the Inspector's.

"Good afternoon, Mr. Gooch—and again—thank you." Anthony shook hands, too. As they turned their back on the forge, the smith motioned to his son and they bent to their task again. The music of hammer on anvil followed Anthony and MacMorran down the street of Magdalen Verney. "Clunk . . . clink . . . clink . . . clunk."

"All I missed," said Anthony, as they passed the vicarage next to the ivied church, "was the chestnut-tree."

"If you aren't careful," replied MacMorran, "you'll miss the return train as well."

6

In the train from Aldersford, Anthony and MacMorran exchanged notes.

"I kept quiet in the bus," said the Inspector, "because conversation wasn't easy. I had four people standing on my feet and another one almost sitting on my lap. To say nothing of a box of kippers on my eyebrows."

"Was a bit congested, I admit," smiled Anthony, "those afternoon village buses nearly always are. But what were you about to say?"

"What do you make of it all? Personally, I doubt if we've picked up very much."

Anthony was silent. MacMorran came again.

"Don't you agree?" he insisted.

Anthony found a more comfortable position in his corner-seat and folded his arms.

"Frankly, Andrew—no. I incline to the opinion that we've picked up a good deal." The testing question which he knew he had invited came at once.

"Exactly *what* have we picked up?"

"Don't know, Andrew. Yet. But it's there—the clue we want—and it's our job to sift and to sort until we find it, and having found it, recognize it."

"I don't share your optimism."

Anthony shook his head. "Oh—it's all right, Andrew. You need have no qualms with regard to the truth of that. But *what* it is exactly, as you just asked—sorry—at the moment, I don't know."

He shrugged his shoulders. MacMorran found pipe and pouch. He slowly and deliberately packed the tobacco into the bowl of the pipe and pressed it down with his thumb.

"Why are you so confident? What is it that gives you such confidence?"

Anthony unclasped his folded arms. He turned to MacMorran and leant forward with his elbows on his knees.

"If I had any doubts, Andrew—and in a way, I suppose, I still retain some—they would nearly all be dissipated by one fact. By one thing that we *know* happened. And I'll put it to you in the form of a question. What did John Gooch do after he called on his uncle at the forge in Magdalen Verney? There he was—discharged from the Air Force—and he calls for the letter which he's been instructed to call for—his uncle hands it to him—and what's he do? First of all, Andrew, answer me that."

MacMorran puffed stolidly at his pipe. The compartment grew thick with smoke.

"I get you," he replied at last, "you mean that he signed up for a job with the Wynyards at High Fitchet."

"Exactly, Andrew. But why?"

"Search me," answered the Inspector, "that's the part I can't get."

"But can you see the unexplainable hiatus?" responded Anthony.

MacMorran shook his head. "Don't get that one. Tell me more."

"Well, Andrew—as I see it—what was it that made Gooch go to High Fitchet in September—we'll take September as read—but which doesn't send Medlicott there until Christmas Eve? That's the part that I simply can't satisfactorily explain to myself. What happened in the course of those three months?"

MacMorran still puffed away at his pipe. Anthony waited for him to reply.

"I think you're making a mistake," he volunteered eventually. "I think you're barking up the wrong tree. Why should the Christmas visit of Medlicott the solicitor have any relation whatever to the engagement by Sir John Wynyard of Gooch, the chauffeur?"

"I can give you an excellent reason, Andrew," came Anthony's quiet reply, "and one, I think, that you're rather carelessly forgetting."

"I'm listening," said MacMorran imperturbably.

"They each went to their death, Andrew. Medlicott, the solicitor, and Gooch the chauffeur. And they each heard from Mr. Levi."

MacMorran heard Anthony out. His pipe was going well now. The compartment was warm and cosy and he had enjoyed his day. And he loved an argument—especially with Anthony Lotherington Bathurst.

"H'm," he said, "I see your point—but I don't know that I'm altogether convinced."

"You're not?"

"No."

"But, my dear Andrew—"

MacMorran waved an authoritative hand. "You wait a minute. Before you run on quite so fast. How about Sir John Wynyard himself? Didn't he also hear from Mr. Levi? You answer that one."

Anthony smiled. "All right, Andrew. I suppose that's a point to you. Although, in justice to myself, I can assure you that I hadn't overlooked it. No, Andrew"—Anthony shook his head—"I'm sorry to appear so cock-sure—but Medlicott went to High Fitchet because Gooch was there."

"I don't agree. To my mind it's a pretty sure thing that Medlicott didn't know Gooch was there until he got there. And that's why he was so upset when he saw him. Don't forget Miss Grenville's story."

MacMorran sat back again. Then he caught sight of the look which had come on Anthony's face.

"What is it?" he asked.

"Andrew," said Anthony slowly and gravely, "I believe you've given me something there. Let me sit still and think."

Anthony sat back and closed his eyes as the speed of the train increased and they began to roar through various stations. Mac-Morran had certainly given him an idea—but even admitting this—the old query still reasserted itself. Why the interval between the autumn (September) and Christmas Eve? If Medlicott knew—why should he be surprised to see Gooch when he went down there? Unless Gooch had deceived him, too—which Anthony thought, bordered on the unlikely, if Gooch had acted as Anthony thought he had done in the first place. And why "hand over the diamond"? Even a diamond ring could scarcely be referred to as "a diamond". Of course, it would have to be a diamond ring which Lady Verney left to Mr. Medlicott. Did the murderer know that? Or was it that—Anthony felt that his thoughts were running riot. Rushing helter-skelter, as it were, in too many directions.

But from the medley, and out of the general mental alarms and excursions, one or two important points did eventually emerge. And not the least of these was that he must ask Sir Nicholas Wynyard, or his brother Quentin, a certain definite question with regard to John Gooch and his movements. There were also one or two additional questions, which he felt he should have to put to Stephen Adderley, but MacMorran would be getting in touch with that gentleman again and Anthony would attempt to do some 'clearing up' at the same time. That was the worst of these interviews when you were pressed for time—it was so easy to forget things when one's mind became temporarily diverted. Even though the said diversion was entirely legitimate.

Anthony opened his eyes. He saw MacMorran facing him and smiling at him. The pipe was still going strong.

"Well?" queried the Inspector, "got anywhere?"

Anthony shook his head. "I don't really know, Andrew—and that's being perfectly frank. When I sat back just now I thought I had—but there are still many parts of the puzzle that I simply can't fit in. They all seem so thoroughly out of place. Your point about Gooch and Medlicott certainly gave me an idea—but upon reflection I can see there are knobs on it."

He tried to rub the mistiness from the carriage windows. "Where are we? Have you noticed?"

"Just through Bicester," replied MacMorran, "and it made me think of a night I once spent at the 'Crown'."

"Good?"

"Wonderful," answered MacMorran, in a tone of deep conviction. "I was never so beautifully canned in all my life." Anthony sat back again. He wanted to concentrate on Gooch—James Gooch, the smith of Magdalen Verney. Particularly on the various statements that the same Gooch had made. Because Anthony had noticed one peculiar thing. He had noticed it when he and MacMorran had stood in Gooch's forge, quite early during the interview. And because of what he had noticed, he had listened most carefully from that moment to every word that Gooch had said. All the way through, with regard to this particular point, the smith had been consistent in the terms of his reference. Anthony re-capitulated as closely as he was able what the smith had told them in the smith's own words. And re-capitulation satisfied him. The omission had been consistent. But why? Even if what Anthony was beginning to think was true—why should the smith have dealt with it as he had—and why in the name of goodness should Medlicott and John Gooch have met murder in the way they had?

And then, in the shimmering of a second, Anthony saw the light. And he chided himself for having been so blind for so long. Yes—that set of circumstances would account for the whole thing. He felt that at last he knew 'why'. His problem now, became of one dimension. It had reached the stage of comparative simplicity. 'Who?'

Anthony thought of the Inspector's interview with Lillywhite, of the way Copplestone had changed colour at a certain moment during *his* interview . . . and then he thought of what Catherine Poulton had told them—how she had seen Gooch and Medlicott and Ebenezer Isaacs in close conversation in the early part of the afternoon of Medlicott's murder . . . and of how Guy Stansfield had found Gooch . . . strangled . . . lying across one of the cars in the garage . . . how Gooch had been prevented from telling his story to Nick Wynyard . . . the killer must have felt that matters were desperate in the extreme . . . and then Anthony smiled . . . for he remembered how Elisabeth Grenville's suitcase had been ransacked . . . and he now knew that he also knew 'who'.

He leant forward and tapped MacMorran on the knee. "Got some news for you, Andrew. Important."

"What is it?" demanded the Inspector eagerly.

"We shall be in to Paddington within a couple of minutes."

CHAPTER XI

1

ANTHONY and MacMorran travelled back to High Fitchet at noon on the following day. The Inspector was waiting by the door of the compartment when Anthony arrived on the platform at Liverpool Street.

"Here you are," he said. "I've been lucky enough to snaffle a couple of corner seats."

"Very nice of you, Andrew. Very nice indeed. But there—you invariably do the right thing. It's second nature with you by now. How long have we got?"

MacMorran looked at the time. "Couple of minutes or so. Not much more. I rather expected you to get here first."

"To tell the truth, I didn't feel like hurrying, Andrew. In fact, I've spent best part of the morning in deep contemplation. I've been meditating on the cult of murder."

"Lucky to have the time," countered the Inspector, "but get in and make yourself comfortable. I think we're almost 'off'."

Anthony took his seat and MacMorran followed him into the compartment. It was about half full.

"Why, what have you been doing," continued Anthony, "breakfast in bed, I suppose?"

MacMorran favoured him with a withering glance. "While you've been meditating, as you call it—probably a euphemism for wasting time—on the other hand, I've been hard at work."

"Good man, Andrew," murmured Anthony.

The train began to move. "Yes," continued MacMorran, "I got to work early and I've cleared two matters which arose out of our yesterday's trip down to Aldersford. You'll be interested in each of them."

"Which two, Andrew?"

"One—the question of Medlicott's estate and two, the little matter of that pre-Christmas telephone call of his."

"Andrew, I'm all attention. Tell me all you know."

"First of all, I put a call through to Adderley—from the 'Yard'. Medlicott's executors are his bankers."

"I guessed they would be. Which bank?"

"The Midland Counties. Adderley gave me the address I want. Their executorship work is administered by their Trustee Branch. I've written to them concerning his keys, the diamond ring left him by Lady Verney, and finally the contents of the Wynyard deed-box. I should have an answer in two or three days' time—at the outside."

"Give 'em a week," rejoined Anthony.

"All right. Give 'em a week. Now for the second little matter. I got on to the local telephone people. I expected a fair amount of delay here—but taking everything into consideration, I didn't do too badly. I got shoved about a bit. You know—pillar to post sort of business but, ultimately, due in the main to perseverance and persistence, I managed to get what I wanted." MacMorran leant forward towards Anthony and lowered his voice a little. "The telephone-call was put through to Sir John Wynyard *by* Medlicott. Sir John did *not* ring through to Medlicott. How does that go with you?"

"My dear Andrew," said Anthony, "nothing that you could have said could have pleased me better."

"That's all right, then," said MacMorran.

The train stopped. The station was Stratford. People got out, leaving Anthony, MacMorran and one other.

"Fast from here to Witham," remarked the Inspector, "good job—I loathe crawling trains."

Anthony forsook his corner seat and went to sit at MacMorran's side. "Has it occurred to you, Andrew, to ask yourself the question as to why Sir John Wynyard left his bed on what we'll call Boxing Night and made his way downstairs to his writing-room?"

MacMorran fumbled in his overcoat pocket and produced his pipe. It was his inevitable refuge at all questioning times.

"Well," he replied, after a few seconds' thought, "I take it, from the opinion put forward by Dr. Beddington, his medical adviser, that he felt ill and got up. But when he arrived downstairs, the heart-attack which had come upon him proved too much for him and ended fatally. Before—and so quickly—he could obtain help. I've put that badly—but you know what I mean."

Anthony shook his head. "Sorry, Andrew—but I don't get it."

MacMorran frowned at Anthony's reply. "Why not?"

"I base my reception of your version, Andrew, on several things. I'll endeavour to show you what I mean. When Sir John Wynyard was found dead in his *writing-room*, Andrew—mark the significance—by the maid Carter, in front of him were these articles." Anthony ticked them off on his fingers. "One—his fountain-pen. Two—a supply of his own personal writing-paper—and three, a copy of the Holy Bible, open at the Psalms. The Psalms of David, Andrew."

"I've considered all that," countered MacMorran, "and I admit that there are significances there. But I consider, too, that they're all explainable. There is no evidence to show that he took them downstairs with him when he left his bedroom, with the intention of using them then and there. The top of the fountain-pen, by the way, was not unscrewed. I was careful to ask Sir Nicholas Wynyard about that. Did you think of it?"

"No, Andrew, I didn't. That's one to you."

MacMorran chuckled. "Many thanks for the compliment. But to get back to where I was. Take the incident of the open Bible. You don't know *when* Sir John opened that. And you'll never put it into me that you do. Again—what point can there be in where the book was opened at? No—I shall maintain that Sir John Wynyard came over ill and got up. And that the various things were on his desk (which was their proper place, don't forget) when he got to it. It's a common thing for people to get up—when they wake up and feel bad."

Anthony grinned benevolently. "And one of these days, Andrew," he said, "you'll wake up—and if you feel bad, it'll serve you jolly well right. Now you listen to me. I'll give you my version of what happened. Sir John Wynyard got up when he did to write a letter."

"Whom to?" cut in MacMorran quickly.

"I'm not sure—yet," replied Anthony slowly. "It might have been to Lady Wynyard, it might have been to Mr. Medlicott. I'm not certain. I *think* it was to Lady Wynyard."

MacMorran became contemptuous. "To his wife? I'm sorry, but this time *I* don't get it. Why on earth should any man write a letter to his wife who was in the next room all the time—Gertcher! Tell that to the Marines."

"And when he had written the letter, Andrew," continued Anthony quietly, "I think he wanted or rather *intended* to do something else. But he died—before he could do either. Fate stepped in at the critical moment."

"And to do that something he required the Psalms of David—eh? I'm sorry again—but I—"

"Yes, Andrew," intervened Anthony, "to do that simple thing as you call it, he *chose* the Psalms of David. Because *now* Andrew, let me call your attention to the letter found in the pocket of Sir John's dressing-gown, emanating from Mr. Levi. Haven't you been inclined to overlook that? Is that, do you think, what had caused him to feel ill?"

MacMorran didn't like the look of the pit towards which Anthony had led him. He did his best in the circumstances to extricate himself.

"Er . . . it doesn't necessarily follow," he said, "that because Sir John Wynyard became ill and died at . . . er . . . that particular time, the Levi message was the cause. Although it may have shaken him up a bit when he first received it. I'm not prepared at this stage to go any further than that. Still, what do you think yourself? I haven't heard that. I suppose you're ready to argue that it was through receiving the Levi message that he went down to the writing-room to write his letter either to Lady Wynyard or to Medlicott?"

Anthony smiled and shook his head. "No, Andrew. I don't think that. But I'll tell you what I *do* think. I don't think that Sir John

Wynyard's action, or Sir John Wynyard's death, was anything to do with the 'Mr. Levi' message. In fact, if Sir John Wynyard hadn't given up the ghost when he did—I doubt if our friend 'Levi' would ever have wanted his diamond or even thought about it. Where are we?" Anthony looked out of the compartment window.

"Just through Chelmsford," MacMorran informed him. "Good!"

The Inspector thought over what Anthony had said. It struck him for the first time that day that Anthony had been speaking rather confidently. Before he could translate the thought into words, Anthony spoke again with a smile.

"A good deal hinges, of course, Andrew, on just how well Sir John Wynyard knew his Bible." His smile broadened.

After a longish period of silence, MacMorran determined to test his recently-formed opinion. "Are you definitely on to something? Or am I imagining things?"

"I hope, Andrew," replied Anthony, "to put the criminal in your hands within forty-eight hours from now. So, you see, you may not be imagining a vain thing—after all."

The train began to slow down. "Running into Witham," he added.

"What have I missed?" asked the Inspector.

Anthony laughed. "But don't reproach yourself, Andrew. I've missed nearly as much as you."

MacMorran shook his head. "That's bolony. Kid stakes. What have I missed?"

"What have you missed? Well, you've missed why Copplestone was worried, why, if Medlicott died, Gooch had to be murdered too, why Gooch was anxious to talk to Sir Nicholas Wynyard, on the night that Medlicott was killed, why Miss Grenville's things were ransacked—" Anthony stopped. There was a twinkle in his eye.

"Go on," said MacMorran bitterly, "why Quentin Wynyard's camera was stolen, why the snow was disturbed on the way to the pond-gate, why—"

"Don't reproach yourself, Andrew. I'll say it again. I'm far from clear myself on those points—although I have hopes that some little thing may give me the vital key to them. That's why I made the time forty-eight hours. By the way, I suppose we can get into touch with

Copplestone, Isaacs, Stansfield, Lillywhite and Co., directly we want to? Should we so desire?"

"Yes. They're all being looked after. Can be picked up at once. I've arranged all that with Burrows."

"That's all right then." Anthony paused for a moment and then went on again. "There are several matters I want to attend to when we get back to High Fitchet. As a result of what happens there, I hope to be in a position to round off the case. If things go wrong, however, I may be forced to start all over again."

"What are they?" queried MacMorran.

"Well, I want a word with Sir Nicholas with regard to the little matter I mentioned just now—his father's knowledge of the Bible. I want to see Miss Grenville again—that, perhaps, will be the most important thing of all. Much will depend, Andrew, on how I fare with her. Then there are those other peculiar incidents which we discussed a little while ago. Quentin Wynyard's lost camera and the strange disturbance of the snow." Anthony stopped again. "By the way, Andrew—how far from High Fitchet would you say Percival Comfit's place was?"

"To walk it, do you mean?"

"Yes—I didn't mean as the crow flies."

MacMorran made the necessary mental calculation. "I should say," he said eventually, "almost a matter of five miles."

"You think it would take about an hour and a half to walk it?"

"Just about—I should say," answered the Inspector.

2

Anthony found Sir Nicholas Wynyard in his father's writing-room, towards the latter part of the afternoon.

"May I come in, Sir Nicholas? I'd like a word or two with you."

"Certainly, Bathurst. Come in and make yourself comfortable. That chair over there's not too bad—for a man of your physique."

"Thanks." Anthony seated himself.

"What can I do for you?"

Anthony smiled. "Well, I'm afraid the question I'm going to ask you, Sir Nicholas, may strike you as being somewhat whimsical. But I'm back on the Bible again. Your late father's Bible."

Nick shook his head. "There isn't a sign of it anywhere, Bathurst. I've searched everywhere. So has Quentin. So has my mother. And my aunt. It's a complete mystery where it's gone to."

"That's all right, Sir Nicholas. It isn't the book itself that I'm after now."

Sir Nicholas Wynyard raised his eyebrows. "I'm sorry if I was precipitate. Tell me what it is you want."

"It's a question that you may or may not be able to answer." Anthony paused. "It's to do with your father. Was Sir John a keen student of the Bible?"

"A keen student? Of the Bible? I don't know that I altogether follow you, Bathurst."

"Well, had he—I'll put the question in a slightly different form— had he a sound knowledge of the Bible?"

Nick smiled—but the smile held sadness. "That's a bit of a poser, isn't it?" He rubbed his nose with the tip of his finger. "I'll try to answer you, Bathurst, to the best of my ability. Because I'm not foolish enough to imagine that you haven't an excellent reason for asking me the question. I know something of your reputation— you see. Helen Repton has seen to that. My father was a religious man. I think that I can assert that with confidence and with little fear of contradiction. But he wasn't *religious*. He liked to play fair, act decently *and* he liked to go to church." Nick paused. "You'll be thinking that I'm not answering your question. I know I'm not—and yet I think I am—in a way. My father, as far as my knowledge goes, didn't *read* the Bible. And I've seldom heard him quote from it. I should say that his sole knowledge of the Bible was what he heard of it, when it was read in church. The first and second lessons and things like that. And, of course, he'd have recognized the more famil- iar . . . what do you call them . . . texts, I suppose, is the word. Things like . . . dash it, I can't think of anything because I want to . . . well . . . like Pontius Pilate washing his hands . . . you know what I mean, Bathurst. When you've gone, I expect I shall think of any amount of them." Nick turned and faced Anthony. "Now—have I given you the information that you wanted?"

Anthony smiled this time. "Sir Nicholas," he said, "I don't think, for my purpose, that you could have possibly answered me better."

"I'm so glad to hear you say that. But tell me—I'm a little out of my depth—is it frightfully important?"

"As an integral part of a theory with which I'm toying, Sir Nicholas, it has a certain importance. Which, I think, assumes even greater importance by reason of the terms of your answer. Had you answered me altogether differently, much of the importance would have been lost. As it is—I'm rather more than satisfied."

Sir Nicholas smiled. "Well, I'm glad to think that I haven't said the *wrong* thing. So we're both by way of being satisfied. Which makes it more comfortable for both parties."

Anthony returned his smile. "By the way, how are things with Miss Grenville while the Inspector and I have been away? Has she been subjected to any more unpleasantnesses?"

"Haven't heard of any, Bathurst. So I suppose things have been all right with her. Hope so—at any rate. But she's gone."

"Gone? Gone home, do you mean?"

Nick nodded. "That's the idea. She stayed on for a day or so at the request of my sister. But, of course, she wasn't able to stay indefinitely."

"When did she actually go?"

"This morning. There was a train from Colbury somewhere about eleven o'clock. I took her down to the station in the car." Nick stopped. "A very charming girl, Bathurst," he added, as though by way of an afterthought, "and I'm too sorry for words that she came here for such a foul Christmas. Still—we weren't to know—and I suppose nobody can be blamed. Except the murderer," he concluded bitterly.

"That's true enough," said Anthony, "and, of course, none of us is able to foresee these things. If we could—"

He broke off and shrugged his shoulders.

"Is there anything more at the moment that I can do for you, Bathurst?"

"No, Sir Nicholas, I don't think there is. And many thanks for what you have done."

"Is the Inspector back?"

"Yes. We returned together."

"Any developments?"

"One or two, perhaps. No—I'll go further than that. We have definitely made some sort of progress. In fact—there may be an arrest within the next forty-eight hours."

Nick looked at him almost incredulously. "Really, Bathurst? Well, that's excellent news. I was afraid that you fellows were baffled. Personally, I couldn't see a ray of light anywhere."

Anthony shook his head. "The luck's turned. It often does, if you've the patience to wait long enough. But don't forget, Sir Nicholas, whichever way it goes, it's not going to be exactly pleasant for any of you."

3

Anthony went out to find MacMorran. He ran the Inspector to earth in the larger garage.

"I've had a set-back, Andrew," he said at once.

MacMorran scanned his face for possible enlightenment. "Why? What do you mean? What's happened?"

"Elisabeth Grenville's gone—scurried back to town. I hadn't been expecting that, by any manner of means, I can tell you."

"What's the idea then?"

"Well, I wanted another chat with her rather badly. It's necessary for me—if I'm to round off the case properly and satisfactorily."

"Now look here," said MacMorran, "come clean. Do you mean the girl's let you down—and skedaddled?"

"No. Doubt if it's that. Maybe, of course. But somehow, I don't think so."

"What's happened, then—to cause her to clear off?"

"I tell you—I don't know. But I rather fancy she's scared of something. And I'm afraid I rather asked for it, Andrew."

"How come?"

"Well, you and I were away from here yesterday—weren't we? The coast was clear. The mouse made hay while the sun shone in the pussy-cat's absence. Get the idea?"

MacMorran let go a low whistle. "Oh-ho! So that's your idea, is it? I didn't know that was how the land lay."

"The worst feature of it, Andrew, is this. It's thrown a spanner into *my* works. All the plans I'd made were based on the supposition that Elisabeth Grenville would be here when we got back."

"H'm. Awkward that. All the same, it won't be impossible to get in touch with her, will it? I suppose that the people here can tell you where she's gone. Can't they?"

"I shall have to *publish* the fact that I want her, shan't I? Which, my dear Andrew, is just what I didn't want to do."

"I see. Makes a difference, I agree. Still, I've no doubt that your ingenuity will find a way."

"There's still something after all that. As I hinted to you just now I'm not at all comfortable in my mind as to *why* the girl's gone. If you cast your mind back a little, you'll remember that we left her here more or less in Miss Repton's care."

"I know. But that precaution we took hardly amounted to keeping the girl here against her will. Which is a position that might have arisen. So it seems to me."

MacMorran's last remark seemed to give Anthony an idea. "Where is Miss Repton? Have you seen her since we got back?"

"No. But she's about somewhere, you can rest easy on that."

"Unless she's had an attack of nostalgia too, and followed the example of Miss Grenville. That would be about the last straw."

MacMorran shook his head. "Don't you worry. Cast your mind back to what Helen Repton told us when we first arrived down here. That she'd applied for a special week's leave and had got it. She won't shift! Not if I know her."

Anthony felt a trifle reassured. What MacMorran had just said was perfectly true and he also knew that Helen Repton was of the type that saw things through. He came to a decision. "Let's find her. That'll settle the matter."

"You go," said MacMorran, "I'm just on a little job of measurements. I'd like to see it through, if it's all the same to you."

"O.K., Andrew, but I'm warning you—this has made a difference. At the best, I'm afraid, it must spell delay. I'm not so confident as I was in the train this morning."

MacMorran grinned. "I had a mind to warn you at the time. Chicken-counting has always been an awfu' risky business."

4

Anthony now went to find Helen Repton. But he didn't find her as quickly as he had found the Inspector. Eventually, he ran into Carter, the maid.

"Miss Repton?" said the latter after Anthony had made his enquiry, "she's gone out for a walk, sir. I saw her going. But I couldn't say for certain where she's gone or how long she's likely to be. If I happen to catch sight of her as she comes in, shall I tell her you'd like a word with her, sir?"

"If you would, Carter," replied Anthony, "I'd be very much obliged. Thank you."

The result was that Anthony was forced to wait some considerable time before he was able to establish contact with Helen Repton. Actually, the time was almost on the stroke of half-past four when Helen returned. On her way through the house she met Carter, who at once passed on to her Anthony's message. So she went straight up to her room, took off her outdoor attire and immediately came downstairs again, to try to find him. She was soon successful for the reason that Carter, always sensible, had done the intelligent thing and sealed up both ends. That is to say, she contacted Anthony and told him that Miss Repton had returned from her walk and had been given his message. He therefore guessed that Helen Repton would seek him out at once and contrived to be ready for her.

"I'm so sorry that I was out," she said on meeting him, "but I had no idea that you were back. As a matter of fact, I've been rather more than worried."

"I guessed as much, Helen," replied Anthony, "you mean in the matter of Elisabeth Grenville?"

Helen Repton nodded. "That's just what I do mean. You see, Elisabeth decided to go back home this morning. Which, of course, made me anxious on account of the instructions I'd had from you and the Inspector when you went away yesterday. But what could I do? I argued with her and did my very best to keep her here until you and the Inspector came back again. But it was no good. Elisabeth had made up her mind and back home she went. Still, it isn't as bad, perhaps, as it may seem at first blush."

Helen did some snappy work with her jumper. She produced a letter which she handed to Anthony. "Elisabeth was most insistent that I should give you this. *You!* I was to place it in your hands myself."

Anthony's face cleared perceptibly. He took the letter from her. "This, Helen, is good news for me. For, frankly, I was beginning to think I was up against it. Before I open it, tell me, Helen—why did Miss Grenville leave as she did? Don't answer me too quickly, because what you say may be of the highest importance."

"I think," said Helen carefully—and slowly, "that she was frightened. You see, acting on what you had told me, I was sticking to her closer than a sister—which, naturally, she was pretty quick in spotting—and also, her room was interfered with again. Not as badly as the time before—but Elisabeth told me she had no doubt whatever that somebody had had another rake round in it."

Anthony showed signs of surprise. "But this is strange, Helen. I asked Sir Nicholas this afternoon as to whether anything like that had happened and he said 'no'."

Helen interrupted him. "He was telling the truth. As far as he knew. Because Elisabeth didn't tell him of the second occurrence. That was on my advice. After she'd come and told me, I told her not to breathe a word to anybody else about it. That's why Sir Nicholas didn't know."

"I see. Well, I suppose that explains it. When did this second disturbance of her room take place?"

"Yesterday morning. Between breakfast and lunch-time." Helen Repton stopped and looked him straight in the eyes. "Mr. Bathurst, tell me please, do you think that Elisabeth herself is in danger? Because if so—hadn't we—"

Anthony cut in. "I wouldn't be surprised, Helen. And the point is that by removing herself as she has, she has made it so difficult for us to help her. But anyhow, let's see what she has to say for herself in this letter she's written me."

He slit the envelope. Elisabeth had written as follows:

Dear Mr. Bathurst. Please forgive my writing to you like this and please forgive me also, for deciding to go home this morning.

I shall ask Helen to give you this when you return. But my bedroom was interfered with again yesterday morning between breakfast-time and lunch-time and altogether it's beginning to give me the creeps. So I've decided to be a coward and clear away from it all. You seemed to think that I'm involved in the whole ghastly business, and although it's all a mystery to me, I'm inclined now to think that you must be right. Anyhow, I've had enough of it all. More than enough. Hence my somewhat early departure from High Fitchet and hence, also, this letter to you. If you should desire to communicate with me again, with regard to anything, I shall be found at 39, Greene Mansions, Wimblefield Park. My flat is almost opposite Sir Rowland Farrar's monument. I am in, most hours of the day, for the next week, at least. After that, if you should want to come, please 'phone Wim 3462. I remain, yours very sincerely, Elisabeth Grenville.

Anthony handed the letter to Helen Repton for the latter to read. Helen read it and then commented:

"Well, you know where she is and how to get in touch with her. That's something, at least. You're better off than you were." She handed it back to him. "What will you do?"

Anthony hesitated a few moments before replying. "I think," he said eventually, "that I shall have to go up to Wimblefield Park to see her. There's at least *one* point that I must clarify and, as I see things now, Miss Grenville's the only person in the world from whom that clarification can come. In the meantime I'll repeat the advice, Helen, that you say you gave to Elisabeth. And thanks for all you've done already. And now you'd better make yourself scarce while I run along and have a word with the Inspector. I'll see you again, though, before I go to Wimblefield Park. Which will probably be to-morrow."

Anthony re-read Elisabeth Grenville's letter and then found MacMorran and showed the letter to him. MacMorran's comments in the main were similar to those of Helen Repton. Anthony told him what he proposed to do. MacMorran concurred with the suggestion.

"To-morrow, you say?"

"I think so, Andrew. And as early as I can get away. The matter, certainly, will not brook delay."

All that evening, certain phrases from Elisabeth Grenville's letter ran riot in Anthony's brain. And every time he repeated them, in an attempt to discover something in them, possibly, which he had missed in his first readings, he found that he was saying as a conclusion, "Sir Rowland Farrar's monu-ment," because in her writing Elisabeth Grenville had divided the word 'monu-ment' in that fashion, doubtless, owing to the fact that it had been the last word of a line and she couldn't write the whole word in the space the line had left to her. "Sir Rowland Farrar's monu-ment."

When Anthony went to bed that night the absurd reiteration was still exerting its tyranny over his mind, and in the last few moments which preceded sleep the phrase still possessed him, almost to the point of being on his tongue. He was acutely aware that it reminded him of something. Of something which was similar in that the word "monu-ment" was written as Elisabeth had written it. He had both seen the word in that particular form and heard it. But the vital clue for which he almost frantically searched persistently eluded him. He knew only too well, from previous experience, that he mustn't *chase* it. To do so would be courting failure. He must dismiss it from his mind and let it come back to him of its own free will. So Anthony relaxed his efforts and drifted into the blessed haven of sleep. But at twenty-two minutes past two he woke up. And as he woke up, the allusion for which he had searched came to him. Effortlessly and spontaneously.

"Good Lord," he muttered, "how blind I've been! And from Elisabeth Grenville of all people."

As he composed himself for sleep again, elation came to him. For he knew now that his case was complete—save for the evidence—and he knew also why Quentin Wynyard's camera was missing.

5

When Anthony reached Wimblefield Park station it was just on four o'clock on the following afternoon. After a certain amount of deliberation, he had decided not to telephone to Elisabeth Grenville, to inform her that he was on his way to see her. It didn't take him long to find Greene Mansions, and of course the monument to Sir Rowland Farrar, the famous Colonial Governor, was big enough for all to see.

Anthony looked at his wrist-watch. The walk from the station had taken him about a quarter of an hour. He always liked to check times and distances. Then Anthony received his shock. He located number 39 and as he walked towards the flats, whom should he see coming out, obviously from Elisabeth's, but Doctor Copplestone?

Copplestone stopped on the step for a moment or so, looked round the landscape as though he were feeling very pleased with himself, gave a slight touch to the point of his trim brown beard and then walked smartly away.

"So we arrive together," muttered Anthony, "strange," but then he remembered that this was the first clear afternoon which Elisabeth had had since she returned from High Fitchet. Which, of course, made a difference. Possibly Copplestone had attempted to communicate with her before this and had been unsuccessful. Hence the call this afternoon.

Anthony waited for Copplestone to get well away from the fiat before he went to the entrance to Number 39. Elisabeth Grenville answered his ring immediately. Almost, in fact, as he rang the bell.

"Why—Mr. Bathurst," she said, her eyes full of pleasure, "it's you of all people! Come in—do. I hadn't the least idea when I opened the door. So you got my letter? Helen gave it to you?"

Anthony followed her into her little sitting-room, cosy and most tastefully furnished.

"How else could I have got here, Miss Grenville? In so short a time? You returned yourself only yesterday. Did you think it was Doctor Copplestone coming back for his gloves or something?"

He sat down in the chair Elisabeth placed for him. But she remained entirely unperturbed at his remark.

"Why did you see him? Just fancy that now. Don't things work out strangely? Sometimes I go on for days and never see a soul— and then this afternoon I get two visitors who almost tread on each other's heels."

"I was certainly surprised to see friend Copplestone in this neighbourhood. I had no idea that you and he—"

This time the lady did colour a little. But the sapphire-tinted eyes she turned on Anthony were innocent and guileless.

"Absurd man," she said, "what *do* you think he came to tell me? And I gather it's his third visit, too."

Anthony shook his head from a dictation of sheer policy. "Haven't the foggiest, Miss Grenville."

"Well—I'll tell you—while I make some tea. I'm sure you'd like a cup."

Anthony murmured conventional thanks. Elisabeth busied herself with tea-cups and explanation.

"As you probably know, Mr. Bathurst, the Grenvilles (my family, that is) and the Copplestones are connected. They're by way of being distant cousins. Cousins, too, with a sort of never-ending feud between them. We're all taught from the cradle upwards that there's always a state of miniature war between the two families. Now you listen to this. When Dr. Copplestone and I were introduced to each other at High Fitchet on Christmas Eve, I, very naturally I think, jokingly called his attention to the relationship between the families—but to my utter surprise the joke fell on absolutely stony ground. It did really. Doctor Copplestone's face was a complete blank. It was obvious to a blind man that he hadn't the slightest idea what I was talking about. And he realized that I *knew*! So directly afterwards, and in the most lame attempt to cover up his confusion, he openly pretended that he had understood my allusion all the time. And the pretence, Mr. Bathurst," concluded Elisabeth bitterly, "wouldn't have deceived the veriest simpleton who ever walked out of a rustic Sunday-school."

Elisabeth poured hot water on to tea. "That's episode one," she went on, "and before I proceed, what does Mr. Bathurst think about it? I'd love to hear."

"Well," said Anthony, "there may be several explanations, including the most obvious one. Which is that Doctor Gregory Copplestone is not in the true lineal descent of the pukka, blue-blooded Copplestones and that his Mummie and Daddie never crooned to him of the crimes of the black-hearted Grenvilles. Which, continuing, was something the Herr Doktor was most undesirous of admitting. Explanation by Anthony L. Bathurst." Elisabeth's eyes opened wide. "Well now," she said, "I think that's absolutely wizard."

"Oh, Miss Grenville, and how's that?"

She handed him a cup of tea. "I'll tell you. Doctor Copplestone called on me to-day to apologize for what he called his discourtesy on Christmas Eve. I told him not to be ridiculous. But he insisted that he had behaved most improperly and that his action had worried him ever since. He had called here twice before to apologize but of course I hadn't been in. Then he gave me his explanation. What he described as his 'apologia'. Would I regard it as a strict confidence and keep the dread secret locked within my bosom? I said 'of course'. But I must tell *you*, Mr. Bathurst, if only to assuage your curiosity at seeing Doctor Copplestone leaving my flat. It's this. He's a German by birth and his real name is Koppelstein. Which Lady Wynyard, of course, was quite ignorant about when she invited him to High Fitchet for Christmas. He further explained his visit by saying that he was a gentleman first and a German second. There! You have the whole thing in a nutshell."

Anthony put his cup on the little table and docketed his story for future reference.

"Most interesting," he said, "and a little incredible. But let's pass from Koppelstein to Bathurst. As to the reason why I'm here."

Her blue eyes were lovely as she looked at him. "Yes, is it about what I told you in my letter?"

"Partly. Now tell me—what happened to your room on the second occasion of the interference?"

"The drawers had been—I won't say 'turned-out'—but rather 'turned over'. Things like handkerchieves and scarves which I hadn't packed in my suitcase. Some had been unfolded and shaken out."

"Certain?"

"Positive." Elisabeth's answer was cool and competent. "Right. Well, that makes an excellent jumping-off point for me. I'm going to take you back to the last conversation we had at High Fitchet. Please keep your mind as clear as possible, Miss Grenville. And think, please, as carefully as you can, before you answer. Is that understood?"

Elisabeth nodded. "Yes. Quite."

"Good. Now—at the risk of repetition—I want you to fix your mind on the late Mr. Medlicott. Got that?"

"Um," said Elisabeth, "Mr. Medlicott. I'll think of him and of nobody else. Is that the idea?"

"It is. Now are you still absolutely positive that he didn't *say* anything to you, while you were at High Fitchet, that on second thoughts and after serious reflection, mightn't be right out of the conventional conversation and assume—from a certain angle—say—a grave importance?"

Elisabeth closed her eyes. After a time she slowly shook her head. "There was nothing. I'm convinced of that. Nothing at all."

"Right. Well, that disposes of possibility number one. We'll try possibility number two. Are you equally positive that he didn't communicate with you in writing in some way? By a note—say—no matter how hastily scribbled? Or by a letter which he might have put into one of your drawers? You remember the envelope addressed to you which I showed you? Think over all that, will you, Miss Grenville. So much hangs on your answer."

"So much or so many?" murmured Elisabeth. She repeated her previous technique and closed her eyes. This time Anthony's period of waiting for her reply was not so long. Again—she slowly shook her head.

"I am as certain as one can be that even if Mr. Medlicott made an attempt to write to me, that the letter, or note, or whatever it was, *never* reached me. He certainly didn't give it to me. And if he had put anything of that kind in my room, I should almost certainly have found it. Always allowing, of course, for the contingency that the kind soul who has been so interested in my bedroom at High Fitchet didn't appropriate it before I could."

"I see. Well that disposes of possibility number two. And I'm beginning to know disappointment again. Now I must think. What else might there be? Because we've exhausted all the more likely contingencies."

Elisabeth cut in impulsively. "But, Mr. Bathurst—why *should* Mr. Medlicott do any of these things? I can't see the reason for it. I was nothing to him. Just somebody he'd met for the first time at a Christmas 'do'. That's the part of it all which I can't understand. Why pick on me? It doesn't seem sense."

Anthony shook his head. "I won't pretend to say that I know why, Miss Grenville. All I have at the present is a succession of rather shadowy ideas. Which, I fancy, however, in the end, will add up to something. But you interrupted me."

"Sorry," said Elisabeth, "while you're thinking, I'll pour you out another cup of tea. I'm sure you can drink it."

Anthony resumed his mental exercise. Elisabeth handed him the cup of tea.

"Thank you, Miss Grenville. Now just leave me alone for the next few minutes. Let me see if I can solve this problem in another way."

Anthony sat back in his chair, lifted the left leg and clasped the knee-cap. Elisabeth sat opposite to him and waited in patience for whatever he would have to say to her.

"I give it up," he announced at length, "I can't think of anything that will fill the bill. Not the proper bill. And it's awkward," he added, "because so much depended on it."

Elisabeth still remained silent. She had interrupted him once and she had no intention of doing so again.

"I suppose," said Anthony eventually, "that you can't recall Mr. Medlicott giving you anything? *Any* thing? During the time you were at High Fitchet with him?"

"Nothing at all," responded Elisabeth promptly. "I can give you my word of honour that during the whole of my stay at High Fitchet, nothing whatever, with the exception of ordinary everyday conversation, passed between Mr. Medlicott and me."

"Nothing whatever," repeated Anthony after her. "It beats me," he went on. "It beggars my intelligence. Because if that's true, what the blazes is the murderer looking for?" He relapsed into silence. Elisabeth broke it.

"What makes me even more certain of what I say," she said, "than anything else, is this. While I was at High Fitchet I lent Mr. Medlicott a book. At his request. And he didn't even return it. Of course it wasn't his fault. He was killed before he was able to. I had to go to his room to get it."

She was amazed at the look which had taken possession of Anthony's face. "What?" he yelled, "you prize idiot! Why in the name of thunder didn't you tell me all that before?"

Elisabeth gasped.

6

"Yes," she nodded, "you're quite right. I *am* an idiot. I *should* have thought of it before. But I feel there are excuses for me. You see—I considered your questions in the exact terms of what you asked me. And I never gave that book a thought."

Anthony beamed on her. "Never mind, lady. You've repaired the omission by thinking of it at the psychological moment. But where's the book now? Don't tell me for the love of Mike that it's gone back to the Free Library or even to the Booklovers of Boots. Tell me it's here, that you can put your hand on it and that you'll be passing it over to me within the next few minutes."

Elisabeth grinned. "Don't be so impatient and don't be in such a hurry. It's here—I can get it—you shall have it in less than five minutes—but let me tell you a little story first."

"Lady, this is not the time for stories."

Elisabeth pouted. "It is—and it's going to be. It won't take a minute. Listen! It all started when Mr. Medlicott and I were in the train together. I was reading. He saw me, of course, and asked me what the book was. I told him. It was the *Summa* of St. Thomas Aquinas. He said how much he admired it—had done so for many years—and then asked me if he could borrow it when he got to High Fitchet if at any time he felt like reading it. I said 'yes', of course. Well, to cut the story short—I can see you're absolutely fuming—he borrowed it one night down there, didn't return it, and as I told you before, I went into his room and got it. So there you are—that's the whole story—and I'm sure I'm very, very sorry to have been such a prize idiot as you called me and not to have remembered it when you asked me. And if you give me time, I'll assume the appropriate sackcloth and ashes."

Elisabeth sat back in her chair with her blue eyes looking more lovely than ever.

"Please get the book," said Anthony, "that will be the full, perfect, and sufficient act of repentance. You needn't bother about the sackcloth and ashes."

"Master," returned Elisabeth, "your slave obeys!"

She whisked herself from the room in a flash.

7

Anthony waited patiently for the return of his hostess. He forced himself to this condition by an exercise of sheer self-discipline, for only he himself knew how impatient he really could have been. The interval, however, between Elisabeth's going and Elisabeth's returning was but short-lived and soon the door of the little sitting-room opened and Anthony was privileged to behold a rather breathless Elisabeth, clasping a book, the title of which showed plainly: the *Summa* of St. Thomas Aquinas.

"There you are, my lord," said Elisabeth, rather provocatively, "there's the book you're so anxious to get your claws into. And I've brought it straight down from my bedroom. I haven't stopped on the way to search for any secret messages."

Elisabeth handed the book to Anthony. The latter placed a finger at each end of the binding at the back of the volume and allowed the leaves to flutter downwards. An envelope floated to the carpet.

"Voilà," said Mr. Bathurst.

8

For some seconds he let it lie there, and a smile played round the corners of his mouth and in his grey eyes. Elisabeth thought how attractive he looked.

"I'm disappointed," announced Miss Grenville, "there doesn't seem anything particularly exciting about that. Aren't you going to pick it up?"

She indicated the envelope with a quick gesture.

Anthony still smiled at her. "Miss Grenville," he said whimsically, "I am but human. I'm permitting myself to enjoy the thrill of triumph and the elation of success. Because, down there, lying in that envelope, on your own strip of Axminster, Wilton or Aubusson—have it how you will—is just what I wanted to see."

"Sure?" she asked quizzically.

"As good as."

She returned smile for smile. "You make me frightfully conscious," she said, "of the frailty and inferiority of my sex. Which, I'm usually *very* chary of admitting. If I'd been in your place and felt as you do I should have snatched that envelope from the floor long before this. The sublime patience of the man," she declaimed.

Suddenly she stooped to retrieve the envelope. Anthony intercepted her.

"Not for a minute or two, Miss Grenville—please!"

His hand held her wrist. "Before we pick that up—you and I, and examine the contents, I'm going to tell you what they are. Within certain limits, of course. And I'm sorely afraid that you aren't going to like what you're about to hear."

Elisabeth looked a trifle scared, nodded and then sat quiet and still.

"In that envelope, Miss Grenville," went on Anthony, "I declare solemnly that you will find . . ."

He talked to her for many minutes. When he had finished, Elisabeth Grenville was white-faced, tear-eyed and shaking like a leaf.

"We'll now put my statement to the test, Miss Grenville," said Anthony; "will you be so good as to look inside the envelope?"

Elisabeth obeyed him with trembling fingers. She looked at the contents of the envelope and handed them to him.

"You are right, Mr. Bathurst," she said simply.

Then the strain she had undergone proved too much for her and Elisabeth Grenville gave way to uncontrolled weeping.

9

Anthony wisely resisted the tyranny of tears and let her cry. "I'm sorry," she said at last, "please forgive me."

"That's all right. I understand." He rose and stood before the fire. "I've thought it all out," he said, "several times. And I can't let you off. Because I think this is the only way. You must write a letter—confessing that you had these in your possession all the time."

"Why?"

"You'll see why when you've written the letter. I'll dictate it to you."

"I think I begin to see. Shall I do this now?"

"Yes. Best now."

"I'll get my pen and some paper." She suited her action to the words.

"I think we'll put it like this," began Anthony. He dictated sentences to her. Elisabeth wrote them down like a girl in a dream. Sometimes she nodded to herself as she wrote, as though she found herself in full agreement with what Anthony was dictating. Suddenly she queried something.

"On the Friday evening?"

"Yes—don't you think so?"

She thought it over. "Perhaps you're right. Yes—perhaps so—in the circumstances."

Anthony went on relentlessly to the finish.

"How shall I sign it?" she asked—"my full name?"

"Put your usual signature," replied Anthony, "That will be the most fitting, under the conditions."

"Do you take it, Mr. Bathurst?"

"Please, Miss Grenville, and I'll see that it reaches the proper quarter."

She handed it to him. He placed it in his pocket. "That's that—then. Now let me discuss something else. Will you please listen to me carefully?"

Elisabeth smiled a wistful smile. "That's all I seem to have been doing for some time. All right. Carry on!"

Anthony went on talking.

CHAPTER XII

1

WHEN Anthony got out of the train at Colbury late that evening, MacMorran, in accordance with a telephoned request, had a car waiting for him at the station. When they reached the comfort and comparative tranquillity of the Montfichet Arms, Anthony put certain evidence in front of the Scotland Yard Inspector.

"There you are, Andrew," he said, "something to gladden your hard and stony heart. And procured at enormous personal expense. In the words of the classics, 'have a dekko'."

MacMorran handled the explosive and then whistled. "Miss Grenville?" he queried.

"Ah-ha."

"And she had it with her all the time?"

"Even so, Andrew."

MacMorran whistled again. "Good Lord. That's a staggerer. I wouldn't have considered such a possibility." His eyes showed unmistakable signs of trepidation. "I say—have you followed this to its logical solution? Because as I see it, it means only one thing. It means that—"

"Exactly, Andrew. It means all that. You see—I followed the trail backwards, as it were. And that's where it brought me to. Nice kettle of fish, as you say."

MacMorran emitted his third whistle. "What do we do?"

"I'll tell you what I think, Andrew, and also what I've arranged. Listen to me carefully and let me know what you think about it. Criticize it as much as you like—if you think it necessary."

MacMorran nodded and listened to what Anthony had to say. "We're running a risk," was his final comment.

"Too big a risk, do you think?"

"I don't know. You've sprung it on me rather. I'd have liked more time to think it over."

Anthony went and ordered drinks and put a comfortable-looking pint tankard in front of the Inspector.

"See if that will assist the grey matter, Andrew. It has a certain reputation, I believe, in that particular respect."

MacMorran sat and drank and thought. Suddenly, he turned to Anthony. "Both of us, of course? Not you single-handed?"

Anthony nodded. "Both of us, Andrew. Four arms are better than two."

"How big's the place?"

"Quite small. Below average. Well below average."

MacMorran said nothing. He drank more beer and then had recourse to his pipe. "There's going to be some 'stink'," he announced after a somewhat lengthy period of silence.

"I agree. But can it be avoided? Personally—I don't see how it can."

MacMorran puffed away at his pipe. "No—neither can I."

"Taking it my way," went on Anthony, "should effectively remove all doubt."

"Oh, I know that. I knew the idea when you first put it to me. You can't kid me. After all these years that we've worked together." MacMorran drained his tankard. "What was the camera for did you say?"

"What can cameras be for? To take Medlicott's photograph, of course. By special invitation."

MacMorran stared. "To take—no—I still don't get you."

"Think, Andrew, think."

"Yes—I see. Of course. That would simplify things. And you say that this Levi fellow did much the same thing—eh? Well, well, we live and learn I must say."

Anthony began to talk again. Until MacMorran leant over the table and knocked the dottle from his pipe. He also took out his watch and looked at the time.

"I'm for Uncle Ned. I'll talk it over with you again in the morning." He went to the door and turned to Anthony. "I'll agree to the plan," he said, "but why the hell I always let you have your own way in everything, I'm hanged if I know."

Anthony grinned at him as he called out "Good night".

2

At breakfast on the following morning, Anthony announced his intention to MacMorran of running over to High Fitchet for what he said he hoped would prove to be the last time. MacMorran nodded a somewhat nonchalant acquiescence and then stated that he would accompany Anthony.

"When do you want to go?" he asked. "At once?"

"Leave here about ten, Andrew. That will give me time to do all I want to do before lunch. That suit you?"

"Yes. That'll do for me all right."

"I might," said Anthony musingly, "go to the pond again. I might. I'm not sure. After all, perhaps it's not vital. The countryside's extensive and needles are difficult to find when they're hidden in haystacks. Still, Andrew, we'll see. Ten o'clock then. Meet you outside. In the meantime, I'm going to the writing-room to write a letter."

When they reached High Fitchet, after narrowly averting a collision with a fast-driven car, the driver of which had favoured them with a really magnificent effort of profanity mixed with blasphemy and obscenity, Anthony spoke to the Inspector.

"I want just one word with Sir Nicholas Wynyard. Failing him, with brother Quentin; failing him, with Mrs. Poulton. As I'm in the fortunate position of having three strings to my bow, I shouldn't be disappointed, should I?"

"You should not," replied MacMorran. "And even then, there's still Lady Wynyard to fall back on."

Anthony shook his head. "I don't wish to trouble her. O.K. then, Andrew, I'll be with you again before lunch."

Anthony made his way to the house to see if he could run across Nick. He tapped on the door of the room where he knew Sir Nicholas was usually to be found at this time of the morning.

"Come in," cried a voice. Anthony entered, to find to his surprise somewhat, not only Nick, but Quentin Wynyard, Ebenezer Isaacs and Percival Comfit.

"Ah, Bathurst," said Nick, "I had an idea it was you. What can we do for you? Is it urgent—or can you leave it, say, for half an hour?"

Anthony bowed to the company in general. "My sincere apologies for the intrusion. Had I known you were in conference, Sir Nicholas, I shouldn't have dreamed of bothering you."

Before Nick could reply, Quentin Wynyard broke in, almost laughingly. "Glad to see you've got over your motoring 'incident' of a few minutes ago."

Anthony grinned. "Why, were you there?"

"My car was just behind yours. I had the felicity of hearing that bloke's oratorical efforts. Very fruity!"

Anthony grinned again. "It *was* a good show, wasn't it? For a modest country hamlet? He must have been one of the 'rude forefathers'. I don't know how MacMorran felt, but from what I could hear of it, 'never was heard such a terrible curse!'"

Quentin laughed again and the three other men joined in the laugh, Isaacs being particularly boisterous. Nick Wynyard took it up.

"But I expect—like all those spontaneous curses—nobody seemed one penny the worse."

"I expect so, Sir Nicholas. As you say—it usually works out that way. Still, it's all over now. We'd best forget it. Perhaps the driver has reached Billingsgate by now. That was obviously his destination. What I wanted to ask you, Sir Nicholas, was this. I'm still on the track of your late father's Bible. Have I your permission to look round the library before lunch?"

"Certainly, Bathurst. By all means do so."

"Then I'll go now, Sir Nicholas, and apologize once again for having disturbed you."

"That's all right, Bathurst. These gentlemen and I have a little matter in hand with regard to my father's estate—I'm sure you understand."

Anthony nodded his understanding. "Let's know if you have any luck," concluded Nick.

"Certainly, I will." Anthony bowed again and withdrew.

He walked towards the library, a prey to many and conflicting thoughts. So Comfit was here and Ebenezer Isaacs had also turned up again. But not Alfred Lillywhite, who had been one of the late Sir John Wynyard's oldest business associates. All the same, though, the scene in Sir Nicholas's room had not disturbed him. He had found, to a certain extent, that he could still trace the pattern of the crime.

Anthony opened the door of the library and went in. Sir John Wynyard had been old-fashioned rather than modern in his care of books. There were no artistically arranged shelves running round the walls. Sir John had no book-cases of modern design or type. He relied on tall, heavy book-cases with glass doors for the custody of his literature. There were three of these. Two on one side of the room and one on another. Anthony made his way towards the largest of these three cases. He ran his eye over the lines of books. But evidently, the late Sir John Wynyard had arranged his stock of books with a certain definite regard to classification. For the books at which Anthony looked in this case were all of the variety that might reasonably be described as 'Fiction'.

Here were Dumas, Dickens, Scott, Thackeray, Trollope, Balzac, Zola, France, Tolstoy and Dostoieffsky, cheek-by-jowl with Galsworthy, Bennett, Wells, Shaw and Priestley. Anthony gave the entire contents of the book-case a quick, comprehensive glance and decided, at least temporarily, that the book for which he was seeking was not there. He therefore passed on to the first of the smaller cases, on the other side of the room. This second book-case was better placed, from the point of view of light falling on it, and Anthony was able to see the contents of this case much better and more easily than he had those of the first book-case. But the books herein contained were mainly philosophical, with the exception possibly of those on two shelves, where they chiefly belonged to the technical class.

Again Anthony shook his head and somewhat regretfully moved on to the third book-case. He was not altogether despondent, however, for it had become increasingly obvious that the late Sir John's books had been cased methodically, and it might well be that the volume of his special desire would be found at his third attempt. He moved towards the case, and the instant he saw the contents he knew that here was a distinct hope. He grasped the handle of one of the glass doors and pulled it open. The light here was good and he was able to distinguish the various titles with comparative ease. First of all, therefore, he looked at the top shelf. Yes—the 'A's' had it. To look for his 'B' somewhere near the top shelf was a simple task and, heaving a sigh of relief, Anthony saw the book for which he had come, and took it from its place. It showed clear indications of constant usage. He turned the pages rapidly to test his theory and at last reaped his reward. Yes—there it was—clearly written. He had been right in his association.

Anthony smiled to himself as he replaced the book, closed the door of the book-case and made his exit from the library. Sir Nicholas Wynyard had no doubt told the truth. The Bible his father had used on the morning of his death was no longer in the house. Now for MacMorran, lunch, and the further preliminaries to the last round-up.

3

At three o'clock on that same afternoon, MacMorran and Anthony informed Sir Nicholas and Lady Wynyard that they would be leaving High Fitchet, for the time being at least. Anthony let the Inspector do most of the talking. Lady Wynyard said but little in response to MacMorran's statement and explanations. Every now and then she merely nodded her tacit acceptance of what he had said or of the particular point he had made. His concluding remarks, however, very naturally caused a stir to both her and her elder son.

"And I should say," remarked MacMorran as a sort of conclusion, "that we are not devoid of hope of making an arrest. That will all depend on what turns up, say, in the next week."

Sir Nicholas, however, reacted differently to MacMorran's statement from his mother.

"Well, I regard that as good news, Inspector," he said, "although I realize, at the same time, the inevitable and no doubt painful implications. But until the whole thing's cleared up, there will always be something like a cloud on all of us." He turned to Anthony. "By the way, Bathurst, did you have any luck in the library this morning? I meant to have asked you before?"

Anthony hesitated for a second before he answered. For more than one reason he felt that he couldn't give Nick Wynyard his full confidence in the conditions as they were at the moment. He finessed, therefore.

"I regret to say that I was unable to find your father's Bible, Sir Nicholas. I looked in the library as a last resource. I thought that perhaps somebody might have replaced it there. But to no avail. So I've decided to call it off."

Sir Nicholas nodded. "I was afraid you'd draw a blank. As I've told you, I've hunted everywhere." He turned to his mother. "So have you, haven't you, Mother?"

"Yes. And I can't find it anywhere. The whole thing's an absolute mystery to me."

Lady Wynyard said her piece and then subsided again. MacMorran was all for getting away from High Fitchet. This fact was obvious even to the two Wynyards. Sir Nicholas gave the impression the practical interpretation.

"Well, gentlemen, I've no doubt you're eager to get away. My mother and I understand. If we say that we aren't sorry to see the back of you, I know you'll also understand. But before you go, Inspector MacMorran—and this, of course, goes for you, Bathurst, as well—let me say how much all of us at High Fitchet appreciate the courtesy you have shown us and let me thank you for it on behalf of everybody. I know full well the difficulties you've had to work under and I know equally well how much more unpleasant you might have made things for everybody concerned."

Nick favoured both MacMorran and Anthony with a charming smile. The Inspector made suitable acknowledgment and a few moments later he and Anthony left the house.

"There's a train to Liverpool Street just after six o'clock, Andrew. My suggestion is that we catch it. We've comfortable time."

"What about dinner? It'll mean missing dinner at the 'Red Lion'."

"I'd thought of that. But we'll get something in town. I'll tell you what, Andrew—I'll stand you a supper at Murillo's. Is the idea attractive?"

MacMorran was heard to observe that it had attractions.

"Another thing, Andrew," went on Anthony, "I want a heart-to-heart talk with you in the train on the way to town."

MacMorran eyed him somewhat suspiciously. "What about this time? Don't tell me you've changed your mind."

"Don't say 'what about', Andrew, say 'whom about'."

"Well, 'whom' about then?"

The answer that came was surprising.

"The person who took a chance and made the bad mistake of assuming the name of 'Levi'."

4

Anthony Lotherington Bathurst waited outside the station known as Wimblefield Park. But he waited in the shadows. He had good reason for this, for he had no wish to be recognized by anybody other than Chief Detective-Inspector Andrew MacMorran. He considered, however, that he was on reasonably safe ground as he had allowed a generous margin of time between his meeting with the Inspector and the time of that other meeting which he knew was due to take place later on that evening.

The evening was cold and dark and there was a chill wind which flung itself hungrily at the ribs of men and women and made them long for the warmth and comfort of the fireside. Every now and then, this mordant wind had the companionship of sheets of icy rain which swept tempestuously, and with almost savage cruelty, against all which they found in their way.

Anthony cursed the climate, cursed the incidence of his unhappy choice and huddled in the lee of the wall for physical protection. He registered at the same time a fervent prayer that MacMorran would put in an appearance very soon and that nothing serious had happened to delay his transport. But a few minutes later, Anthony's prayer was answered and he saw the bulky figure of MacMorran approaching him.

"S'truth," declared the Inspector, "what a night! You do pick 'em—I must say. What a beauty."

"Andrew," replied Anthony, "I'm in full agreement with you. 'Mine enemy's dog, though he had bit me, should have stood this night, against my fire'. But seriously, Andrew, don't blame me—blame the atrocious English climate. And *don't* tell me what old Rowley said about it. Well—are you fit?"

"Fit enough," growled MacMorran, "how are we off for time? Plenty in hand?"

"Ample. We've a margin of an hour and a half. I think that should make us safe enough."

"Should do. What do we do—walk?"

"Yes. Safer to walk."

"Yes—and so bloody comfortable, too. Mustn't overlook that. If there's a month in the calendar I hate and loathe, and shall always hate and loathe, it's perishin' January. How far is it?"

"Take us about a quarter of an hour—if we don't loiter."

MacMorran turned up the collar of his overcoat. "Loiter," he repeated indignantly, "I like your choice of words, I must say. Go on. Lead the way."

"We'll take as little chances as possible," said Anthony, "so we'll make for the trees over there. And mind the drips. When the wind blows—"

"I know," said MacMorran, "so spare the details. And cut out the cradle bit as well."

They walked over to the shadow of the trees. At regular intervals, Anthony could hear MacMorran murmuring. When a particularly abundant supply of ice-cold water found its way between his coat-collar and his neck, the murmur increased in measure to something in the nature of an ardent expostulation.

"Not far to go, now, Andrew," said Anthony encouragingly, "the worst is over."

MacMorran nodded. "Did you bring a revolver, Mr. Bathurst?"

"Yes. Did you?"

"Yes. I'm afraid we shall find them necessary. And there's nothing like being prepared."

In this way, Anthony and MacMorran came to Greene Mansions.

5

"I suppose," said MacMorran, as they waited for admission, "there's no chance of a double-cross, is there?"

Anthony shook his head. "Don't worry, Andrew. You'll find that everything will be in order. I've made the arrangements and I'm prepared to stand by them. The main trouble is the lack of room, but we shall have to look round and see what we can do to get over that. But here's the lady coming to let us in, Andrew."

A pale-faced, heavy-eyed Elisabeth came to the door and let them in. Anthony cut short all the preliminaries. Elisabeth Grenville, now that the game was up, had but little to say and both Anthony and the Inspector could see that she was in a state of high nervous tension. Anthony turned to her with a question.

"Is everything in order, Miss Grenville?"

"Yes, Mr. Bathurst."

"Nothing of any kind has transpired since you 'phoned me this morning early?"

"No, Mr. Bathurst. Nothing at all."

Anthony looked round the little sitting-room.

"There's nowhere in here," she said, as though giving voice to his thoughts, "it will have to be in the lounge, I think."

"May we see, please?" asked Anthony, looking at his watch.

Elisabeth beckoned to them to follow her. She took them into the room she had furnished and decorated as a small lounge. MacMorran nodded to a door.

"What's in there, Miss Grenville?"

"My bedroom," replied Elisabeth.

Anthony thought he saw the plan. He began to talk. "Look here, Andrew. I've been thinking things over again. We must give Miss Grenville protection. After all, she knows pretty well all there is to know. And—we mustn't forget this—the murderer knows she knows! Which fact alone places her in very definite danger. I'll stay here in the bedroom. I can hear what goes on and I may be able, after a time, to see something as well. I'll see, too, that Miss Grenville comes to no harm. You wait outside till the quarry comes out. You can find cover somewhere—and you can't miss him when the time comes. How many men have you warned?"

"I shall have three officers here at seven o'clock. There will be one at each end of the road until our man comes. And Chatterton will have the place under observation from the other side of the road. From almost directly opposite. There'll be four of us to deal with Miss Grenville's visitor. You needn't worry about that part of it. There's only one thing—"

"Yes. I know what you mean. You're alluding to my end. Now look here—if for any reason I want the arrest held up I'll come out before our friend does and give you the tip. How's that? Everything covered?"

"O.K.," said MacMorran. The Inspector looked at his watch. "It's just on seven o'clock. My chaps'll be in position in a few minutes from now. And we've half an hour to wait. I'll go and check points. Cheer-o, Miss Grenville—and good luck. See you later, Mr. Bathurst."

MacMorran gave Elisabeth a sympathetic glance and then made a quick and quiet exit.

6

It was very dark now and although the gusts of rain had ceased, the wind, if anything, had increased in violence and whipped the pools of water that lay in places on the pathway into miniature turgid lakes. The coast had been clear when he had left the apartment, so MacMorran walked quickly across the road to see if he could find Chatterton. Not that he really harboured any doubts. Chatterton, who had worked under him at the 'Yard' for years, was reliability itself. No sooner had MacMorran's feet found the opposite pavement than the rain started to fall again. MacMorran cursed aloud.

"All the same though," he admitted to himself, "I'd rather have my job than the one Mr. Bathurst's picked. There *is* elbow-room out here."

He looked to see if he could see any sign of Chatterton. There was a courtyard of sorts with an arched entrance facing him. MacMorran moved nearer to it. Then he stood motionless on the pavement and peered through the curtain of rain. He thought he saw feet. He was right. The feet belonged to Chatterton. The latter came out from beneath the archway and became visible to his superior officer. He saluted—from force of habit.

"Good evening, sir. All clear so far. Nothing arrived at No. 39. Directly it does, I'll proceed to carry out instructions."

"O.K., Chatterton. You'll join me later, then. Keep yourself warm."

"Yes, sir—and dry," responded Chatterton, "some hopes!"

7

The plain-clothes man at the further end of the block wanted a cigarette badly. He felt in his pockets and couldn't find the usual packet which he habitually carried in the left-hand pocket of his overcoat. After trying other pockets equally unsuccessfully, the sickening realization came to him that he had either left the packet in the station or had lost it.

Sergeant Buckridge swore. The fact is regretted, but must nevertheless be recorded. Then, almost on the heels of this revelation, came a second distasteful realization. It had begun to rain again! Buckridge pressed his back into a doorway. Good job that perishin' wind had dropped a bit. He thrust his hands deeper into the empty pockets of his overcoat and pushed his chin as far as he could into the comforting grip of his turned-up collar. Why the hell had he ever been such a B.F. to join the blasted Police? It was just his ruddy luck to have clicked for this special job. It *must* be a special job, he argued to himself, for the Super, to have put a sergeant on it. He held up his wrist to look at the time.

"H'm—ten minutes past seven. And God knows how long he'd have to wait before anything happened."

It was at that moment that MacMorran slipped out of the murk and accosted him. "Good evening, Sergeant."

Buckridge jerked himself to the alert.

"Good evening, sir."

"If you can call it that," added MacMorran.

They conversed in low tones for a few minutes.

8

At the other end of the row of flats known as Greene Mansions, waited Detective-Sergeant William Cullis (C.I.D.). He was of different temperament from his colleague, Buckridge. For Cullis took the rough with the smooth, almost everything in his stride, and contrived to remain unfailingly cheerful. He knew, from what MacMorran had thought fit to tell him, that they were on one of Mr. Bathurst's 'do's'. That fact meant a lot to Bill Cullis. It meant that it was almost enough to eliminate completely for him everything in the nature of unpleasantness.

When he spotted MacMorran appear out of nowhere, as it were, Cullis's enthusiasm gave him a thrill. He *knew* that they were after big game that night. He listened attentively to what the Inspector had to say.

"I understand, sir," he replied. "And when the time comes, I'll move in accordance with instructions. Very good, sir. You can rely on me, sir."

Andrew MacMorran, having covered his three points, now began to consider again, his own movements. He decided to have another word with Chatterton. So he moved off again in the wind, rain and darkness, towards the archway over the entrance to the courtyard opposite to Number 39. The time was now twenty-five minutes past seven, and as MacMorran moved down the street towards his auxiliary, the long black shape of a car slid smoothly and almost silently past him. MacMorran watched it—almost fascinated. He saw it pull up outside Elisabeth Grenville's. MacMorran took a few paces forward so that he was in the lee of the Sir Rowland Farrar memorial. Where was the car going to park? He hoped Chatterton would efface himself completely and then thanked whatever gods there be for the black darkness of the night.

Then he heard the slam of a car door and saw a figure walk quickly up the steps of the entrance. MacMorran slid into the archway-entrance and made contact with the indefatigable Chatterton. The latter elevated his thumbs.

"O.K., Chief," he whispered. "'Is nibs is in! Did you see him?"

"Yes," replied MacMorran shortly, "not being blind, I did. I was afraid you'd stick your fat head too far out and that he'd see you."

Chatterton shook the fat head with supreme confidence. "Not 'im, Chief! I had the old 'bushel' craned round the side there. Didn't give 'im an earthly. Besides, you can always duck."

Chatterton grinned at his own pleasantry. MacMorran gave him no immediate answer. He stood and watched the flat which now housed Elisabeth Grenville, Anthony Bathurst—and a double murderer. When he eventually did speak, he brought Chatterton back to a realization of duty.

"As far as this place is concerned, Chatterton, you've had it. We know now where our man is and all we have to do is wait for him to come out. You get along to Buckridge and Cullis. Contact them both. Tell them you've taken further orders from me. Cullis saw the car—he knows the bird's in the nest. Buckridge should have spotted the car, too. Tell them to move up from each end and work nearer to Number 39. They're to keep as inconspicuous as possible, so that all of you can be ready to join me at an instant's notice. Is that clear, Chatterton?"

"That's all O.K., Chief. I'll push along at once and give 'em the lay-out. We'll all be in our places when you want us." Chatterton slid off into the darkness.

CHAPTER XIII

1

ELISABETH Grenville had answered the ring at her bell by summoning all her courage. She had to discipline herself severely to screw that courage to the sticking-place. But she found some degree of comfort in the knowledge that Anthony Bathurst would be but a few yards away from her during the ticklish ordeal which she would soon be called upon to face.

The murderer bowed to her as she opened the door for his admittance. "Good evening, Miss Grenville. Mr. Levi—at your service. You see that, among my vices, I can at least parade one virtue. The virtue of punctuality. May I come in? After all, I am here, this time, at your invitation."

Elisabeth knew that she was trembling, that her fingers were quivering and she hoped that the man who had just spoken to her wouldn't be able to see that her knees were knocking—for she had a wild, frightening suspicion that they were.

"Come in, please," she said. Her voice, too, was unsteady.

"Why," he said, "what's the matter? Don't tell me that you're a bundle of nerves. I regard that as distinctly uncomplimentary."

She shook her head and showed him into the tiny lounge. "Please sit down," she said.

The chair she indicated to him had its back to the connecting door and to Anthony Bathurst. Elisabeth knew her instructions and was determined to follow them explicitly. The murderer appeared to harbour neither doubt nor suspicion. He took the chair Elisabeth had offered him.

"Well," he said, "I got your letter. I won't say that I wasn't surprised. But why didn't you tell me before that Medlicott had confided in you? That's the point that puzzles me. Why didn't you connect us in that way?"

Elisabeth knew that she simply *must* pull herself together. "I thought my letter made that point clear," she said. "I only found the papers when I got back here. I don't think Mr. Medlicott did confide in me. I don't think that for one moment. He had simply slipped the papers between the pages of a book which I had lent him when we were at High Fitchet."

"No wonder I couldn't find them. I did my best."

The murderer's tone was grim and almost sullen. Elisabeth remembered the words that she had been told to say.

"What I can't understand," she said haltingly, "is that you should have brought yourself to . . . to . . ."

"To murder both Medlicott and Gooch—eh? That's what you mean, I presume?" His voice was savage and sore. "Don't you think those documents would have delighted the eyes of, well—whom shall we say? Well—suppose we say Sir Nicholas Wynyard. *Sir Nicholas Wynyard!*" He repeated the title in tones of the utmost contempt and of what sounded to Elisabeth like bitter loathing and indignation.

"I'll say they would," he added truculently. "Still," he went on, "what's done can't be undone and it's no use crying over spilled milk. But I'll say this, Miss Elisabeth Grenville, I appreciate what you've done. I do really. Because I realize that you *might* have chosen other and much more unpleasant alternatives. That is to say from my point of view. What did occur to me was this. What made you pick on me so unerringly? Mere feminine intuition?"

Elisabeth hoped that he was unaware of her gratitude for his suggestion.

"I suppose it must have been that. Yes—I can't think it could have been anything else."

The murderer's look changed a little. He eyed her shrewdly. "I suppose that I *can* trust you? You told me the truth in your letter? You've kept all this to yourself? Not told anybody else? Be careful!"

The threat was now unmistakable. Again Elisabeth remembered the exact words of the reply which she was to give him.

"Should I have invited you here this evening as I did—if I had told anybody else?"

"I suppose not. No, I don't think you would have. Well, talk's all very fine in its way—but it doesn't get one very far. What's wanted at most times is action. You'll now hand over to me what I came for. Two extremely valuable commodities." The murderer extended his hand. Elisabeth went and picked up a book.

"I have them here," she said quietly, "exactly as Mr. Medlicott must have left them. Look—you can see for yourself."

She put the book in his hands. He took what he wanted and his eyes lit up.

"At last," he said with grim satisfaction. He opened out two papers. "Yes," he said thoughtfully, "this gives the full story. It's all here." He looked up at Elisabeth. "Pretty valuable—eh? For the gentleman whom you and I know as Sir Nicholas Wynyard. Could anything be *more* valuable?" He chuckled softly to himself. "Hand over the diamond—or else." Ha-ha—not bad that—though I say it as shouldn't. Put the police off the scent properly—including the great and wonderful Bathurst." 'Mr. Levi' chuckled again. "And Samuel Levy gave the chapel people a handsome sum of money—how I laughed when I heard *that* yarn go round! How handy that newspaper cutting was! I believe I'm right in saying that our friend Bathurst of all people was most attracted by it. What a sucker! It's marvellous how some people will fall for anything sensational or out of the ordinary and neglect the everyday things which are almost invariably the most important. Well, all good things must come to an end and I must be getting along."

He placed the documents he had taken from Elisabeth's book in a compartment of his wallet and stood up.

"Before I go, young lady, there's one thing I *must* say to you. Circumstances compel me. This interview must remain for ever a secret between you and me. You understand that, don't you? Your sending for me, as you have done, and your handing over to me of these documents proves to me that you desire to act as a sensible little girl. And, of course, I now possess all the proof, and if you talked who would believe you?"

'Mr. Levi' patted his breast-pocket. Then he came straight up to her and looked at her straight between the eyes.

"And there's another angle, isn't there? Dead girls tell no tales. But you've thought of that, too—I feel sure. Well, *au 'voir*. No—on second thoughts—good-bye. I have a mind for a somewhat lengthy stay on the continent."

The murderer went to the door of the lounge and turned.

"I say," he remarked, "what a show-up for the Wynyards! Don't you agree? As a family they've never impressed me." The front door slammed, and as the noise echoed through the apartment something seemed to snap in her brain and a fainting Elisabeth fell into Anthony's arms. The strain had at last proved too much for her.

2

MacMorran saw the door open and the light shine through to the road. He saw a dark figure come running towards him. He stepped out of the shadows and, as he did so, his three subordinates obeyed their orders and moved up in support. 'Mr. Levi', always on the alert, saw the danger at once and his quick brain told him at least some of the truth. With him—to think was to act. With a sudden sharp swerve he avoided the Inspector's extended arms and at the same time butted Buckridge in the solar plexus.

Before Cullis or Chatterton could move to take a hand, 'Mr. Levi' turned and ran. Not towards his waiting car but straight across the dark patch of road. He ran fast and fiercely with his head down—

which was probably the real cause of his undoing. For the night was dark and the road was wet.

3

As the murderer swerved away from MacMorran and effectively removed Buckridge from barring his way, Cullis and Chatterton tore after him. But whereas he went to the right of Sir Rowland Farrar's memorial, they attempted to cut across him from the opposite direction. It has already been written that he ran fast and fiercely. So fast and so concentratedly that he neither saw nor heard the car which hit him. The car was travelling fast . . . there was a grinding scream of brakes . . . and 'Mr. Levi' had no chance at all. The car hit him and hurtled him away in the distance. His cry was smothered as the life was smashed out of him.

When MacMorran came up, Cullis and Chatterton had already reached him. Chatterton knelt down by the prone figure. Neither the Inspector nor Cullis spoke for some seconds. They each seemed to rely on Chatterton to tell them all there was to tell. The driver of the car, looking as though he had seen a ghost, stood a few yards away. A uniformed constable, who had arrived on the scene, was spoken to by MacMorran and effaced himself. At last Chatterton looked up. He shook his head at MacMorran and his face was grave.

"No good, Chief. He's had it."

The driver of the car essayed explanation. MacMorran heard him out and then replied.

"That's a great relief to me," said the driver, "I was afraid that—"

"All the same," said MacMorran, "you're lucky. Because you were exceeding the speed limit."

He handed the car driver over to the constable with instructions to the latter to do the necessary. "And then put the body in an ambulance. Where will it go to, Wimblefield?"

"Yes, sir."

"O.K. Expect me along there later."

MacMorran had further words with his own men and then walked slowly back to 39, Greene Mansions. A quarter of an hour later the body of Nick Wynyard was on its way to the mortuary at Wimblefield.

CHAPTER XIV

1

A WEEK later, Anthony and Chief Detective-Inspector MacMorran sat with Elisabeth Grenville in the same little lounge at Number 39, Greene Mansions. They had partaken of a really excellent dinner, in the planning and preparation of which Elisabeth had surpassed herself; and had now settled down to coffee. Elisabeth had just served Anthony and had handed him the tiny sugar-basin.

During the meal, all talk of the Medlicott case had been taboo, but now that dinner was over and done with, Elisabeth knew that the barriers would be removed and she would be permitted to ask questions which Anthony Bathurst would answer. But Elisabeth was at great pains to know how and where to start, and a feeling of relief came to her when Anthony presented her with an appropriate opening.

"Feeling better than about this time last week?"

"I'll say," replied Elisabeth, "but I can't believe it's as long ago as a week. It seems to me much more like the night before last. How's your coffee?"

"Excellent, Miss Grenville. Worthy of the dinner we've just eaten."

Elisabeth flushed with pleasure at the compliment. "And yours, Inspector MacMorran?"

"Couldn't be better, Miss Grenville. And it's all very appropriate. The case started with you, it finished with you, and you're the only one of the cast present at the Bathurst inquest." He winked slyly at Elisabeth. "Very-very informative—these Bathurst inquests," he added.

"He must have his little bit of fun," said Anthony, "and on the whole it's a good sign. It shows he's in a good temper. Which occurs about every other Coronation Day. Seriously, though, Miss Grenville, your part in the case has been much bigger even than my good friend Andrew realizes. And, I think, perhaps, more than you even realize yourself. For at least two of my most vital clues emanated from you entirely."

"Well then, sit down both of you and make yourselves thoroughly comfortable and tell me all about it. And—and this means *a lot* to me—satisfy me for all time that, acting as I did, I did the right thing."

"You need find no reproaches for yourself with regard to that, Miss Grenville. Tempted though he may have been, the man you helped to his doom had been guilty of two most dastardly killings for which I can find but little extenuating circumstance, and certainly no forgiveness. And if my opinion doesn't altogether satisfy you as to the integrity of your own conduct, ask Andrew MacMorran here for his opinion."

MacMorran was quickly into the breach. "I'm with Mr. Bathurst all the way, Miss Grenville. You have no call to reproach yourself at all. Not only did you do the r-right thing, but you also did a very plucky thing. It isn't every girl who'd have found the nerve to face the ordeal that you did."

"I'm glad," said Elisabeth quietly, "to hear you say that. Glad—and you don't know *how* relieved. Now, Mr. Bathurst, go ahead with your story and I'll promise not to interrupt you again."

Anthony smiled. "I wonder if you'll stick to that. Anyhow I'll have a go. Where shall I start?"

"From the right place, of course. From the beginning."

"Well, if anybody should know all about the beginning—it's you yourself. Still, I think I know what you mean and I'll do my best. If you think I'm going off the rails—pull me up." He finished his coffee and they lit cigarettes. That is to say he and Elisabeth. MacMorran produced his ancient pipe.

"First of all," said Anthony, as he began his explanation, "I was struck by this fact. That the murders occurred *after*—and almost *immediately* after—the death of Sir John Wynyard. That fact intrigued me. I felt that it had—that it *must* have had—an *importance* far beyond what we may call the 'normal'. So I began to search in my mind for what I called to myself 'reasonable' importances.

"While I was engaged mentally in this way, I ran up against something else which tended strongly to corroborate this opinion. I refer, of course, to the visit to High Fitchet for the Christmas holiday of Walter Medlicott. Who, permit me to point out to you, was Sir John Wynyard's solicitor, in addition to being a very old personal friend. Now, in relation to that, you will both recall what Lady Wynyard told us. Can you remember it?"

"Very well," answered the Inspector, "she told us that the visit was entirely unexpected and that she herself had no inkling of it until Sir John Wynyard himself suddenly came and told her that Medlicott was coming. I think, from memory, that she told us that this took place somewhere about a couple of days prior to Christmas Eve. Yes, I follow your reasoning there."

"Well, I deduced from that," continued Anthony, "that Medlicott went to High Fitchet, much more as Medlicott, the solicitor, than as Medlicott, the friend. That, in other words, he went because he had something to communicate to Sir John Wynyard which, not only had come out of the blue as it were, but which, in addition, was of such paramount importance that he actually took it to his old friend, Sir John, *for Christmas*! We have since confirmed that Medlicott 'phoned Sir John from his office at Aldersford on the Saturday morning before Christmas and, no doubt, made this arrangement. So there we have—the stage all set.

"When Medlicott arrives at High Fitchet he naturally breaks his bad news to Sir John Wynyard. And Sir John, as he was bound to, as you will see later, confides in his son—and heir—Nick Wynyard. I'm fairly sure, in my own mind, that Nick, when he first heard the news which Medlicott had brought, begged Medlicott to keep his mouth shut. But, of course, Medlicott was a solicitor of the old school and a man of the very highest principles and all Nick's entreaties for 'hush-hush' fell on empty air. And then—when both sides were 'sparring', as you might say, the blow fell. Sir John Wynyard died. And the sword of Damocles which, up to that moment, had been merely *suspended* over Nick, *fell* right on him! His problem, had become acute! You both know now—but I will tell you in greater detail—what that problem actually was."

Anthony took another cigarette and lit it.

"This is an account of what happened—as I see it. Either on the Saturday which preceded Christmas, or a few days before that—we shall never know when exactly—a young man called on the old-established firm of Medlicott, Stogdon and Medlicott, at their offices in High St. Aldersford and asked to see Mr. Walter Medlicott personally."

"Just a moment," interrupted Elisabeth, "Please forgive me—I promised I wouldn't do this again—but are you certain of this? I mean—have you been *told* that this happened? Or is it that you're—"

"I haven't been told, Miss Grenville," replied Anthony, "but I'm as certain as if I had been told. I'll go on. That young man called himself John Gooch, which was the name he had always been known by."

"My turn," said MacMorran, "why didn't Adderley tell us this?"

"For the simple reason that Adderley didn't know. Gooch didn't give his name. He asked to see Medlicott. And if Adderley knew about the call—which I doubt—he attached to it no importance whatever."

"Right-o," said MacMorran, "I'll pass."

"That young fellow," went on Anthony, "had been discharged from the Air Force a few months before. He had served abroad for something like six or seven years. Don't overlook that last fact, because it's tremendously important."

MacMorran looked up enquiringly.

"You'll see the force of that later on, Andrew. Young Gooch—as we'll continue to call him, produced to Mr. Medlicott something in the nature of a thunderbolt. Once again, you must remember that Gooch, Medlicott and the Wynyards, *père et fils*, are all dead, which means that we shall never know the precise details, and that I'm constructing the picture as I see it. As I am convinced that it so happened. But to go on.

"Gooch placed in front of Medlicott undeniable evidence that he was the eldest and legitimate son of the late Sir John Wynyard. His two pieces of evidence were the marriage certificate of his mother, Sarah Gooch, and his own birth certificate. You've both seen these two certificates so you're familiar with their terms. Medlicott was flabbergasted. He realized the implications. Not only what it meant to the Wynyards but also the path which he himself would be compelled to pursue. Gooch left the evidence with him and Medlicott gave him his word that he would see the matter through to its authentic termination."

"Just a minute," interjected MacMorran, "there are one or two points here which are far from clear to me."

"I know," said Anthony, "you're asking questions as to why this should have been the first indication of it all. And I think I can dispose of all your difficulties. Let me trace what I think occurred. I'll give you the story as I'm pretty sure it took place. Absolutely from the beginning. If you then *still* harbour doubt or difficulty, tell me. But I don't think you will." MacMorran nodded his acceptance of Anthony's offer. "Although the Wynyards now reside at High Fitchet, they have old associations with Aldersford and the adjoining village of Magdalen Verney—the home of the Gooch family. Sir John, in his youth, no doubt, when visiting Aldersford, met and fell in love with Sarah Gooch of Magdalen Verney. He married her secretly. You know that—we have the marriage certificate. But soon after the marriage, probably, they realized that passion had been the inferior part of discretion and they agreed to part. Sarah Wynyard, as she now was, and helped, doubtless, financially by her husband, went to Ireland, where her son was born. That you also know, because you've seen *that* birth certificate. But what Sir John didn't know, what Sarah had deliberately kept from him, was the fact that *he* was the father of a son. It may seem strange that she should have acted in this way. But I think she loved Sir John and wanted to spare him, *in his life*—mind that—all the embarrassment she could.

"After her son was born, Sarah returned to live with her elder brother at Magdalen Verney. She kept her secret. He, no doubt, thought that the boy was illegitimate, shrugged his shoulders, made no enquiries, kept quiet for the sake of his sister's reputation, and brought the boy up as one of his own family. Then Sarah died suddenly—and Sir John Wynyard was free to marry again. Which he did—still not knowing he was the father of a son. When Sarah died, I suggest, she left two letters, to be dealt with after her death. For her brother to deliver to the appropriate quarters. The first was to Sir John informing him of her death. The second to her son. To be *handed* to him by his uncle upon reaching the age of twenty-one, or on the death of Sir John Wynyard—*whichever occurred first*. This letter told the boy all the truth, enclosed her marriage-lines, told him where he could obtain a copy of his own birth-certificate (I'm entering the realm of conjecture now, I admit) and told him *to place* the whole position in the hands of Mr. Medlicott, whom she *knew* she could trust. She was a Magdalen Verney girl—you see—and knew all that the firm of the Medlicotts stood for. You see—although Sarah was willing to spare Sir John while he lived—she wasn't going to see young John deprived of his lawful rights when her husband had been gathered to his forefathers." Anthony broke off. "Well, how am I doing?"

"All right," said MacMorran, "but there's still an awfu' lot to explain. For instance why—?"

"Wait for it," said Anthony, "it'll come. I'll endeavour to help you. I'll try to explain two matters which are possibly troubling you out of what I have just said. Number one may be this. Why didn't Gooch come forward until he was nearer twenty-seven than twenty-one? A good point—but I'm confident I have the right explanation. It's this. When he came of age he was serving in the Far East—difficult to contact—and any documents sent to him would stand an excellent chance of not reaching their destination. His uncle knew that and played for safety. He knew how his sister, Sarah, had impressed upon him the supreme importance of his nephew receiving her letter—so he waited until the young chap came home. I can't say that I find any criticism of that action. Can you, Andrew?"

MacMorran shook his head. "No. Go on."

"Now I'll try to deal with what may be your second point. What happened between young Gooch coming home, somewhere about late summer or early autumn, and the time he went to Medlicott? Which we're fairly certain must have been, say, round about the third week in December. Well, I've given that matter a good deal of attention myself and I fancy that again I've been able to hit on the true explanation. My suggestion is that he was waiting *for a copy of his birth certificate to come to him from Ireland*. His mother had supplied him with the necessary details for him to make the application. You observed that he was born in Dublin. It's possible, I think, that there were certain difficulties—I've run against them before where Irish registrations have been concerned—and Gooch was kept waiting until the December. He wasn't going to Medlicott with his story until he carried with him the full rounds of ammunition." Once again Anthony appealed to his two hearers. "How are we now? Moving along?"

MacMorran nodded. Anthony's answers had obviously impressed him. But Elisabeth had a query.

"There's one little point, Mr. Bathurst, I'd like to put to you, if I may. May I?"

"Certainly, Miss Grenville. Delighted. What is it?"

"Well," said Elisabeth nervously, "I'm afraid I must begin by asking you what they might call a supplementary question. But am I in order in thinking that what upset Mr. Medlicott, when he and I arrived at High Fitchet on the Christmas Eve, was seeing Gooch?"

Anthony rubbed his hands with pleasure. "You are in order, Miss Grenville. You are absolutely dead right and I must congratulate you on having picked up the point. I should, of course, have come to that point later. But that's by the way."

"Oh, but I haven't finished yet," continued Elisabeth—"and I'm sorry to have anticipated you over it. I think I've got a bit of a poser for you."

"Let's have it, Miss Grenville. Don't spare me—or MacMorran will swear that I'm spoiled."

"It's this. If Gooch called on Mr. Medlicott at Aldersford, as you've just said he did, and told Mr. Medlicott who he was, and put all his trump cards on the table—and made Mr. Medlicott bolt off to High Fitchet so that you couldn't see his . . . er . . . heels for dust—why, then," exclaimed Elisabeth triumphantly, "was Mr. Medlicott so upset when he saw him again? Surely he expected to see him?"

"Good girl," said Anthony, "I asked myself the same question. But isn't the explanation both obvious and simple?"

"Not to me." She shook her head.

"It's excessively simple," said Anthony. "Gooch concealed from Medlicott the fact that he already had obtained employment in the house of the Wynyards at High Fitchet. Gooch went there on purpose. And, no doubt, concealed from Sir John all information which might have aroused his suspicions. It was highly exciting for him—there was the vista of possible hopes—and—in addition—he could also get the 'lie of the land'."

"You win," said Elisabeth, "and I'm a priceless idiot not to have thought of it."

"I can now cover something else," continued Anthony, "at least I think I can—and that is why Medlicott was perturbed when you and he were in the train. Do you remember?"

"Very well," said Elisabeth.

"Medlicott saw Dr. Copplestone," she went on, "but why that fact disturbed him, I haven't the foggiest idea."

Anthony shook his head at her. "You've got it wrong, Miss Grenville. Look at it from the other angle. It wasn't seeing Copplestone that worried Medlicott. It was seeing the other man—the man who walked along the corridor behind Copplestone."

"Why—who was that? And how do you know?"

"I don't know. But my conjecture is that the other man was Nick Wynyard. When Medlicott saw him—it made him realize more fully the nature of his errand—it brought home to him more poignantly than ever before what it would mean to Nick Wynyard—and Medlicott was affected."

"But Nick never admitted that he came on my train!"

"Exactly—he kept it dark. But I'm pretty sure he did. It was he who drove off in the first car from Colbury station with Dr. and Mrs. Copplestone and Lillywhite."

"But what was the point of keeping it dark?"

"I incline to the opinion that he thought it might tend to confuse the Police. You get the idea? Who was the sinister stranger that frightened the murdered man in the train?"

"I think you're right, there," volunteered MacMorran.

"Well," continued Anthony, "there's the position as it was when you, Miss Grenville and Medlicott arrived at High Fitchet. Quentin and Catherine welcomed you and while that was going on, Medlicott spilled the beans to Sir John. Sir John told Nick—*but not Lady Wynyard.*"

"Why not?"

"I think, Andrew, that he got cold feet and funked it. I'll tell you how I arrive at that conclusion."

"Look here," exclaimed Elisabeth, "this is an appropriate moment for drinks. I managed to get some beer in. Yes? Both of you?"

"Lady," said MacMorran, beaming on her, "count us both in."

Elisabeth slipped out and they heard the comforting tinkle of glasses.

2

"I feel better," said MacMorran a few minutes later, "in fact I can say I feel distinctly better."

Elisabeth smiled at him and put down her tankard. "Now, Mr. Bathurst—you have our permission to continue with what Inspector MacMorran called earlier on 'your inquest'."

"Command me, Miss Grenville! Well—things 'simmered', I suggest, until the early hours of the day after Boxing Day. The worry which had gnawed at Sir John, eventually became his master. He left his bed in those small hours and repaired to his writing-room. He took with him a copy of the Bible. Has either of you any idea why?"

"I think I get it," replied MacMorran, "you've helped me, of course, by the way you've told the story. He went to the writing-room to write a letter to his wife. You hinted as much to me a day or so before we broke the case wide open. That letter amounted to a confession. Am I right?"

"Yes, Andrew. That's exactly what I think. Some men are like that. They'll put a confession on paper which they haven't the guts to put into speech. In other words, Sir John was about to write, what he jibbed saying to his wife, Lady Wynyard."

"But what did he require the Bible for?" demanded Elisabeth, "he wasn't such a pious man as that would seem to suggest." For a moment Anthony was silent under her query. He sat and stared into the flames of the fire.

"I'm not sure. I should hate to assert that I was anything like sure. But I *think* I've found the answer even to that question. At any rate, I *like* to think I have."

"Well, what is the answer, Mr. Bathurst?" rejoined Elisabeth. "I think it was this. Sir John felt that there had come a slur on his moral character. In this respect. I fancy that he had been guilty, as far as his second wife was concerned, of a *suppressio veri*—he had told her nothing whatever about his previous relationship with Sarah Gooch. He felt that Lady Wynyard would take the news badly—it meant, you see, that her son, Nicholas had an elder and legitimate brother. Of which fact previously, she hadn't had the slightest suspicion. Now Sir John's Bible was opened at the Psalms of David. And this is what I think he had in his mind. He was about to confess to his wife, in writing, what his troubled mind regarded as his dark past. I think he wanted to cite David as a standard of comparison. David, who had been 'a man after God's own heart', had also been guilty of much worse conduct than he had. David's affair with Bathsheba combined the elements of both murder and adultery. And yet David, despite his moral shortcomings, had found favour with the Lord. Sir John felt it would palliate his own conduct, so to speak. Do you get my line of argument?"

Both MacMorran and Elisabeth nodded.

"Now Sir John Wynyard was not a close student of Holy Scripture—I've satisfied myself on that point—and he thought he would probably find the Biblical references he wanted, in connection with David—in the Psalms, instead of in the Book of Samuel. And then came the end. Before he could write the confession which he intended to write, he had a heart-seizure and died."

There ensued a silence. Anthony tried to force an opinion. "Well, does my explanation get by?"

Somewhat to his surprise, seeing that neither of his hearers had commented, both Elisabeth and the Inspector were in agreement.

"Is that the reason," asked the last-named, "you purchased that copy of the Bible?"

Anthony shook his head. "No, Andrew. At that time I was coquetting with the idea that Sir John Wynyard himself was the author of the Levi messages. You see—I was moderately certain that the word 'Levi' in each instance, had been cut from a Bible. I explained to you before why I thought that. But I couldn't satisfy myself from memory that the word 'Levi' occurred in the Psalms at all. So I checked the point. I had to buy a Bible to do it. As far as I've been able to see on a rapid run-through, it occurs only twice. So I felt that Sir John, probably, had not turned to the Psalms of David for that particular purpose."

"Good," responded MacMorran, "you pass."

"I think then, now," continued Anthony, "that we've dealt with the 'genesis' of the crimes. So I'll pass on to the actual murders themselves. And I'll endeavour to take you along the paths of my reasoning which led us ultimately to a successful solution. Yes?"

Both Elisabeth and the Inspector signified their assent.

3

"Let me," went on Anthony, "put myself in Nick Wynyard's place. From Christmas Eve until Boxing Day he had been facing a problem. Facing circumstances which completely transformed his life and his future. But they were *most* important *then* by reason of their *future* implication. He had a certain amount of time, as it were, to look round and to take stock of the position. But then, in the twinkling of an eye, his father dies and the threat of the future becomes the raw gnawing menace of the present. Medlicott has told them who Gooch is and of what he holds that Gooch has given him. But *only* Medlicott and Gooch know Medlicott has intimated that fact as well. If they could both be eliminated, Nick Wynyard, all the Wynyards, and the traditional possession of High Fitchet and all that that possession entailed could be put back, as it were, in *statu quo ante*. So the murder resolve is born in Nick's heart. All that he has to do is to perfect the details of the commission. And surely, if he play his cards cleverly enough, he would be almost the last person in the world to be suspected. So he broods over his black resolve. He has little time—be it remembered. If he is to act, he must act quickly or Medlicott, the solicitor, will set the Gooch ball rolling. He can't kill Medlicott in the house. He must get him outside somewhere. He knows that the country near the house, at such a season of the year and in such weather conditions as were then prevalent, is given to privacy and comparative solitude.

"He waits for his chance. The sunshine that followed the snow was the means of giving it to him. Medlicott thinks of taking a walk over to Sturton Ridge—across several lonely fields and through a number of lonely spinneys. To meditate, doubtless on the unpleasant nature of the task which faced him. In the matter of John Gooch. So Nick begins to plot and his plot was something of this sort, I suggest. He has no lethal weapon handy and the time for action is so short that he has to abandon any idea he may have had of obtaining one. He happens to see his brother Quentin's camera lying on a table in the hall. And another idea flies into his quick and receptive brain. He will find out which way Medlicott goes, catch him up in a carefully selected spot, and offer to take his photograph, because all the time that Nick was thinking thus, he was toying with the idea that he could kill the weakish, non-robust elderly solicitor by a most unusual method. I'll come to that, however, later."

Anthony paused, but Elisabeth and MacMorran were far too enthralled by his story to think, even, of interruption.

"I rather think, too," continued Anthony, "that Nick *knew* that Medlicott couldn't swim."

This time Elisabeth came in eagerly. "You're absolutely right there. He *did* know! Because at dinner one evening I happened to overhear Mr. Medlicott tell him that he was no swimmer at all—I think he said he couldn't swim a stroke."

"Good," replied Anthony, "then that makes me feel more certain than ever that I'm on the right track. Well, Medlicott went out for his walk and Nick Wynyard followed him armed with Quentin's camera, his own field-glasses and wearing running-shoes, appropriately spiked. He followed him until he came to the place where he intended to disclose himself. What happened subsequently, I'm pretty confident, was this. Nick, having used his field-glasses and made certain that there wasn't a living soul within distance, joined Medlicott and declared that he had come out with the intention of taking some photographs. The weather was so glorious, there was so much sun, the scenery was magnificent, etc., etc. Could he have the pleasure of taking Mr. Medlicott's? Where would be the best place? From the point of view of the light and of a really picturesque setting? What about the gate (near the pond—mark you—with a good depth of icy water and only thin ice on top)? If Mr. Medlicott, say, leaned over the gate and faced this way? And he himself stood here by the pond? Excellent! Should make a really charming picture.

"Medlicott naturally agreed. Why shouldn't he? He had known Nick ever since he was born. So there we are—all set for the first murder. Have you got the full picture in your eyes? Because I want you to have, so that you can understand fully Nick's next move."

The Inspector and Elisabeth assured Anthony that they had.

"Medlicott then," went on Anthony, "leaned over the gate—hat on and pipe in mouth. Nick, with camera, finessed for the best place to take it from. He wasn't altogether satisfied that he was in the most suitable position. No—he'd try one or two other places—the light wasn't quite right. And then, I suggest, Medlicott missed 'the photographer' who had slipped through the hedge and was now approaching his victim from the rear. And almost noiselessly—remember—by reason of the carpet of snow. But with no camera in his hand! With murder, rather, in his heart."

Anthony stopped—to proceed more slowly. "You are both aware that Nick Wynyard was an accomplished athlete. His speciality was the long jump. When he won this event for Oxford against Cambridge at the White City last Spring, he had cleared over twenty-two feet. He killed Medlicott by jumping on his neck from behind and fracturing the top of the spinal vertebrae. If he'd merely knocked him out, Medlicott's body was then destined for the pond. But Nick killed him all right and then began his search for the vital certificates. To his infinite chagrin, however, they weren't on Medlicott's person. So he was faced with the fact that half his job was still undone. However, for a moment or so I'll get back to the murder itself. I'll tell you how I was assisted towards my deductions concerning the manner of the murder.

"Feeling as I did as to the reason of Medlicott's visit and to the murders occurring *after* the death of Sir John, it had seemed to me from the first that to find the killer we must look for somebody in the Wynyard family. There were six. Lady Wynyard, Miss Amy Wynyard, Nick, Quentin and Catherine and Henry Poulton. But look at it how you will, anything vital which affected the property or the estate, seemed to me to indicate Nick, perhaps, first of all. Let me put it like this. He seemed a *likely* suspect. Now let us glance at two main features connected with the way Medlicott died. The first was the disturbed track of snow leading up to the gate which gave entrance to the second field. The field of the pond. And the gate over which Medlicott leaned to have his photograph taken. Remember that his pipe, knocked from his mouth, fell into the *second* field. That disturbance suggested to me that somebody had run hard along the path at a quick speed and I found myself wondering why a person should run in such a manner straight towards that gate.

"Then there was the cut on Medlicott's cheek—or if you prefer the word—the scratch. That puzzled me for a long time, but when I began to sketch in the whole of Nick's background and discovered his athletic prowess with regard to 'Long-jump' proficiency, I began to think that I had definitely arrived somewhere at last and that the scratch had been caused by a spike on one of Nick's shoes. Which is a fair jumping-off place (no pun intended) to get to the gentleman who, I'm afraid, dominated our thoughts, certainly Andrew's and mine, for so long a time. I refer to 'Mr. Levi'."

Anthony paused and looked at Elisabeth. "Tell me, Miss Grenville—I'm interested. Did that name filter through at all to you people in the house at High Fitchet? I've often wondered?"

"Just vaguely, Mr. Bathurst. You know—as a sort of nebulous rumour that there was a mysterious person of that name mixed up in the case somehow. But we had no more than that."

"Show her, Andrew," said Anthony, "the form in which the 'Levi' problem first came to us."

MacMorran took out his pocket-book and handed her a slip of paper. "This is what Mr. Bathurst is referring to, Miss Grenville. One of these was found in the pocket of Medlicott's overcoat, one in Gooch's overalls, and one in the pocket of Sir John Wynyard's dressing-gown."

Elisabeth took the paper curiously. "What on earth does it mean? 'Hand over the diamond'." She shook her head. "Explain, please—I'm simply dying of curiosity."

"That piece of paper," said Anthony, "was the murderer's first attempt to throw the police off the scent. He tried others subsequently. But this first attempt was by the introduction of two *very* scarlet herrings. A diamond and 'Mr. Levi'. Neither of which really existed. All the words with the exception of 'Levi' were cut from the letterpress of the *Daily Telegraph*. I am completely satisfied as to that, by the way, as I took steps to prove it, as far as was reasonably possible."

"How were you able to do that?" asked Elisabeth.

"By co-operation with one of the maids at High Fitchet I was enabled to have access to the used and discarded newspapers from the house. My eyes had already told me that the letter-press of the *Daily Telegraph* had been used for all the words except 'Levi', so I took a chance. It came off. I discovered that three fairly recent copies of the *Daily Telegraph*, which paper was in daily supply at the house, were missing. I found that fact extremely eloquent as, once again, the finger of suspicion was pointed at the Wynyard family, plus possibly

Percival Comfit who, as a neighbour, *might* have been aware of the domestic arrangements at High Fitchet. Which left me with the word 'Levi' only, to trace—if I possibly could. But therein I failed. Although I think I can tell you what happened with regard to that. Nick cut the word from the copy of his father's Bible—the book which had been found in the writing-room when Sir John Wynyard had his heart-attack and died. Having done this, he destroyed the book—probably wrapped in the mutilated copies of the *Daily Telegraph*."

Elisabeth nodded. "I had been intending to ask you another question, Mr. Bathurst, but since you've been talking, I think I can see the answer myself."

"What was the question, Miss Grenville?"

"Well—what I had been wondering was this. Why was a 'Levi' message put in Sir John's dressing-gown pocket? He died a natural death—I presume that there's no possible doubt about that?"

"None whatever, Miss Grenville. We took special steps with the Doctor to confirm that as certain. No—that was Nick again, doing his best to bring confusion to the Police authorities. What he was endeavouring to do was to proclaim through the medium of these mysterious 'Levi' messages, with their strange and cryptic references to a non-existent 'diamond', that there was a killer abroad who was committing a chain of murders, actuated by avarice and lust of possession. Besides—Nick would never have been suspected of killing *his* father—their affection was not only evident—but real."

"Yes—I was right, then. Actually that was the explanation I had found for myself."

"Good. I will now pass on to the killing of John Gooch. Consider the stage as it now was with the curtain down on Act I. Gooch hears that his 'friend' (remember the terms of his mother's letter) has been killed. Remember, too, that Gooch had put his whole case into Medlicott's hands. So Gooch, very understandably, smells a rat. And having smelt it, he repairs at once (mistakenly of course) to Nick Wynyard. Nick told us this himself. But deliberately—and with definite reason. Because it served to bring Gooch into the Medlicott orbit. Nick calculated and to some extent, at least, he calculated correctly—that if the Police knew this, they would form the inevitable opinion that Gooch was killed because he knew something about Medlicott. To keep his mouth shut. Whereas, the reverse was the truth—Medlicott was killed because he knew something about Gooch. Thank you. Miss Grenville."

Anthony took a cigarette from the case which Elisabeth held out to him.

"This approach, however, of Gooch to Nick Wynyard, gave the latter the opportunity for which he had been looking. He made an appointment with the chauffeur for the following morning, and in the garage. 'Where', he said, in all probability, 'you and I can be alone and talk quietly over whatever it may be you wish to discuss with me'. And then Nick's cunning mind saw another implication. He realized that if he removed Gooch, he would be able to pretend that the death of Gooch had deprived him of an alibi support for the afternoon of the Medlicott murder. Which he knew he would be bound to be asked about. His subtle argument was, 'if I make Gooch necessary to my alibi for Medlicott, I shall be the last person to be suspected of his murder'. And I'm bound to admit that the point weighed with me at times and gave me quite a considerable amount of difficulty."

Elisabeth looked very white as she spoke. "How did he . . . kill Gooch?" she asked.

"Very simply, I should say. He timed matters to let Gooch arrive in the garage first. And naturally, as a chauffeur and mechanic, Gooch's attention was directed to a car. He might as well do something while he was waiting for Nick. When Nick did enter, he went in, I should imagine, wearing light shoes and, as in the case of his previous victim, Medlicott, approached Gooch noiselessly from behind. A coil of rope was flung round the man's neck and twisted tight. He was throttled. A piece of real authentic 'Thuggee'. It was the work of a few seconds. Then he slipped the second Levi note into the pocket of the overalls, and was back in bed in less than a quarter of an hour."

Elisabeth knitted her brows. "The second 'Levi' note? You mean the third, surely?"

Anthony shook his head and smiled. "No, I don't think so, Miss Grenville."

"But what about—"

"Sir John's?"

"Yes."

"I think that was by way of being an afterthought. I don't think it got into the dressing-gown pocket until both these others had *been* placed. I fancy it occurred to Nick later to do that—it *must* have—after all, he didn't know his father was going to die, did he?"

"No—of course not. I should never make a detective."

"Well there you are, then—the curtain has descended on Act II. Medlicott and Gooch have been silenced—but the full problem is as yet unsolved for the murderer—he is still without the two certificates which must be destroyed before he can feel safe. But where are they?"

Elisabeth poured out more beer. Anthony was grateful and drank.

4

"Where could they be? The first place of search was obviously the room which Medlicott had occupied and any other clothes of his which might be in there. But the search which our murderer made, revealed none of the evidence which he so badly needed. The certificates were not there. He knew that Medlicott had them. For the simple reason that when Medlicott arrived at High Fitchet on Christmas Eve and was closeted with his father, he had been sent for, informed of this terrible new position which had been opened up, and had actually *seen* the two certificates which had then, when the interview terminated, gone back to Medlicott's possession. Where could they be, then? They hadn't been on Medlicott's person, and they aren't in Medlicott's room. He felt moderately certain that Medlicott hadn't handed them back to Gooch. Because he knew Medlicott, he knew his methods of business, and he knew the exact angle from which the solicitor regarded Gooch. And then," said Anthony, "a rather remarkable thing happened. Have you any idea to what I allude?"

He seemed to address his question to Elisabeth. She shook her head.

"You ought to have," declared Anthony. "Nick found in one of Medlicott's drawers, an envelope addressed to you, in Medlicott's handwriting."

"So it *was* Mr. Medlicott's?"

"I think so. In fact I'm almost sure it was. And here's the remarkable part about it. The envelope was empty. It was empty, I think, because Medlicott addressed it to you before going out for his last walk, and then found he hadn't time to write the little note he had intended writing. So he decided to put off that part of it until he returned. But he didn't return, so all the murderer found was an empty envelope."

Elisabeth broke in. "But what I can't understand, Mr. Bathurst, as I told you before, is what Mr. Medlicott should write to me about?"

Anthony smiled. "But there's where Fate took a hand in the game, Miss Grenville. In fact, all through the drama, you figured something like a *dea ex machina*. Can't you see how Nick regarded Medlicott's envelope addressed to you?"

"No. Indeed I can't."

"He thought that for some reason which he couldn't fathom, Medlicott had passed the Gooch certificates into your keeping. If you can 'see' a thought, I visualize his on these lines. You had become friendly with Medlicott on the way down in the train. Medlicott, in his turn, had become nervous of what he had in his possession. After all, you must remember that Nick had lived for days, hag-ridden by his own murderous thoughts. Conscience took a hand, you see, in shaping the picture he was painting. Medlicott he argued to himself, had intended to pass the certificates to you, for temporary safety, in the envelope, but he had subsequently changed his mind and handed them to you! From that moment, Miss Grenville, *your* room became the target of Wynyard's search-attentions. You are aware of what happened. Your personal belongings and your room generally were all turned over. And yet, although they were there all the time, both you and he missed the vital Gooch certificates." Anthony smiled.

"But I still don't see," reiterated Elisabeth, "I know that Mr. Medlicott had left them in my book—but even so, you haven't told me what Medlicott was going to write to me about. Has he, Inspector MacMorran?"

"He will tell you," said Andrew MacMorran, "you don't know him as well as I do."

"Only Medlicott could do that, Miss Grenville," said Anthony. "I'll tell you, though, what I *think* was his intention. Can't you guess yourself?"

Elisabeth cupped her chin in her hands. She stayed like that for some little time. "I think," she said eventually, "that I can hazard a guess. But please don't howl at me if I'm hopelessly wrong. You've no idea how sensitive I am."

MacMorran grinned.

"Go on," said Anthony, "nothing venture, nothing howl."

"He was going to write to me to thank me for the loan of the book. Yes?"

Anthony nodded. "We think alike, Miss Grenville." Elisabeth coloured with pleasure. "I'm beginning to re-establish myself. I expect it was about time."

"We've now," said Anthony, "reached Act III. You've told me what's happened in your room and I'm beginning to fit the pieces together into the entire pattern. And, naturally, I turn my attention to the matter of 'Mr. Levi' himself."

Anthony stopped. "How about a cigarette? Try one of these." He handed round his case and MacMorran produced his lighter. He worked on it for more than a minute.

5

"In the matter of 'Mr. Levi'," Anthony continued, "the murderer had two pieces of luck. One good—one bad. They ironed themselves out. But the bad piece enabled me to break the case wide open. I'll deal with his piece of good fortune first. It emanated from that interesting personality, Mr. Ebenezer Isaacs. Although I strongly suspect that 'somebody' who should have known better—Nick himself in all probability—had put Isaacs wise to the 'Levi' messages which had been found on the two victims. Isaacs—shrewd and 'full of brotherly love'—has an element of mischief strongly entrenched in his mental constitution, and as luck had it, he was enabled by means of a newspaper cutting he happened to be carrying about with him, to toss a dear little 'spanner' into the official works. And for a time 'Samuel Levy' looked like something that would eventually require a Phenacetin powder. I'll tell you about it."

Anthony recounted for Elisabeth's benefit the Levy Bequest incident.

"But it passed," he continued "and once again our producer, Miss Elisabeth Grenville, pulled another rabbit from her seemingly inexhaustible hat."

"What on earth was that?" inquired Elisabeth.

"You wrote me a letter," said Anthony, and at this, MacMorran looked up. "After you took fright and hared away from High Fitchet. You left it with Helen Repton for her to give to me upon my return to the house. Remember?"

"I'm not likely to have forgotten it. I was scared stiff as I explained to you. But what was so specially noteworthy about my letter? I can't think of anything."

"Nothing noteworthy, perhaps, but something was tucked away in it which probably provided the very stimulus this lazy brain of mine required to make it function properly. Can you recall writing the word 'monument' and finding that you weren't able to get the whole word into the one line? So that you were compelled to disarticulate it to 'monu-ment'?"

"No. I can't say that I do. But what was so important about that?"

"Nothing, perhaps, *per se*. But it caught my eye, I suppose, and having succeeded in doing that, it proceeded to crawl into my brain. I found myself repeating 'monu-ment'—'monu-ment'. I'm like that. Words or phrases or even snatches of music sometimes take up their residence with me and stay for days. And after a time, after I'd repeated 'monu-ment' to myself several times, it suggested to me a phrase from somewhere—I had no idea where—which also contained the word 'monu-ment' in the same form as you had written it. It took me some days to track this fellow to his lair but I knew that if I relaxed and let it come to me, it inevitably would. Well—one night it did. And the couplet was this. Listen to it carefully and you may get something of a jolt. You'll also get the reason why my brain started working as it did and recognize the spark which had ignited it.

"The couplet in question is a quotation from the Rev. Richard Harris Barham who, over a hundred years ago, tossed off the famous *Ingoldsby Legends*. This is now it goes. It's taken from an effort entitled 'Misadventures at Margate'. 'And now I'm here, from this here pier, it is my fixed intent, To jump as Mr. Levi did, from off the Monu-ment'!"

"Good Lord!" exclaimed Elisabeth while MacMorran whistled.

"Then," said Anthony, "you may guess that I was feeling very warm. I began to study psychology. Why had the murderer deliberately provided a clue—to anybody who was sagacious enough to find it? Because there *is* a clue there. With 'Levi' there's the key-word 'jump'—which to anybody who knew his athletic reputation, *must* suggest Nick Wynyard. I think the answer to the question is that most ancient of all answers perhaps—vanity. The murderer's vanity was such that although it might prove to be a finger-post with his name on it, he was prepared to take a chance on it."

"I think you're right," said Elisabeth, "I knew Nick, you see—and I also think you're wonderful."

"Spare my blushes," said Anthony, "and let me continue. For a query arose in my mind. Was Nick acquainted with the 'Ingoldsby Legends'? They're hardly normal reading for the modern Oxonian. They might, however, I concluded, have belonged to his adolescent days. I decided to put the matter to a test. One day the chance came to me. Andrew here, and I, motoring to High Fitchet one morning, narrowly averted a collision with another vehicle. The driver of the vehicle regaled us and our driver, of course, with a highly meritorious effort in the vernacular. In point of fact, one of the choicest and juiciest it's ever been my fortune to hear. When I was shown into Nick's room a little later on, Quentin, Comfit and Isaacs were with him. They were there, I believe, in connection with Sir John's estate. At any rate, that was his story. I told them of the little road incident which had just taken place and I finished up the account of it by quoting one of the most familiar of all the Barham lines. I have no doubt that you both know it. It comes from *The Jackdaw of Rheims*. You'll recognize it, I'm sure, immediately you hear it."

Anthony stopped to press a cigarette-stub into the ash-tray. "'Never was heard such a terrible curse'. Then, to my entire satisfaction, and quite spontaneously, Nick partly finished the line for me. 'But what gave rise to no little surprise, Nobody seemed one penny the worse'. Nick, mind you, not Quentin! Not Isaacs! Not Comfit! Nick! And the words tripped from his tongue so smoothly that I knew for certain that he had real knowledge of the Rev. R. H. Barham's famous work. To make assurance doubly sure, I asked his permission to look in the High Fitchet library, under the pretext that I was still searching for his father's mislaid Bible. And there, on the shelf, with its pages well-worn and much-used, stood a volume of the *Ingoldsby Legends*. I felt certain then that I had done the right thing because I had already come to you and dictated the letter that I wanted you to send him."

Elisabeth nodded. "I wasn't too sure that he'd come. I thought he might fear it was a trap."

"No. I never thought that. And the terms of my letter were such that he couldn't intelligently think it, either."

"I was dead scared all the time he was here. And if it had lasted much longer than it did, I should have fainted in his arms instead of in yours."

Anthony shook his head. "No—you wouldn't. You played a good show, Miss Grenville. Not only at that last interview, but all the way through the piece. You played a 'blinder'."

MacMorran knocked the ash from his pipe. "And now," he said, "now that you've finished payin' each other compliments, there are one or two questions that *I'd* like to ask. O.K.?"

"O.K., Andrew. Go ahead, man."

6

"There aren't many," said MacMorran, "and none of them is by way of being important. They just stick in my mind a bit, that's all."

"Right-o, Andrew. Let's have them, by all means. No spoiling the ship for a ha'porth of tar."

"Well, then," went on the Inspector, "here's Number One. It's to do with Copplestone. Dr. Koppelstein, to be more precise. As I've since been given to understand that that's his real name. We noticed, you and I, that all through the piece, the gentleman appeared to be very worried. From memory, I rather fancy that you mentioned the matter to me as being of some significance. You were more than ordinarily concerned about it. Now here's my question. If the Herr Doktor comes out of it all with a nice clean sheet, as he undoubtedly has, what was causing him the head-ache? For that he had one, I haven't *any* doubt."

MacMorran sat back and waited for Anthony's answer. Elisabeth, who had listened to all that the Inspector had said, looked across at Anthony.

"If you like, Mr. Bathurst, as it happens, I can answer that question. And I feel sure that my answer will satisfy Inspector MacMorran completely."

"Go on, then, Miss Grenville. Any answer I might give would be merely my own ideas on the matter. Whereas yours, as you say, is going to be authentic. I shall be as interested in it as Andrew here."

"I got this from Catherine," said Elisabeth, "so that you need have no qualms about accepting it. Lady Wynyard had met the Copplestones—I'll continue to call them that—at a B.B.C. studio. Last summer, I think it was. But I wouldn't be sure about that. She's a very great devotee of music. The Copplestones, I should say, were inclined to exploit this—especially Dr. Copplestone himself. Now although he's managed to get his choir under the notice of the B.B.C. and they'd already had several broadcasting and Radio engagements, he is none too strong from a financial point of view. In short, the doctor of music had a nose for money and he managed to extract from Lady Wynyard a sort of half-promise that he could look to her for some considerable financial support. The Christmas invitation to High Fitchet was to clinch the deal. Do you get it now?"

"I see," said Anthony. "For, of course, when Sir John died, the Wynyard financial situation became a little obscure—sons are often different propositions from their sires and Copplestone (with both eyes on the bees and honey) saw his favourite's chance beginning to look much more like that of an outsider. Hence the long face and care-worn look. Thank you, Miss Grenville. Once again, you see, you fill the bill. No real detective should ever be without you! Does that satisfy you, Andrew?"

"Absolutely," replied MacMorran.

"Come on, then. What's your next one?"

"Only one more. And it isn't really in the nature of a query. It's more that I'm seeking information again. When, in your opinion, were the 'Levi' messages constructed—or prepared, perhaps, is the better word?"

"Well, of course, that's a sticky one to answer. But I should say that something like this happened. When Nick formed the resolve to destroy Medlicott and Gooch, he at once looked round for something in the way of a 'smoke-screen'. Something which would place the crimes in a vastly different category from that to which they really belonged. So he thought up the 'diamond' red-herring. Then the message from 'Mr. Levi' suggested itself—and he devised the particular means of preparation. I should say that he got the first one ready directly he knew for certain that Medlicott intended to go out for his walk. The others followed—the one for his father, of course, was, as I previously hinted, what he considered, doubtless, a subtle afterthought."

"I think I'm more or less in agreement," said MacMorran, "but I felt I'd like to know how you thought about it."

"Well?" inquired Anthony, "how do we go now? Any more for the *Skylark*?"

Elisabeth looked at MacMorran and MacMorran looked at Elisabeth. They shook their respective heads.

"No," said the lady, "all clear as far as I'm concerned. And I expect you'd like one for the road. Yes?"

"I don't mind if I do," replied MacMorran, "the night air does strike cold when you've been sitting in the warm."

Anthony winked at Elisabeth behind MacMorran's back. "The last time I heard him say that, Miss Grenville, was on an August Bank Holiday when the temperature was in the nineties."

Elisabeth poured out the last drinks. "There's one thing," she said, "I'll think twice about where I spend next Christmas. I don't want another one like the last has been."

"You never know, Miss Grenville, there are as bad fish in the sea as ever came out."

MacMorran gave a half-smothered exclamation. He had upset some of his beer.

"If you ask me, Andrew," said Anthony, "the night air in the last few minutes has become even colder."

THE END

KINDRED SPIRITS . . .

Why not join the

**DEAN STREET PRESS
FACEBOOK GROUP**

for lively bookish chat
and more

Scan the QR code below

Or follow this link
**www.facebook.com/groups/
deanstreetpress**